SNOW MOUNTAIN MISFITS

SNOW MOUNTAIN MISFITS

Cold War Tales of the Super-Secret Army Security Agency

Jeremiah Davis

ISBN: 9798657489187

Cover sketches by Arielle Combs

DEDICATION

This book is dedicated to all those who served in silence, particularly to the men and women of the Army Security Agency, and especially to absent comrades.

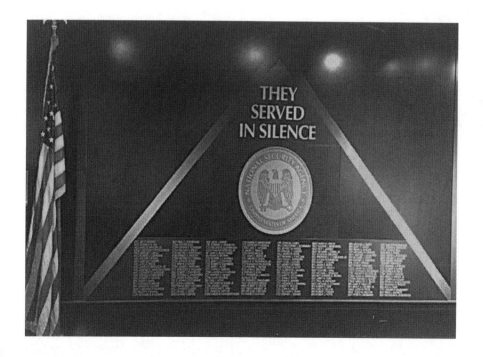

Table of Contents

INTRODUCTION

The art of intelligence is often referred to as the world's second oldest profession. However, some intelligence practitioners might argue that the collection and analysis of intelligence have been more essential to mankind's survival than the services of courtesans. Only after basic physiological needs are met and one's safety or the safety of his group is assured that man can entertain his desire for sexual intimacy. The debate over this point can be saved for another time, but it is clear that the two professions date back to the beginning of time and have on some occasions been interwoven. The Old Testament tells us that when the Hebrews were encamped at Shittim in the Jordan valley opposite Jericho, ready to cross the river, Joshua sent out two spies to investigate the military strength of Jericho. The spies stayed in the house of Rahab, who was described as a harlot who hid them when soldiers came to capture them.

Throughout the course of history, human groups have sent men to high ground to watch for signs of an approaching enemy and to assess the threat. Schneeberg, a mountain in northeastern Bavaria, was first used for that purpose more than 500 years ago when the Margrave of Bayreuth, a prince of the Holy Roman Empire, directed Captain Kunz von Wirsberg to establish a chain of observation posts at strategic locations to the north and east of the city.

Schneeberg was an ideal, but sometimes inhospitable site for such an outpost. Its summit stands nearly 3,500 feet above sea level. It is the highest mountain in the Fichtelgiberge range of Upper Franconia. True to its German name which means Snow Mountain, it is crowned with snow for more than half the year. A watcher there has a commanding view of the surrounding area, particularly to the east toward the Czech lands of Bohemia, less than 20 miles away. The villagers from nearby Weissenstadt were required to establish a permanent watchtower there as

1

early as 1520, and sentries no doubt manned positions there during the 30 Years War in the early 17th Century.

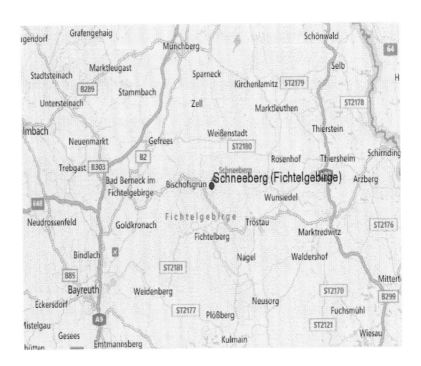

In more peaceful times, outdoorsmen and winter sports enthusiasts frequented the mountain top. In 1879 the Fichtelgebirge branch of the German-Austrian Alpine Club built the first simple platform on the rock summit; at the same time a rude stone hut was erected. In 1904 a log cabin followed and in 1926 the Weissenstadt branch of the Fichtelgebirge Club built an observation tower called the *Backöfele* or baking oven from oak logs. Legend has it that the very first *Backöfele* was constructed back in the early 1600s when people fled the conflict in surrounding villages and came to Schneeberg to bake their bread. The tower became a popular destination for hikers prior to WW II and remains one to this day.

The winds of war blew across Schneeberg in the late 1930s as Nazi Germany prepared to annex the Czech lands of Bohemia and Moravia. The *Luftwaffe* built a wooden tower more than 100 feet high atop the mountain in 1938. The purpose of the tower was kept secret, but it no doubt served to monitor activity on the Czech side of the border. It was razed in 1942 for unexplained reasons, perhaps because it was no longer needed once the Czech lands had involuntarily become part of the Reich.

Immediately after the end of WW II in 1945, the U.S. Army Signal Corps established a monitoring post atop Schneeberg to track the troop movements and activities of our erstwhile Soviet allies. This signal reconnaissance team initially operated from the *Backöfele*.

And then came the Cold War. By the end of 1951, the signals intelligence (SIGINT) collection station on the mountaintop had become a permanent site operating around the clock. The U.S. forces requisitioned part of the summit, established a small base there, and began erecting various buildings as well as steel structures for antennas. A wooden frame building was built on the summit in 1952. It housed an operations area, troop billets, and a small kitchen/mess area. Two stone wings were added to the building a year or two later as the site expanded in scope and manning.

A small log cabin was erected sometime prior to the mid-1950s a few hundred yards downhill from the summit. Around 1959 or 1960, the "Cabin," was significantly enlarged with a long, concrete and brick extension containing several sleeping rooms which accommodated six to ten men each. The extension also included a modern latrine with toilets, urinals, sinks, and showers.

Most of the single troops stationed on Schneeberg were billeted there until the site closed years later. A small number (mainly equipment maintenance, communications center operators, and administrative troops) continued to be housed in a wing of the original wood and brick building at the summit which became known as "Topside." The other wing of the

4

Topside building initially contained the operations area, armory, and orderly room.

Three corrugated metal buildings were erected on Schneeberg in 1961. Each one measured approximately 25 by 60 feet. One was built within the compound on the summit, and two were set up near the Cabin. The operations area was transferred to the new steel hut on the summit. The one directly across the Cabin's parking lot became the detachment mess hall. The other was built opposite the mess hall and Cabin on the other side of the one-lane access road that led to Topside. It would become the Club, the watering hole for site personnel and the locus of many a poker game and foosball contest. Once operations had shifted to the new building on the summit, the old operations area in the Topside building became the "kino room" where films from the Army and Air Force Exchange Service (AAFES) movie circuit were shown by whoever knew how to run the 16mm projector.

In 1961 the West German armed forces (the *Bundeswehr*) took over the area to the north of the summit and adjoining the American presence. The joint *Bundeswehr-Luftwaffe* communication Sector (*Fernmeldesektor*) "E" became fully operational in 1967 and took up its surveillance role in a modern new reinforced concrete tower which could be seen from many miles away. The top of the mountain became a military out-of-bounds area and the *Backöfele* was now "behind the wire."   (*Preceding photos courtesy of Phil Ward's Schneebergvets.org*)

The single-lane access road that ran to the summit from Route 303 near the foot of the mountain was paved for the first time in 1965, thereby bringing to an end two decades of dust, mud and potholes and providing a more comfortable link to Bischofsgruen and the rest of the outside world. The new road was narrow, and the asphalt layer was thin. In later years, the road was improved and given a good layer of asphalt, probably to accommodate *Bundeswehr-Luftwaffe* comings and goings.

U.S. Army operations on Schneeberg were discontinued in the early 1970s, and the American site was closed. Plans called for the former U.S. compound to be turned over entirely to the German government. However, the Army Security Agency reportedly "rediscovered" Schneeberg in 1974 and decided to reactivate the site. SIGINT operations resumed on a permanent basis by October 1975. By then, the buildings had deteriorated from neglect. The Cabin had become uninhabitable because part of the roof had caved in. Assigned personnel had to live on the economy in Bischofsgruen, renting rooms or small apartments. By the end of the 1970s, new technology enabled most signal collection activity to be remotely forwarded to Field Station Augsburg, thus allowing for a substantial reduction in the number of personnel assigned to Schneeberg.

The wood and stone Topside structure was renovated in the late 1970s or early 1980s and a kitchen was added. U.S. Army authorities at Grafenwoehr oversaw the construction of a new gym and other structures at the site. The old Cabin, the Club, the former mess hall, and the old metal operations building were all torn down along with other dilapidated wooden structures.

Operations were gradually phased out as the Cold War concluded at the end of the 1980s and start of the 1990s. The last operations personnel were pulled off Schneeberg during Operation Desert Storm (1990-1991). Later, a small unit of engineers took up temporary residence and dismantled all structures previously used by the American forces except for the wood and stone building and a few antenna masts.

The *Bundeswehr* followed suit in 1994 and abandoned its massive tower. Schneeberg was totally deserted. The local county government (*Landkreis* Wunsiedel) finally succeeded in purchasing the real estate on the summit in 1996. Schneeberg again became accessible to the public. A few years later, the *Bergwacht* (mountain rescue service) built a cabin on the site of the 1960s-era Cabin and mess hall. The German tower still stands deserted, but the Americans' wood and stone building was removed in late 2003 or 2004. Despite the abandonment of the old site, some of the local citizens claim that on cold winter nights when the air is still, they can hear American music and raucous laughter coming from the top of Schneeberg.

Who were the Americans who lived and worked on Snow Mountain during the peak of operations in the 1960s?

Nearly all were members of the Army Security Agency. The United States Army Security Agency (ASA) was the Army's signals intelligence (SIGINT) and communications security (COMSEC) organization from 1945 to 1976. The Latin motto of the Army Security Agency was *Semper Vigiles* (Vigilant Always). ASA was the successor to Army Signal Corps intelligence operations dating back to World War I. It was under the operational control of the Director of the National Security Agency (NSA), located at Fort Meade, Maryland; but ASA had its own commander at ASA Headquarters at Arlington Hall Station in Virginia. During a wartime situation, planning called for most ASA units to come under the control of field commanders. For example, an ASA battalion would support a corps-level formation, and subordinate ASA companies would provide direct SIGINT support to army divisions. ASA ceased to exist as of 1 January 1977 when it merged with the Army's Military Intelligence component to create the Intelligence and Security Command (INSCOM).

The vast majority of ASA personnel were enlisted soldiers, non-commissioned officers (NCO), and warrant officers who were trained in military intelligence skills including: foreign languages; Morse code, voice and teleprinter intercept operations; intercept and analysis of radar and telemetry signals; cryptanalysis (i.e., codebreaking); communications analysis; intelligence reporting; radio direction-finding; and other skills such as electronic equipment repair, and communications center operations.

ASA field elements were tasked with monitoring and analyzing the military communications of the Soviet Union, the People's Republic of China, their allies and client states, and other nations around the world. The field stations gathered information that was often time-sensitive in its value. Depending on its importance and classification, SIGINT data was passed through intelligence channels within hours of intercept for the lowest-priority items and in as little as 10 minutes for the most critical information.

"The King has note of all that they intend by interception which they dream not of" (Shakespeare's *Henry V*, Act II, Scene 2)

ASA personnel were stationed at locations around the globe, wherever the United States had a military presence and sometimes where there was none. Although not officially acknowledged at the time, ASA had a significant presence in Vietnam beginning at least as early as 1961. Rather than serving under the ASA name, these elements were designated as radio research units. ASA personnel of the 3rd Radio Research Unit (RRU) were among the earliest U.S. military personnel in Vietnam; the 3rd RRU later grew to become the 509th Radio Research Group. The first ASA soldier to be a battlefield fatality of the Vietnam War was Specialist 4 James T. Davis from Livingston, Tennessee, who was killed on 22 December 1961, near the old French Garrison of Cau Xang. He had been assigned to the 3rd Radio Research Unit at Tan Son Nhut Airport near Saigon, along with 92 other ASA members.

A regular Army recruiter once told a potential ASA enlistee in mid-1964 that ASA was "an army within the Army." ASA had its own training facilities (most notably at Ft. Devens, Massachusetts), military police (MP) elements, communication centers, and chain of command. Nearly all ASA military occupational specialties (MOS) required a top-secret security clearance which necessitated an in-depth background investigation which was conducted by FBI agents or other federal investigative officers. The purpose of the investigations was to determine if the prospective ASA member had weaknesses or character flaws which would disqualify him from having access to "special compartmented information," that is, SIGINT. During the 1960s, the Army considered homosexuality and the use of illegal drugs as serious character weaknesses that would automatically bar a person from having the necessary security clearance.

Very few ASA members except for some clerks, MPs, cooks, and support personnel were draftees. Most ASA soldiers had at least a high school diploma and had very high scores on military aptitude and IQ tests. Many had a year or two of college, and some even had earned a baccalaureate degree prior to joining the Army.

Beginning in the mid-1960s, volunteers for ASA were required to sign a four-year enlistment contract rather than the normal three-year commitment signed by other volunteers or the two-year active duty commitment to which draftees were obligated. Many men considered the extra year's commitment a fair deal since they believed they would be avoiding service in a combat arm like the infantry and that they would have relatively easy duty. It was not unheard of during the Vietnam War for an Army recruiter to assure a potential ASA enlistee that there were no ASA units in Vietnam. This was technically true, but as many ASA men learned the hard way, the radio research units in Vietnam were in fact ASA.

Some ASA training, particularly language school, could result in significant college transfer credits, which was another enticement for many potential volunteers. ASA members liked to consider themselves the top 10% of Army enlistees, and some ASA linguists were known to brag that they were the top 10% of the top 10%. This did not always endear them to their comrades-in-arms, who referred to the linguists as Monterey Marys – a sobriquet referring to their having received language training at the Defense Language Institute (DLI) in Monterey, California. It also recognized that many of the linguists were far more bookish than they were athletic – and that a few even had some notably effeminate traits.

Operational (as opposed to administrative) elements of ASA field units usually worked rotating shifts, 24 hours a day, seven days a week, 365 days a year. ASA troops were not allowed to discuss their operations with outsiders. In fact, they could not talk among themselves about their duties unless they were in a secure location. Even today, decades after the fact, some of the missions still cannot be discussed. Owing to the sensitivity of the information with which they worked, ASA soldiers were subject to travel restrictions during and long after their time in service. ASA activities have only been partially declassified to this date. In fact, to ensure that it contains no classified information, the contents of this book had to be reviewed by the National Security Agency before it could be published.

During the 1960s, the primary ASA command in Europe was the 507th USASA Group headquartered in the I.G. Farben Building in Frankfurt. It had three subordinate battalions (bn): the 318th USASA Bn at Herzogenaurach (Herzo Base) near Nuremberg, the 319th USASA Bn at Rothwesten near the city of Kassel, and the 320th USASA Bn at Bad Aibling in southern Bavaria. The 319th Bn had several small detachments or "outstations" along the West German border with East Germany. The 318th Bn had a few outstations along both the East German and Czechoslovak borders. Detachment J at Schneeberg was one of them. Another was Det K, a summer-only site at Hohenbogen, a mountain near the village of Rimbach in the Bavarian Forest, a few miles west of the

Czechoslovak border. (Det K became a year-round site following the August 1968 invasion of Czechoslovakia by the Soviet Union and its Warsaw Pact allies.) Herzo Base was re-designated the 16th USASA Field Station in the mid- to late 1960s as part of a reorganization of ASA facilities and units in Europe.

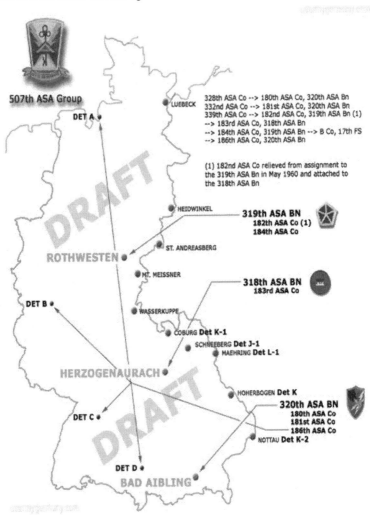

328th ASA Co --> 180th ASA Co, 320th ASA Bn
332nd ASA Co --> 181st ASA Co, 320th ASA Bn
339th ASA Co --> 182nd ASA Co, 319th ASA Bn (1)
--> 183rd ASA Co, 318th ASA Bn
--> 184th ASA Co, 319th ASA Bn --> B Co, 17th FS
--> 186th ASA Co, 320th ASA Bn

(1) 182nd ASA Co relieved from assignment to the 319th ASA Bn in May 1960 and attached to the 318th ASA Bn

319th ASA BN
182th ASA Co (1)
184th ASA Co

318th ASA BN
183rd ASA Co

320th ASA BN
180th ASA Co
181st ASA Co
186th ASA Co

Note: The unclassified map above shows the location of various ASA units in Germany during the early 1960s. It and links to other historical

12

information on the ASA in Europe can be found on the following website:
https://www.usarmygermany.com/Sont.htm?https&&&www.usarmygerm
any.com/Units/ASA%20Europe/USAREUR_ASAE.htm

The sites at Coburg, Schneeberg, Maehring, Hohenbogen, and Nottau were subordinate to the 318th ASA Bn at Herzo Base. Coburg, Maehring, and Nottau closed around 1964. Det A is shown on the map as somewhere in the Bremerhaven area. However, other sources put Det A at Goeppingen near Stuttgart and identify it as supporting the 4th Armored Division in the mid-1960s. Det B was at Wurzburg and supported the 3rd Infantry Division.

The sites at Luebeck, Wasserkuppe, Mt. Meissner, Heidwinkel/Bahrdorf, and Wobeck (south of Heidwinkel but not shown on the preceding map) were subordinate to the 319th ASA Bn at Rothwesten during the early to mid-1960s.

Assignment to a border site was considered hardship duty by many career ASA soldiers, particularly married personnel, senior NCOs, and officers. The border detachments were small – usually 50 to 100 men. The commander was normally a 1st lieutenant or a junior captain who was unmarried and probably not intending to make the Army his career. There was relatively little for the commander to do other than supervise the administration of the detachment. Most detachment commanders had little interest in or knowledge of the detachment's SIGINT operations. These were normally the responsibility of a warrant officer or senior NCO who served as the site operations officer or operations NCO in-charge (NCOIC). Another senior NCO served as detachment first sergeant or NCOIC; he would often be assisted by an admin sergeant and a detachment clerk. If the detachment had a mess hall, a relatively senior NCO would usually be mess sergeant and have a few subordinate cooks. Detachment security was the responsibility of a handful of ASA MPs and sometimes local unarmed civilian guards. The rest of the detachment personnel were either directly involved in SIGINT collection and analysis or they supported those functions with equipment maintenance or by providing 24/7 communications with higher headquarters and with NSA.

Unlike most career NCOs, many first-term ASA linguists and technicians considered an outstation assignment highly desirable duty.

Discipline and strict adherence to military dress and grooming codes were generally far more relaxed at border sites. Outstation personnel were tightly knit groups, with the primary group being the "trick" or shift to which one was assigned. Each site would have four tricks working rotating shifts, usually six days on duty and two days off. The trick chief was often a specialist 5th class (SP5), an experienced E-5 who might be designated an acting buck sergeant and who was nearing the end of his enlistment. Sometimes a trick chief might be a staff sergeant (E-6) on his second or third enlistment.

As mentioned earlier, Detachment J was located on top of Schneeberg at an altitude of more than 3,400 feet (1,051 meters) above sea level. The entire mountain was covered in a thick pine forest, except for Det J and the adjacent German military SIGINT site at the summit. A handful of German military personnel shared the Cabin with the Americans, but there was little interaction between the two groups. Most of the German troops lived in a small casern in Wunsiedel and traveled by military bus to and from their SIGINT tower on the mountain.

The town of Bischofsgruen (population 1,900) occupies a valley between Schneeberg and nearby Ochsenkopf (elev. 1,024 meters), site of ski trails and jumps as well as a major radio and television broadcast tower serving the surrounding region. The men of Det J referred to the town as Bisch and to the young ladies of the town as Bisch bunnies. Relations between Det J personnel and the people of Bischofsgruen were good, unlike German-American relations in some towns or cities near major American military bases serving combat units, such as infantry, armor, artillery, and armored cavalry.

Many ASA soldiers derisively referred to the combat units as "animal outfits" and avoided contact with them as much as possible. Several Schneeberg men had been trained as German linguists at Monterey and could converse easily with the townspeople. Many others learned at least rudimentary German on their own and made a genuine effort to speak German with the locals, an effort that was appreciated by the people of Bisch.

The nearest U.S. military installation to Schneeberg was an armored cavalry squadron (battalion) base, Christianson Barracks, near the village of Bindlach, approximately 15 miles from Bisch. A small artillery unit was located a little further away in the city of Bayreuth, home of the annual Richard Wagner opera festival. Schneebergers went to Bindlach for medical care and to use its small post exchange (PX) or attend chapel services. A few married Det J NCOs resided in U.S. military family housing at Christianson Barracks or in Bayreuth. The U.S. Air Force Security Service (ASA's USAF counterpart) maintained a modest year-round SIGINT facility 30 miles to the north on the outskirts of the city of Hof, not far from where the borders of East Germany, West Germany, and Czechoslovakia met. Other than those installations, there were very few American soldiers or airmen within a 30-mile radius of Schneeberg.

The chapters that follow tell tales of the men who were stationed on Schneeberg in the mid-1960s – the Snow Mountain misfits. (Women did not become an integral part of ASA until the mid-1970s, so there were no female soldiers assigned to Schneeberg or other outstations in the 1960s.) Some of the stories here have been embellished a bit. A few may (or may not) be total fiction or may be based on anecdotes from earlier years or from other outstations. The names of most of our characters have been changed for the sake of privacy, but many of the nicknames represent real Schneeberg vets. The author is proud to be one of them and to have served alongside them. He would like to express his deep appreciation to Phillip Ward, his language school classmate and fellow Schneeberger, who founded and managed the Schneebergvets.org internet group and who assembled and administered an enormous amount of photos and other material which provided significant inspiration and assistance in writing this book and which have kept the memories alive over the years. Finally, a special salute to all the Snow Mountain misfits who have gone on to their final rest. Whenever and wherever we may meet now or in the future, we will raise a glass and drink, "To fond memories and absent comrades. Prost."

Sources
Rainer H. Schmeisser: *Der Schneeberg*, Beiträge zur Geschichts- und Landeskunde des Fichtelgebirges Nr. 1, Regensburg 1979

Dietmar Herrmann: *Lexikon Fichtelgebirge*, Ackermann Verlag Hof/Saale

Rudolf Thiem: *Der Schneeberg - höchster Berg des Fichtelgebirges'* (*Heft 13/2006 der Schriftenreihe Das Fichtelgebirge*) ISBN 3-926621-47-8

External links

http://www.bayern.fichtelgeberge.de/schneeberg/index.html

Information about the Luftwaffe's former communication sector tower at http://www lostplaces.de

Some chronology was provided by Ed Railsback in December 1999 on the Schneebergvets.org website.

https://en.wikipedia.org/wiki/United_States_Army_Security_Agency

https://www.usarmygermany.com/Sont.htm?https&&&www.usarmygermany.com/Units/ASA%20Europe/USAREUR_ASAE.htm

****

(Author's Note: Comments, questions, or constructive criticism may be sent to the author at: Jerry@snowmountainmisfits.com)

THE ADVENTURE BEGINS

The early spring sun reflected brightly off the painted white brickwork framing the main gate to Herzo Base. The MP on duty was busy checking an incoming vehicle and barely glanced at Jack Rutherford and me as we exited the post. Nearly all our earthly belongings were jammed into the trunk and backseat of my black 1951 Mercedes-Benz four-door sedan. I bought it several weeks earlier from a used car lot near the main post exchange in Fuerth. We were glad to be leaving Herzo Base and excited to be heading to Detachment J, 318th USASA Bn, the border site at Schneeberg.

As we headed toward the autobahn near Erlangen, we passed the large Adidas shoe factory on the hillside outside the town of Herzogenaurach. Once on the autobahn, we had to head toward Nuremberg first and then turn north on the autobahn that eventually leads to Leipsig and Berlin. We knew that we would be exiting 20 miles before the highway crossed into East Germany just north of Hof where some of our Air Force Security Service friends from language school were stationed.

The four-lane highway reminded me of the parkways near my home on Long Island. It occurred to me that Hitler was building the autobahns around the same time that FDR's Works Progress Administration was constructing the network of parkways around New York City. The 15-year old Mercedes rode smoothly on the autobahn and negotiated the hills easily as we passed heavy trucks and aging Volkswagens that struggled up the hills in lower gears. It wasn't a luxury car by any means, just a simple sedan based on a pre-WW II design and powered by a 4-cylinder gasoline engine coupled to a 4-speed manual transmission.

A little over an hour after we left Herzo, we passed the exit for Bayreuth and then turned off the autobahn onto eastbound Route 303 at the Bad Berneck exit. Once past Bad Berneck, the road was lined with pine forests and hilly embankments. We soon saw a sign pointing to a road leading into the village of Bischofsgruen. We knew we were getting close to the unmarked turnoff that would lead to our new home. Jack saw a road sign indicating a left turn ahead for a hospital. That was the landmark for our turn as well.

We turned from the well-paved and well-traveled Route 303 onto a narrow road that had seen better days. It had apparently been paved at one time, but the work must have been done cheaply because nearly all the asphalt had decayed into ruts and debris leaving little but the macadam base. The hospital was on the right, a few hundred yards uphill from Route 303, and was surrounded by a six-foot high cream-colored stone wall. It did not bear much resemblance to hospitals that we had seen stateside or even down in Nuremberg. There must have been a parking lot, but it was out of sight somewhere behind the walls. The only entry we could see looked a bit like a gate house for a castle with an adjacent vehicle entrance and one-story building. We learned later that this *krankenhaus* was not a conventional hospital. It specialized in physical rehabilitation and served patients needing psychological or psychiatric treatment. Had we known that at the time, we might have considered it an appropriate omen of what Detachment J would be like.

The road improved markedly a half mile uphill from the hospital entrance where it became a smooth, one-lane asphalt road with narrow gravel shoulders and drainage ditches on both sides. A large metal sign was mounted on a 4x4 post warning that we were entering a military restricted area and that only authorized personnel were to proceed. The sign was printed in German, English, and Russian.

Seemingly impenetrable pine forests lined each side of the road as we cautiously drove up the mountain. The forest shone a brilliant green in the midday April sun. There was no sign of habitation for another mile or two until we saw a pair of almost identical gray corrugated metal buildings on either side of the road. There was a parking lot on the right separating one of the metal buildings from what looked like a log cabin that had been modified by the addition of a long one-story addition that stretched back toward the end of the parking lot some 60 or 80 feet beyond the log-sided part of the structure. A young man our age wearing fatigues was working on the engine of his VW Beetle at the near edge of the parking lot.

Jack rolled down the window of the Mercedes and called out, "Hey, where's the orderly room? "

The guy seemed startled by our presence, but after a quick glance he gestured up a steep incline in the road and said, "Just keep going straight up the hill and stop at the guard shack. The MP there will show you where to park Topside."

The guard shack was only about 200 yards from the parking lot. The gate to the compound was open, and we could see the 8-foot barbed wire-topped fence that extended on both sides of the gate. We stopped and waited as the MP sidled up to the car. Jack had his window open. The MP was wearing wrinkled fatigues with SP4 insignia on his right sleeve. A black and white MP brassard was on his left shoulder, and there was a .45 automatic in a patent leather holster hanging from the olive drab web belt around his ample waist. He wore a simple baseball-style fatigue cap on his head instead of the fancy white helmet liners that MPs at Herzo wore.

He looked at us quizzically, "What's up? Who are you and what do you want?"

Jack responded before I could, "We're Specialists Rutherford and Daniels reporting in. We've been sent up from Herzo Base as replacements."

"Right. Park next to that stone building. The orderly room is on the far side of the building. Welcome aboard."

I thought it was odd that he didn't ask to see our IDs or our orders, but what the heck....

We signed in at the orderly room and had a very brief introduction to the detachment NCOIC, Master Sergeant (MSG) Oliver Henry. Sergeant Henry certainly wasn't an old man, but he seemed old to our 20-year old eyes. He was probably in his early 40s. He didn't get up from behind his desk to greet us, but I could tell that he was a big man in stature and in girth. I guessed that he was probably just a tad over 6 feet tall. He had a ruddy complexion, a full face, blue eyes, and short light hair worn in a "high and tight" crew cut complete with stand-up waxed forelock.

The blue and green three-up and three-down chevrons on the sleeves of his starched fatigues showed that he earned his MSG stripes before 1958 when the Army added two new pay grades for enlisted personnel – E-8 and E-9. Sergeant Henry was a MSG E-7 and was allowed to wear the old olive-drab-on-dark-blue stripes that differentiated him from a post-1958 promotee to MSG E-8. His face was clean-shaven and had a one-inch scar over his left eye and a similar mark to the left of his double chin. He had an unlit stub of a cigar clenched in his teeth.

An embroidered cloth replica of the Combat Infantryman's Badge above the left chest pocket of his fatigues indicated that he had served in active combat as a member of an infantry unit. I assumed that meant that he served in the 1950-1953 Korean War. He was apparently the real deal. The real Army. I couldn't help wondering what he was doing in ASA, but I knew enough from his gruff exterior that now was not the time to ask.

The detachment clerk-typist, PFC Anson, took us to the supply room and issued each of us two sheets, a pillow and pillowcase, and two olive drab wool blankets. Anson was skinny and blond with a boney face and more than a few zits scattered across his young-looking, nearly whiskerless face. His blue eyes tended to dart about a bit and to avoid eye contact with Jack and me. His hair was a longish crew cut that might have been a flat-top once upon a time. He was quiet and seemed like a good person who wanted to be helpful. Maybe he was just a bit shy.

He rode with us down the hill past the MP hut and the perimeter fence and on to the Cabin, our new barracks home. I parked my car in an empty spot and asked Anson, "What's the story with Sergeant Henry? What's he like? I've gotta say that he reminds me a little bit of Sarge in the Beetle Bailey cartoon strips."

"Oh, he's not so bad," Anson replied with a chuckle. "His bark is worse than his bite. He doesn't say too much most of the time, but when he does say something, you'd better listen. A lot of the guys call him Jolly Ollie behind his back, but he ain't too jolly when he's on duty. Never call him that if you know what's good for you. He likes being called Top – as in First Sergeant. Basically, that's what he is. Detachment First Shirt.

"He's in the Club most nights playing cards. You'll get to know him well enough if you hang out in there. He almost never goes down to Bisch or anywhere else as far as I've seen."

Anson led us into the Cabin and down a long corridor flanked by a row of windows on the right-hand side and several doors on the left, including an open door to the latrine and shower area. He opened one of the doors near the far end of the hallway and led us into a room with eight sets of bunks and lockers. The mattresses on two of the bunks were stockaded, indicating that they were unassigned at the moment. He told us that the bunks had belonged to guys who had left the day before, heading back to battalion headquarters at Herzo Base and eventually back to the States for their discharge from the Army. There was no one else in the room, and all the other bunks had been neatly made. Each had a row of combat boots and other footwear lined up beneath it.

Jack asked Anson, "Where are the people who bunk in this room?"

"They're working the day shift in Operations. They'll get off duty in a couple of hours when the shifts change at 1600 hours. Until then, get settled in here. The empty wall lockers by the vacant bunks are yours. You know how to set it up – uniforms to the right and civilian clothes to the left. Put your foot lockers at the end of your bunks and stow your field gear on top of your wall locker. But don't get too comfortable. You'll probably have to move to another room within the next few days, depending on your trick assignment. If Father Pat is around, he'll probably want to give you his traditional new guy orientation speech."

"Who's Father Pat? Does the detachment have its own chaplain? It seems too small for that," I asked.

Anson just smiled and said, "No, Father Pat ain't no chaplain. Not even close, but once upon a time he was in a seminary studying to be a Catholic priest. He's a Spec 6 and one of the senior linguists in Ops. He's a Czech linguist like you guys. Spec 6 Pat Riley. Do either of you know him?"

"Sorta. But not really," I replied. "There was a Spec 5 Riley a few months ahead of us in Czech language school in Monterey, but I didn't know him. I always tried to avoid anyone with more than one stripe back then, even Spec 5s who aren't really NCOs. I remember that Riley drove a two-tone '60 or '61 Olds two-door hardtop with a stick shift on the column. It was hot. He graduated from Monterey at least a year ago, so it's probably the same guy with an extra stripe now."

"That's him! He still has the Oldsmobile. I think it's parked up Topside by the Ops building now. Anyway, welcome to Det J. I'll see you guys later in the mess hall or in the Club."

"Right. Thanks, Anson. Seeya," Jack called out as Anson closed the door to the squad room behind him.

Jack and I lugged our heavy foot lockers from my car. We positioned them at the foot of our newly assigned bunks and checked the contents to make sure everything was arranged according to regulations. The beds were standard-issue metal army cots, olive drab in color. The gray striped mattresses had been folded stockade-style in an "S" shape at the head of the beds. There wasn't much to them. Just like the mattresses we had in basic training and in Monterey. They may have been two or three inches thick, but they were nothing like the thick mattresses that we knew our language school classmates from the Air Force had been issued at Hof Air Station 20 miles up the autobahn. Nevertheless, this was our new home and probably would be for the next couple years. It sure beat the crowded barracks at Herzo Base.

We made up our bunks and had to strain to put the duffel bags containing our field gear on top of our wall lockers. They contained most of the equipment we would need if the balloon went up and we had to deploy to a regular army division in the combat support role for which we had received virtually no training. I couldn't remember everything that was in my duffel bag. I recalled the heavy rubber "Mickey Mouse" boots designed to protect our feet from mud, muck, and Arctic cold. There was a sleeping bag, a shelter half which would mate with someone else's shelter half to form a two-man tent, woolen pants and shirts, long johns, and other sundry items we prayed we would never need. We each put our combat pack on top our wall locker along with our gas mask, entrenching tool, mess kit, canteen, and steel helmet. We would soon be assigned M-14 rifles which were locked in the detachment armory adjacent to the orderly room.

We had just finished making up our bunks when a someone a few years older than us opened the door and walked into the room. Jack took a look at him and called out, "At ease!" Something we were trained to do in basic when an NCO entered our area. He was wearing rumpled fatigues with bloused combat boots like we were, but his had obviously not been shined recently. He had the cloth rank insignia of a Spec 6 on his sleeves. Jack and I were both Spec 4s and still a bit wary of anyone with more stripes.

"Geezy Peezy! What the hell was that for?!" responded the SP6. "I'm not an NCO; I'm a Specialist 6th Class! That may be the equivalent paygrade of a Staff Sergeant E-6, but it doesn't mean shit out here on the Hill. Don't ever call 'At Ease' for me or anyone else out here. We don't do that. This is a border site. An outstation. We do things differently here. You'll figure that out soon enough."

The SP6 was a tad shorter than average, maybe 5'7" and had thick, wavy dark hair and deep blue eyes framed by laugh wrinkles despite his being only in his mid-20s. His eyes sparkled with a hint of Irish mischief and inner joy. He had a naturally relaxed and friendly air about him that made us feel comfortable in his presence.

"I'm Pat Riley. Some people call me Father Pat, but I prefer plain old Pat. I think I remember you both from language school. How're your Czech skills?"

I didn't want to b.s. him, so I was honest. "I think mine are average, Pat. I'd never pass as a native, but I can understand a lot of what I hear. I was in an aural comprehension course that didn't stress being able to speak the language. By the way, my name is Jerry Daniels. This is Jack Rutherford. He and I were at Monterey together and then for training at Fort Meade, and finally at Herzo."

"Uh huh. What about you, Jack? How is your Czech?"

"Ummm…well, it's a little weak, to be honest, but not too bad."

Pat paused thoughtfully for a moment and then said, "Okay. We'll find out about that tomorrow or later in the week in Ops." He looked at our lockers and bunks and continued, "Right. It looks like you two are pretty well squared away already. I want you to come across the parking lot with me now and we'll have a cup of coffee in the mess hall while I give you a little history lesson about the Hill."

The breeze was noticeably chilly as we stepped outside, even though it was late April. We crossed over from the Cabin to the mess hall, a one-story corrugated steel building measuring around 25 by 60 feet. Pat led us into a small vestibule and then through a door into the mess hall itself. There were 12 to 15 tables, each with four wooden chairs with plastic covers on the chair backs which matched the plastic tablecloths on each table. Napkin dispensers, a sugar bowl, salt and pepper shakers, hot sauce bottles, and mustard and ketchup containers graced each table. Pop-out, metal-framed windows lined each side of the building. The kitchen and stainless-steel serving area took up the back third of the building. There were a couple of cooks and three German-looking helpers working in the kitchen preparing whatever was on the menu for the evening meal. It didn't smell bad at all.

A stack of metal mess hall trays and steel cylinders full of utensils were to the left, where the serving line began. Racks of cups and large coffee and hot water urns were to the right of the serving area next to a milk fridge that offered a choice of white or chocolate milk. Bins of plastic drinking glasses were stacked next to the milk dispenser. There was a small alcove in the back of the mess hall near the entrance door which contained a desk, office chair, a file cabinet, and a typewriter. A small sign on the desk read SFC Rayburn, Mess Sergeant.

Father Pat grabbed a cup of black coffee and told us to do the same. Both Jack and I poured two-thirds of a cup of coffee into our brown plastic mugs and added some milk. We had to backtrack a bit to get spoons so we could stir the sugar we added to our coffee. We joined Pat at a table near Rayburn's tiny office cubicle.

Pat looked at us for a minute or two and began to speak very earnestly, almost as though he were a professor addressing his students. "There are two important things that you guys have to remember out here. First, you are guests in this country, and you represent our country to the people of this area. Yes, we won World War II, but that war ended more than 20 years ago. West Germany is our NATO ally now. You will see German Army and *Luftwaffe* troops on this mountain. In fact, there are *Luftwaffe* members billeted in rooms at the front of the Cabin. You'll be sharing the latrine and showers with them. Other than having some of them in the Cabin, we don't have much contact with them, but you have to remember that they are our partners and should be treated with respect.

"The ASA people here on the Hill now are just the latest in a long line of sentinels posted here over the past few hundred years. The first were sent here more than 500 years ago.

"Schneeberg can sometimes get a little nasty weather-wise, as you will certainly learn from first-hand experience in the months ahead. You're lucky to be here in April. The last of this past winter's snow finally melted a week or two ago. We have a great line-of-sight to the east toward Czechoslovakia. It's less than 20 miles from here to the Czech border. That means that we can easily intercept Czech military radio communications. And that's why you're here."

Father Pat paused, sipped from his coffee cup, took a breath, and continued, "ASA has been up here since the end of World War II. The German Armed Forces, the *Bundeswehr,* set up shop here a few years ago. The *Bundeswehr* and *Luftwaffe* are almost finished building that huge new concrete tower that looms over Topside. Most of this mountain is a restricted military area. You probably noticed the signs far down on the access road. So here we are. Detachment J of the 318th U.S. Army Security Agency Battalion. Any questions so far?"

It took a minute or two for us to digest all this information. We knew a lot of it already, except for the history of Schneeberg. Jack broke the awkward silence. "When do we go to work? Back at Herzo we did a little HF radio monitoring and some basic transcription of taped intercept, but we spent more time working in the motor pool and doing other donkey work than we spent in Operations."

"I'll show you around Ops tomorrow morning, and then we'll see what trick you'll each be assigned to. We lost two Czech ops earlier this week, so I know that two of the tricks are a man short. You'll be fine. Everyone knows that you're weeds, so no one is expecting you to hit the ground running."

Jack groaned a little, "Ah crap, I hoped we had finished being weeds when we left Herzo. Everywhere you go they call new guys something different. I've heard them called newbies, nugs, jeeps, and worse. Why the heck do they call new guys weeds?"

Pat laughed, "To be honest, I'm not sure, Jack. I don't know if anyone knows for sure. The folklore has it that new guys are called weeds because up until very recently everyone who deployed to Germany came by troop ship. That's how I came over a year ago. Anyway, the new guys got off the ship and reported to their new duty assignment so soon after arrival that some said they still had seaweed on their boots. It is what it is, guys. You will be weeds for a couple months until someone newer is assigned to your trick."

I had a question too, "What's the C.O. like, Pat? We met Sergeant Henry briefly, and Anson gave us the skinny on him. But the C.O. wasn't in his office. All we know is that his name is Captain Medved."

Pat didn't hesitate, "The Det commander is a good officer. He's a former enlisted man who got his commission from artillery officers candidate school. He's not an ASA officer – I mean he's not in the Army Intelligence and Security or Military Intelligence officer branch, but he is assigned to ASA. He served two tours with an arty unit in Vietnam and as an advisor to ARVN, South Vietnamese, troops. I don't know how or why he got assigned to ASA, but I think we're lucky to have him. He doesn't

26

go into Ops at all and generally leaves us alone, allowing Jolly Ollie to run the detachment. We haven't had any inspections since I've been here and no PT, motor stables, or any of the chicken shit details you probably pulled at Herzo. If you do your job and don't cause any problems, CPT Medved and Ollie will leave you on a long leash."

"Great! It sounds almost too good to be true, but that's why we asked for outstation duty."

Pat finished his coffee and told us to finish unpacking our stuff and then take it easy until chow time. Jack and I went back to the Cabin to work on our lockers and lay low for the rest of the day Maybe we'd meet some of our new co-workers and then see what awaited us in the morning.

****

A TOUR OF OPS

After breakfast in the mess hall the next morning, Jack and I trudged up the steep asphalt road leading from the Cabin, mess hall, and the Club to the gated compound where Topside, Operations, and some auxiliary buildings were located. It was only 200 yards, but the slope made it seem much longer. We passed through the gate, nodding to the MP and German guard who were on duty. No identity badge was necessary. We were wearing fatigues and were clearly part of the detachment team. Just inside the gate on the left-hand side of the road and opposite the guard shack was the fuel dump. It consisted of several large above-ground tanks containing gasoline and diesel fuel for use in Army vehicles and privately owned cars belonging to detachment personnel. If you owned a car like I did, you could buy a monthly ration of gas coupons issued through the Quartermaster Corps and use those coupons to get gas at military installations. You could also buy discounted gas coupons that were redeemable at German-run ESSO stations. Buying gas on the economy like Germans did was much more expensive.

The inner compound road circled the main Topside building housing the orderly room, communications center, and other facilities. We were told to bear left and go to the door to Operations, a mobile home sized, corrugated metal building resembling the mess hall but with the windows boarded over from the inside. A loudspeaker outside was blaring out the static-laden broadcast of the Armed Forces Radio Network (AFN). We knew from our time at Herzo Base that this was "cover music." Basically, it was just noise intended to keep anyone outside the compound from using a listening device to pick up sensitive, ops-related conversations that might disclose our mission's successes or failures. Schneeberg was far from the AFN transmitters in Nuremberg and Berlin, so the reception on the mountain was poor and often blocked by static.

The entrance to the Ops building was on the extreme left side of the structure. The door was always secured with a cipher lock. Only authorized (i.e., cleared) personnel could enter. We pushed the buzzer on the cipher lock and waited for someone to open the door. A bespectacled SP4 in wrinkled fatigues soon opened the door.

"Whadaya want?" he barked.

"Spec 6 Riley told us to report here at 0800. We signed in yesterday, and…."

"Father Pat! Hey, Father Pat! You got two weeds waiting for you at the door. Come and get 'em."

Pat Riley was at the door a few seconds later and told us to come in. We had been in the ops areas at Herzo Base, so we were not in awe of entering a restricted area. We were curious, of course, but it was not a big deal at this point after having spent a few months in training at NSA and a couple months at Herzo.

We entered a 6 foot by 3-foot foyer area with a concrete floor and corrugated steel interior walls. There didn't seem to be any insulation, at least there in the foyer. To the left of the foyer was an 8 x 12 hut, the kind that was usually mounted on the back of a deuce-and-a half-truck. We poked our heads in as Father Pat began his tour guide spiel.

"This is the TR hut. It's where the transcribers do their work. It's my office too since I supervise the Czech transcribers. The operators, which is what you will be, man the receivers, record the intercepted voice, and try to write a hand gist of what they hear. The TRs transcribe it on 6-ply paper which is sent back to Herzo Base via courier along with the tapes. Copies of the scripts go to NSA too. As you can see, there are several AN/TNH-11 reel-to-reel tape recorders and a few MILs. You know what MILs are, right?" He didn't wait for a reply. "They are standard manual typewriters, but they only type in upper case letters. The ones used by the Russian linguists also type in the Cyrillic alphabet"

There was room for two or three TRs to work in the hut among the recorders and MILs. Only one guy wearing earmuff-style earphones was transcribing from a tape when we peeked in, and he didn't look up from his MIL to greet us. Turning right, we entered the main Ops spaces, and Father Pat resumed his guided tour narrative.

"Here on the left you can see three VHF intercept positions. One of the earphone-wearing operators manning that center position is a Czech linguist like you." He pointed at a SP4 and a SP5 who were working the positions. "The Spec 5's pos is for Czech targets, and the other one is for East German. The third is in reserve in case things get busy. You guys will be sitting one of those positions to start out with. You're lucky; we just replaced the old R-220 receivers with new GLR-9s. The GLaRe-9s are nice because they have a scope where you can see signals popping up and down. The R-220s didn't have a scope, and that made it harder to search for signals. You'll record the voice from the signals you intercept on the reel-to-reel tape recorders on each position. Your trick chief or one of the more senior ops will train you." As we moved on, I could hear one of the ops snicker and let out a sneering stage whisper, "Weeds!"

Pat continued as if he hadn't heard the taunt. "Over there on the right you can see two mirror-image UHF multichannel positions. Only one, the one on the left, is used on a daily basis. Each one has a bank of recorders and demultiplexers so you can break out individual channels from any 4-, 8-, or 12-channel system used by the Czechs. The toggle switches activate the individual recorders which are paired with the receiver and demuxers. A rotating dial allows the op to listen to the inputs from the receiver and the different demuxers. It's pretty damned complicated to run, and it's extremely challenging from a linguistic standpoint to understand what our potential adversaries are saying because you never know what they will be talking about. But don't worry, you guys won't be running the UHF position for at least 6 months, if ever. You gotta be good to handle it."

I knew right then that I wanted to run the UHF position and be good at it. Father Pat moved on a few feet and pointed out a kerosene heater which he said was the only heat in Ops. "It gets godawful cold in here during the winter. The heater is not powerful enough to warm the entire building, so plan on wearing long johns, a sweatshirt, and your parka at work when winter comes. By the way, our detachment dog Shadow stakes out the spot right in front of the heater on winter nights. You better pray that you're upwind of him when he farts – which is often." Pat laughed, and we laughed along with him, not realizing then the truth of his warning.

Heading a bit further into the Ops building, Pat pointed at a large waist high counter that was at least 4 feet wide and almost as deep. It was made of plywood and had rolls of brown wrapping paper mounted over it and big rolls of sealing tape on the counter. "This is where you will pack up tapes and other classified material for the twice-weekly courier runs to Herzo Base. Your trick chief will show you how to wrap the packages securely and according to regs. It's gotta be done right. Or else!"

He showed us a couple more intercept positions on the left that looked just like the Czech and East German positions we had passed moments earlier. "These two VHF positions target Soviet ground forces communications and are manned by Russian linguists. They generally don't have a lot to do since the Russians are in East Germany and Poland, pretty far from our site."

31

He pointed out a mass of cables connected to a large panel in the far-left corner of the building. "These are for the antennas connected to the VHF positions. The antennas are outside, of course. Once you learn your jobs, you'll be able to experiment with different VHF antenna inputs to get the optimum possible signal strength. And you'll love it in the winter when the antennas ice up and you have to go out, climb up onto the mounts, and knock the ice off them," he laughed a bit when he said that. "The UHF antennas are controlled right from the UHF position. Since UHF signals are highly directional, the op has to rotate the antenna until he gets the strongest possible signal."

He turned to the right and pointed to a closed door in the far-right corner of the building. "This is the office for the Ops OIC and the Ops NCOIC. We don't have an Ops OIC right now, but we think they'll be sending us a warrant officer soon to fill that slot. The Ops NCOIC is Sergeant First Class (SFC) Karney, with a K. Karney spends most of his time in the orderly room b.s.ing with Jolly Ollie and brown-nosing with CPT Medved.

"OK, you two. That concludes our tour of Ops. If you have any questions, you can save them for your trick chief. Rutherford, you're assigned to Baker Trick. They're working mids now, and you'll join them at midnight tonight. Try to get a few hours' sleep during the day today and then report to Ops at 2345 hours for trick change. Your trick chief is Staff Sergeant (SSG) Jim Hall. He's a Russian linguist. He'll put you to work with an experienced Czech op."

"What about me, Pat? What trick will I be on?" I asked.

"I didn't forget you, Jerry. You'll be on Dog Trick. They start a set of mids tomorrow night when Baker Trick goes on break. Acting Sergeant Will Morrow will be your trick chief. He's a Russian linguist too. You'll find him after dinner tonight playing poker in the club. You can't miss him. He's tall, skinny, has thick black plastic-rimmed glasses, and chain smokes Pall Malls."

"What should we do now?" Rutherford asked.

"You're on your own until your shift starts – midnight for you, Rutherford, and tomorrow midnight for you, Daniels. But first, check in with Anson in the orderly room. Tell him that I've assigned you to Baker and Dog Tricks and see if he can billet you in the rooms where your tricks sleep."

We walked across the road to the main Topside building and the orderly room. Anson was at his typewriter and kinda grunted when he looked up and saw us. "What's up?"

"Spec 6 Riley told us to check in with you and see if there are bunks available in the Baker Trick and Dog Trick rooms," Rutherford replied.

"Yeah, I think I can get you set up. Sit tight for a few minutes. I'll see if the C.O. wants to meet you. You already met Sergeant Henry. You can wait in the kino room." He pointed off to his left, past the arms room to an open room with easy chairs and some bookshelves.

We walked out of the orderly room and into what Anson called the kino room. We knew that *kino* was the word Germans used for movie theater. There were 12 to 15 vinyl-cushioned chairs in the room, most oriented in one direction. Sure enough, the kino room had a movie screen along the wall it shared with the arms room. At the opposite end of the room was a 16mm movie projector. The bookshelves lining one wall held mostly paperback books – a lot of mysteries and action stuff like Matt Helm and James Bond, as well as miscellaneous novels and non-fiction. There was a hand-lettered sign on one shelf that read Take One, Leave One. "This must be the det library," I thought to myself.

We had just begun looking at the book titles when someone entered the room. We looked up and were surprised to see SSG Gray, who had been the admin NCOIC at HQ Company at Herzo when we originally signed in a few months earlier.

"Hey, Sergeant Gray. How's it goin'? Good to see you. Are you permanent party here now?" I asked.

"Call me Rob, as long as Ollie or the C.O. isn't around. OK? Yeah, I just got in here a couple days ago. I'm the det admin NCO. My desk is in there with Anson and Ollie. I wish I could say that I'm happy to be here, but it really wasn't my choice. It's okay though. I'm here. Anyway, it's good to see you guys. You'll have to remind me about your names though." Rob spoke softly and carefully.

33

"I'm Jerry Daniels, and this is Jack Rutherford, Rob. We're both Czech linguists and will be working tricks here. We're waiting to see if the C.O. wants to meet us. We already met Sergeant Henry."

Rob shook our hands. He had a good handshake, but I noticed his hands were very soft. That's a crazy thing to notice in another guy, but that's what I noticed.

"Master Sergeant Henry is essentially the same as a company first sergeant. He likes to be called Top, just like a first shirt. He's old school Army in a lot of ways – not career ASA. I don't know how he wound up here, and I'm not sure he does either. He's getting close to retirement and almost never leaves the Hill. He's got his own room up here Topside in the other wing where Anson, Sergeant Dean Peece the comms center NCOIC, and I bunk. The electronic maintenance and comms center people are billeted up here too. MPs as well. I think Ollie has a wife back in the States, but he doesn't talk about her. He doesn't have a car either, but he'll occasionally sign out a three-quarter if he wants to go to Bindlach to the PX or for sick call. Ollie was with the infantry in the Korean War. He never ever talks about it, but he wears a Combat Infantryman's Badge, so you can bet he saw his share of shit over there."

Just then Anson called to us from the orderly room, "Daniels, Rutherford, get in here. The first sergeant wants to see you."

We went back into the orderly room to meet MSG Henry again. His desk was in one corner of the room, diagonally opposite Hanson's. There was another desk in the room. It had SSG Gray's nameplate on it. We stood casually in front of Sergeant Henry's desk and waited for him to look up. Once again, there was a stump of a cigar in the corner of his mouth. I guessed it was a permanent fixture. He was wearing reading glasses on the end of his nose which he slowly removed as he looked up at us.

"Which one of you is Daniels?" he half growled.

"I am, Top," I replied with a trace of a squeak in my voice. I was intimidated already.

"So, you must be Rutherford, right?" he asked and then continued without waiting for an affirmation from Jack. "Anson tells me that Spec 6 Riley has assigned you to your tricks and that he's gonna set you up in rooms with your tricks."

"That's right, Top."

"Good. I want you to think of your trick chief as your squad leader. The Ops NCOIC is like a platoon sergeant, and Spec 6 Riley is his assistant. They're both married and live off the Hill, so your trick chief is your boss most of the time. If you have a problem, see him first and then Sergeant Gray. Don't bother me with any piddly ass shit. And don't even think about bothering the C.O. Understand?"

"Yes, Top," Jack and I replied simultaneously.

"I hear that at least one of you went to college for a year or two. There's a lot of you college boys here on the Hill. Most of you flunked out and joined ASA instead of waiting to be drafted. Good choice. This is good duty up here. There's no P.T. but there's some exercise equipment over in the supply building if you want to work out. There's no K.P. either. Every payday, you will kick in your share to pay the three Germans that work in the mess hall and do the work you'd do if you were pulling KP. The food in the mess hall is good. SFC Rayburn is the mess sergeant, and he does a great job with the rations we're issued. Military discipline is relaxed, but don't try to take advantage of it. Any questions?"

"No, Top!"

"The C.O. is down at Herzo for a meeting, but he'll be back tomorrow. He usually likes to meet new personnel. I'll let you know when he wants to see you. In the meantime, keep your boots and belt brass shined. Your haircuts look okay for now. Don't let your hair grow too long…. Now go back down to the Cabin with Anson and get settled into your bunk area. I might stop by to check on you later today, so make sure your wall locker and footlocker are standing tall. That's it. Now, get out of here and let me work."

"Thanks, Top," we half whispered as we retreated from the orderly room and met up with Anson in the hallway outside.

The three of us walked back down the road to the Cabin, climbed the concrete steps into the building, and walked down the hallway to the trick rooms. Dog Trick's room was at the end of the hall. We went in expecting to find at least one guy there, but there was no one there. There was an empty bunk in the middle of the room, and Anson told me that it was now mine. He went back up Topside, leaving Jack and me to move

35

my stuff from the room where I spent the prior night into Dog Trick's room. Two guys our age wearing civilian clothes walked in just as we were finishing up.

"Hey, weeds! Watcha doin' in our room?" they asked, but not in a hostile tone.

"Hi, I'm Jerry Daniels. I arrived yesterday. I'm a Czech linguist, and Father Pat assigned me to Dog Trick. This is Jack Rutherford. He'll be on Baker Trick." I explained with a smile.

"Okay. That's sounds good," the taller of the two said. "I'm Joe Parker, and I'm a Czech too. I suppose Rich Roberts or I will be training you on the VHF position. This is Stan Pace. We call him the Bard. He's a Russian op. Welcome to Dog Trick. We start mids tomorrow night, so enjoy your last day of freedom while you can. A couple of the other guys are down in Munich this break. They should be back early tomorrow afternoon."

"That's cool. Hey, Stan, why do they call you the Bard?" I was genuinely curious.

Stan looked a little embarrassed and averted his eyes a bit. "Oh, it's really nothing. Almost everyone up here gets a nickname sooner or later."

"Don't be modest, Stan. Tell him."

"Naw, I'd rather not," Stan demurred.

"Well, if you don't, then I will," Joe half chuckled. "Stan is our resident bard, minstrel, and fine actor. He studied drama in college for a couple years before joining ASA. On special occasions, especially after significant drinking, the Bard has been known to leap up on a table and recite a soliloquy from a Shakespearean play or maybe a sonnet or two. He does it with great elan! Oh, man, and you should hear him do Kipling's '*Gunga Din*.' He even does it with a great cockney accent."

The Bard was clearly nonplussed. "C'mon, Joe, I've only done that kind of thing a few times. Gimme a break!" He shifted gears and looked at Jack and me, "It was good meeting you guys. Welcome to The Hill. I think you're gonna like it here…at least until winter comes. Glad to see you took the bunk in the middle of the room, Jerry. New guys get the bunks in the middle. You can move to one by the wall or the windows when the old-timers PCS back to the world of round doorknobs, the USA.

Hey, the mess hall starts serving in a few minutes, why don't you join me and Joe over there once you finish moving in."

"Thanks, Stan. I'll do that. Jack will probably join us too if that's okay."

"Yeah, sure. See you over there in a little while."
***

WALKABOUT

I finished squaring away my wall locker and footlocker in the Dog Trick room and then walked over to the mess hall with Jack. The main entree was liver and onions – one of my favorites at the time. Not too many people like liver, so there was another nondescript dish as an alternative. Jack and I joined Joe Parker and Stan Pace at one of the tables. Both Joe and Stan harassed me a bit over my liking liver, but it was all good natured. Anson was eating with a few other guys who stopped by our table to introduce themselves on their way out of the mess hall. I was sure I wouldn't be able to remember their names.

After they left, Joe told us that the tall guy was known as Lurch. "You remember Lurch from *The Adams Family*, don't you?" Joe asked. "He was the butler character played by Ted Cassiday. He resembled the Frankenstein monster, minus the bolts."

I had to laugh because the resemblance was striking. "Yeah, I can see why he's called Lurch. Man, he sure has the height for it, and the slightly convex face, big ears, and deep-set eyes really ice the cake. The prominent chin helps too. Does he mind being called Lurch?"

"Not at all. I think he likes it. He's one of the nicest guys on the Hill. He never gives anyone a hard time about anything. He's one of the electronic maintenance techs, so he lives Topside with Anson and the other straight-day ladies. The other guy was Matt Rivington. He's the comms center guy on Dog Trick, so you'll be seeing a lot of him. He lives Topside too, but he spends a lot of time at the Club. He gets a little strange when he drinks too much, but that's not too out of the ordinary around here."

Jack decided to go back to his room to get a few hours of sleep before working the last mid shift with Baker Trick. I didn't feel like going back to my room yet. It was still sunny and pleasant, so I thought it might be a good opportunity to explore the Topside compound.

I made my way back up the steep slope toward Topside and through the open gate by the guard shack and fuel dump. The MP on duty came out of the shack, "Whoa there, buddy. Hold it right there. Who are you and what are you doing here?"

I was surprised that he challenged me, but then I realized that I was in civilian clothes rather than the uniform I had worn the other times I had passed through the gate unchallenged.

"I'm SP4 Jerry Daniels. I arrived here yesterday and will be working on Dog Trick," I said as I took out my wallet and showed him my military ID.

"OK. No problem. I'm Frank DiMartino. I'm the MP on Charlie Trick. Large Louis is the MP on your trick."

"Large Louis?"

"Yep, that's what they call him. He's a very big boy, but a really nice guy too. He hangs out with Anson and Bear a lot of the time. Bear is one of the maintenance guys. He works with Lurch."

"Oh, I just met Lurch down at the mess hall. I won't ask why Bear is called Bear, Frank."

"Hey, it'll be obvious once you meet him. His real name is Barry, but he's built like a bear – short, a little on the round side, but immensely powerful. He looks like he could tear phone books in half without breaking a sweat. I think he was a star wrestler in high school."

"I'll look forward to meeting him. I'm just gonna walk around the compound now if that's okay."

Frank the MP smiled and waved me on, "Sure. Take your time. There's not much to see. The PX, such as it is, is only open when Bill Pierce feels like opening it. There's not much in there anyway other than soda, candy, and cigarettes. You might want to check out the pool room and weight room next to the little PX though. Have fun."

Once past the guard shack, I turned right on the road that circled Topside and walked past the rear of the main Topside building. There was a rear door that led to the boiler room. I poked my head in the door and could see that from the boiler room, you could go into a hallway that led past the comms center and sleeping rooms to the rest of the Topside building. Continuing along the compound road, there was a parking area containing a pair of deuce-and-a-halfs, a jeep, and a three-quarter ton canvas topped truck. They were parked by a large barn-like structure with a sign identifying it as the motor pool. The small PX was in a single-story, wooden building that was painted apple green and housed the supply room, the pool room, and the weight room. No one was around, so I shot some pool for a while before checking out the kino room again in the main U-shaped Topside building.

Unlike most day rooms back in the States, there was no TV in the kino room. I couldn't help wondering why. It would be cool to watch German TV, and it would probably help us learn more German. So much the better if it could pick up Czech TV too. That would really help my language comprehension. But I was thinking like a linguist and not necessarily as a soldier.

A couple guys were reading paperback books, but there was no movie being shown just then. It was after regular duty hours, so the orderly room was empty except for the charge-of-quarters (CQ) who was sitting at Anson's desk reading a book. I stuck my head in the door and said hi, but I didn't hang around to talk or introduce myself. There would be plenty of time for that in the days ahead.

I did take a minute to drop a couple letters in the mailbox hanging on the arms room door. I had dashed off short notes to my Mom and girlfriend giving them my new mailing address and promising to write a longer letter soon. Anson or whoever was available took outgoing mail each morning to the APO at the armored cav casern in Bindlach and brought back incoming mail for det personnel. The round-trip took a little more than an hour, unless the driver stopped at the Bindlach PX snack bar for a burger and a milk shake or to check out the wives of the cav guys who lived on the post.

The mail was also how movies came to and from the site. The detachment was on the movie circuit run by the Army and Air Force Exchange Service (AAFES) which also ran all the post exchanges. We were on the tail end of the movie circuit. The large bases got the movies first. They were old by the time they reached us, and sometimes they were chewed up and patched together with Scotch tape. But, heck, the guys told me that they were free.

(Sketch courtesy of schneebergvets.org. Not drawn to scale or exactly as remembered by the author.)

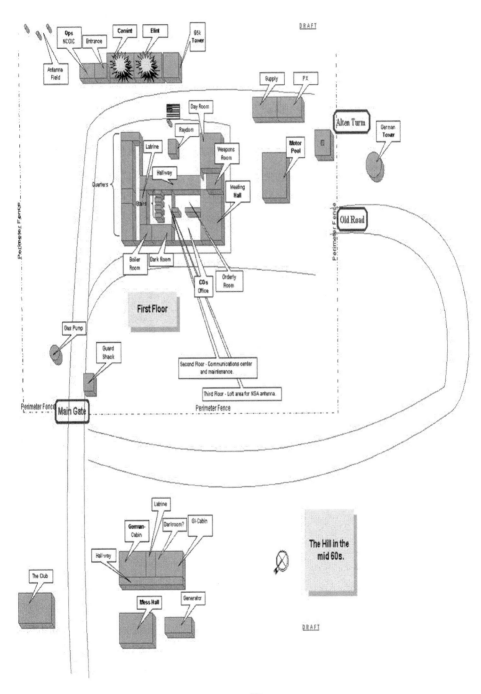

It was coming up on 7 pm or 1900 hours in Army talk. I figured I'd go down to the Club and see what that was like and if my new trick chief, Will Morrow, was there playing cards as predicted.

The walk down the steep slope to the Cabin area gave me a real appreciation of the beauty of the mountain landscape. The access road down from Topside was nearly straight for the first half mile. Once you passed the Cabin/Club/mess hall area, there was nothing but thick pine forest on either side of the road as far as the eye could see. I couldn't see Bischofsgruen at the foot of the mountain or any other sign of civilization except for the road. The evening sun cast shadows from the trees across the asphalt surface and highlighted the brilliant green of the trees. I could only imagine what it must be like in the winter when the trees would be wearing a coat of heavy snow and the road would be almost impassable. *(Photo courtesy of Phil Ward and Schneebergvets.org)*

I was so entranced by the beautiful vista that I almost walked right past the entrance to the Club. It sure didn't look like much on the outside. It was almost a twin to the mess hall directly across the street and a close cousin to Ops. Someone told me that all three buildings had been set up at the same time several years earlier. They already looked like relics from WW II. I think they were considered temporary buildings.

The Club had corrugated steel walls and a similar looking roof. A stove pipe protruded from the right side of the roof perhaps two-thirds of the way toward the rear wall. There seemed to be only one door to the Club, and it was only a yard or two from the road. Two concrete steps led to a windowless metal door with a light fixture above it.

I figured that there would be a bunch of people in there that I didn't know. Since I'm a little on the introverted side, I took a deep breath to settle my nerves before opening the door. As I did, I detected the not so subtle smell of urine. "That's odd," I thought as I opened the door, "There must be something wrong with the sewage system."

There were a dozen guys in the Club. Five or six were playing cards at a poker table on the right side near a kerosene heater. MSG Henry was one of the players. They had all looked up when I opened the door and entered the one-room building, but they quickly looked back down at their cards and didn't offer a greeting or display any interest in my presence. A juke box stood in the near left corner of the room and was playing "California Dreaming" by the Mamas and Papas. It sounded good and made me a little nostalgic for Monterey and language school.

There were several tables scattered around the room. Anson and a burly looking fellow I assumed was Bear were sitting at one table, and Anson greeted me with a wave. Two men were intently and noisily playing on the foosball table that stood near the middle of the room. Three one-armed bandits were set up on sturdy wood shelves along the left wall. The horseshoe-shaped bar took up most of the rear left quarter of the building and had a dozen or more bar stools running from one end to the other. A young man in a field jacket and jeans was the only one sitting at the bar. He was wearing a soft fedora pushed down over his eyes and seemed oblivious to everything around him except for the beer mug in front of him. I remembered seeing him in the mess hall a couple hours before. His name was Matt, but I couldn't recall his last name. (*Photo courtesy of Phil Ward and Schneebergvets.org*)

The bartender looked up at me, gave me a big smile, and waved me over. "Welcome to the Club! You must be one of the weeds who got here yesterday. I'm Doug Broussard. Most people call me Cajun 'cause I'm French and from Louisiana." It sounded more like Loosianna to me. "Like I said, a lot of people call me Cajun, but I'd rather be called Doug."

"Jerry Daniels," I reached over and shook hands with Doug. "What can I get to drink here?"

"Well, I can give you anything you want, as long as it's *Frankenbrau*. It's not too bad a beer. We have an exclusive contract with them for some reason. I don't know why. I manage the Club and tend bar when I'm not on duty in Ops," he chuckled. "The brewery gives us these ceramic mugs as a goodwill gesture. Everyone on the Hill gets one, if he wants one. Oh yeah, we have Coke, Fanta, and 7-Up too, if you don't want to drink beer."

He reached behind the bar and handed me a gray, half-liter mug that had the *Frankenbrau* logo on it. "Here's a magic marker, Jerry. Write you name on the bottom of the mug, and I'll keep it on one of those pegs on the wall for whenever you come in." He pointed at the back wall where 25 or 30 mugs were hung on wooden dowels.

"Thanks a lot!" I took the mug and marker and wrote my name on the bottom of the mug. "So now can I have some beer to christen my new mug?"

Doug took a bottle of beer from the cooler and handed it to me. The glass bottle was dark brown, and it had the standard German lid consisting of a white ceramic stopper with a rubber washer on it. The lid was connected to the bottle by a hinge. You could pour what you wanted from the bottle and then close it securely with the hinged cap to keep it fresh. I filled my new mug with beer. There wasn't much left in the bottle after that.

Doug appeared to be a few years older than me. He had a roundish face with early onset laugh wrinkles at the corners of his eyes and a bit of a cleft chin. His dark hair was combed back and was thinning. He gestured to the guy with the fedora, "That's Matt Rivington. He's the comms center guy on Dog Trick. He's a really nice guy usually, but he's going through a bad patch lately. Girl trouble on the home front, I think."

He paused a moment and called across the bar, "Hey, Matt, say hello to Jerry Daniels. He's a new guy on Dog Trick."

Matt raised his head and looked over at me. I could see from several feet away that his eyes were bloodshot. "Hey! How y'all doin'?" he asked without much enthusiasm and then looked down again at the counter and his beer.

"Good to meet you, Matt," I said. "I'm looking forward to working with you."

Matt sorta grunted in reply and then took a big swallow of beer from his mug.

"Are you a Mary?" Doug asked.

"Yeah, I'm a Czech 98G. Pat Riley told me I'll be an op to start out with. What about you?"

"I'm a 05K. You know what that is? There are only a couple of us on The Hill. Don McGrew is another one. We work together. Usually on straight days."

I knew that an 05H was a Morse code intercept operator. I was quite sure that an 05K was a non-Morse intercept op, but I didn't know for sure what they did in Ops. I knew better than to ask him about his duties while we were in the Club. "Sounds cool," was all I could think of to say. I turned around on the stool a bit and watched the two guys playing foosball.

"Don McGrew is the guy on the left," Doug offered. "He's from the hills of North Carolina. A super smart guy. He helped the ASA engineers design the intercept equipment in the RRCV-4 van."

"Wow. I guess he must have a lot on the ball."

The guys at the poker table finished playing a hand, and a tall skinny guy with thick glasses stood up and walked over to the bar. He was wearing jeans and a flannel shirt. "Hey, Cajun, gimme another beer." I had him pegged as Will Morrow.

"Are you Sergeant Morrow?" I asked

He peered over at me through his Coke bottle lenses, "Who wants to know?" he challenged.

"I'm Jerry Daniels. Father Pat told me I'll be working for you on Dog Trick. I'm a Czech linguist."

47

"Okay. Good to meet you. We start mids tomorrow night. You're already set up with a bunk and everything in the trick room, right?" He lit an unfiltered Pall Mall cigarette and took a deep puff as he waited for his beer. His index and middle fingers were stained yellow from nicotine.

"Yeah, I'm good to go, Sarge."

"Let's get something straight right away. You call me Will or Morrow, but not Sarge unless we're in front of the captain, and then you call me Sergeant Morrow. I'm only an acting sergeant, an "A-Slash" as we're called. I'm not a tread. Not a lifer. I'm a Spec 5 Russian Mary, and I go home next year, and that will be the end of me and the Army."

"Got it," I replied as he turned and went back to the poker table with his beer.

I sat there for a while checking out the room and listening to the juke box. Don McGrew and his opponent were still playing foosball, and the poker players were concentrating on their cards. I noticed that they were using poker chips and that there were no coins or currency on the table. MSG Henry still had a cigar stub in his mouth, but I didn't notice him puffing on it. Every time I had seen him so far, he had a cigar in his mouth. I wondered if it was the same stub and if he slept that way.

After finishing my second beer, I had to pee. "Hey, Doug, where's the latrine?"

He looked at me quizzically, "The latrine? It's in the Cabin, across the street."

"No. Isn't there one here in the Club?"

Doug chuckled, "Oh yeah, it's right out the front door. You stand on the front steps and pee whichever way the wind isn't blowing. And try not to wave your willie around if a car or the German trick change bus happens to be driving by. Wait until they pass."

"Ah, I guess that accounts for the smell of piss by the entrance."

"Wait until winter. The snow on both sides of the door will be good and yellow by then."

"Right. Thanks," I replied, a little embarrassed to be a weed. I walked across the street to the Cabin and used the latrine there rather than using the "latrine" at the Club.

I toyed with the idea of going to the trick bunk room and writing a letter or two or maybe going back up Topside to see if anyone was showing a movie in the kino room. "What the hell," I thought, "I'll go back to the Club and have another beer or two and try to get an idea of who's who.

The poker players were a quiet bunch. They concentrated on their cards and didn't engage in much kibitzing or conversation. I noticed that Morrow had some sort of ledger and seemed to make occasional notations. I asked Doug about it and why there was no money on the table.

"Oh, they play payday stakes. If you play, you run a tab like you would in a bar. At the end of the month, the wins and losses are totaled up. After you draw your pay from the officer who brings the cash up here, you pay your KP dues for the Germans who work in the mess hall. Then at the end of the line is a table where Morrow sits. He'll tell you how much you owe or how much you've won and then you either pay your losses or collect your winnings."

"That sounds good. What kind of stakes do they play for?" I asked.

"Well, it's basically a friendly game, at least most of the time. White chips are worth a nickel, red ones a dime, and blue ones are a quarter. You can't bet more than a quarter at a time, and there can only be three raises per round. You buy in for five bucks, and most times that five dollars will last you a few hours, unless you're a really bad poker player. Do you want me to ask them if you can sit in?"

"No. Not tonight, Doug. I'm not much of a poker player, but I'd like to give it a try once I know more of the guys."

Matt Rivington was still sitting at the bar with the fedora over his eyes. I couldn't tell if he was sleeping or just tuning out the world around him. I decided to give him some space and not try to start a conversation with him. By then, I had a bit of a buzz from the strong German beer. It was still early in the evening, but I decided to go back to the Cabin and get a good night's sleep.

****

DOG TRICK

I slept late the next morning and skipped breakfast. After the morning ritual of a shower and shave, I made my way Topside and staked out an easy chair in the kino room. Although it was Saturday, Anson, MSG Henry, and SSG Gray were in the orderly room nearby. I could hear the clacking of Anson's typewriter and muffled conversations among the three. Captain Medved must have been in his office adjacent to the orderly room because I saw his Triumph TR-4 parked in front of the building. It was a real pretty car – baby blue with a black convertible top and wire wheels.

I sat in the yellow vinyl chair and wrote a short letter to my Mom using a clipboard as a writing surface. Like many military members stationed overseas, I used all-in-one onion skin writing paper that folded up into an airmail envelope with pre-paid postage. Surface mail took a few weeks to get to the States, but airmail letters got there in a few days. I didn't have much news to relay to my Mom, but I knew she liked hearing from me often, so I wrote a couple times each week.

I sealed the letter and put it in the mailbox outside the orderly room. Today's outgoing mail had already been collected and taken to the armored cavalry casern in Bindlach. My letter wouldn't be going out until Monday.

I looked over the bookshelves in the kino room and picked out something by Ian Fleming. I had seen a James Bond film while in Monterey and enjoyed the action and adventure. I heard that the books were as good, if not better, than the movies. I was soon engrossed in Bond's skullduggery and romantic escapades. To be honest, the romance

50

(that is, the sex) was welcome fodder for the fantasies of this soon-to-be 20-year old's brain.

Anson stirred me from my reveries, "Hey, Daniels, it's almost 12:30. Mess hall closes at 1300. I'm goin' down for chow. Wanna come?"

"Yeah! Thanks, Anson. I lost track of time. I missed breakfast, so I'm pretty damn hungry. Anyone else from Topside going down now?" I asked.

"Naw. Bear is working on a piece of commo gear that must be fixed and operational ASAP. He's a hellavu electronics maintenance tech. He can fix damn near anything if you give him a little time."

"Hmmm. That's good to know. He works straight days like you, doesn't he?" I asked.

"Yep. All the maintenance guys work straight days 0800 to 1600, but they're on call 24/7 if they're needed. There always has to be at least one tech up here Topside in case one is needed in Operations or the comms center. The others can go downtown or wherever, but one guy always must be Topside. It's never a problem. This is Bear's weekend on call."

We walked down the hill to the mess hall. The sun was shining on the top of the mountain, but low clouds were blocking the view down toward Bischofsgruen.

****

After lunch with Anson, I went back to the trick room intending to take a nap before working my first mid shift on the Hill. The room was a bit cramped. There were bunks, foot lockers, and wall lockers for eight people in a space better suited for six men. The tight quarters might have been alleviated by using bunk beds instead of regular cots, but no one wanted the hassle of having upper and lower bunks. Privacy and personal space were precious enough without going double decker.

Will Morrow was sitting on his bunk immediately to the left of the door. He was smoking a Pall Mall and reading a paperback book. He looked up briefly and grunted a hello when I entered the room. There was a guy in cook's whites lying on the bunk next to Morrow's. He was wearing cowboy boots and had a Stetson hat covering his eyes. My bunk was next to his. Sitting on the bunk beyond that by the window was a fit looking guy in a crisp white t-shirt and fatigue pants who had his back to the door and was listening to music with earphones connected to a small

51

stereo system set up on a stand in the corner next to his bunk. He turned around and took off his phones when he sensed my presence behind him. He had dark wavy hair a little longer than regulation length, and he was wearing Army-issue black plastic eyeglasses.

"Hey! How's it goin'? You must be the new guy. Daniels, right? I'm Rich Roberts," he said as he got up and extended his hand to me. He had the kind of smile that seems genuine and makes you want to smile right back.

"Yeah. Jerry Daniels. Good to meet you, Rich. I'm a Czech Mary."

"Me too. I work the high side, the UHF position, in Ops. You'll be on the low side, VHF, at least for a few months until you get the hang of things. I'll be training you if I'm not tied up doing another mission."

"Sounds great, Rich. Thanks." I noticed that he had a firm handshake and looked me straight in the eyes when we talked. I got good vibes from him. None of the macho b.s. that some guys project when they first meet someone new, like they are challenging you to see who will be the alpha dog right from the get-go. It always seems stupid to me. Rich seemed to have a good aura around him, if you believe in that kind of thing. I actually do believe in auras, and it usually helps me get an initial fix on who are the good guys and who are the assholes.

"How was your break, Rich? I noticed that you weren't here when I got in here yesterday. Go anywhere interesting?"

He paused slightly and looked away for a second before responding. "Well, yeah. I took the train down to Munich from Bayreuth. I love that city and try to get down there whenever I can. I've got some friends who are students at the university down there. They live in the Schwabing section of the city, which is a little like Greenwich Village in New York. It's a fun place. I can usually find a couch to sleep on. Have you been down there yet?"

"Not yet. I've only been in Germany for a few months and haven't had the time or the money to do much exploring except for the Nuremberg area."

"Put it on your to-do list, Jerry. Save up your money and practice your German. Most people in Munich speak at least a little English, but they appreciate it when we Amis try to speak German."

"Will do. Thanks, Rich."

Roberts turned back toward the window and put on his earphones. I noticed that the record jacket on his bunk was a *Deutsche Grammophon* recording of Ravel's *Daphnis et Chloé* performed by the Berlin Philharmonic. I didn't think much about it, even though most of the guys I knew were into rock or folk music. I learned in Monterey that ASAers have far reaching tastes in music and other stuff.

Joe Parker had the bunk in the corner opposite Roberts. Joe was one of only two African-Americans on the Hill. The other was an MP whom I had seen but not yet met. I think he was on Able Trick. I had noticed that there weren't very many black guys at Herzo either, but I hadn't given it much thought. I did know, or at least I heard, that Joe was one of the best Czech linguists on the Hill and that he had become proficient in German too.

Stan Pace, the Bard, a Russian op, had the bunk next to Joe. Neither he nor Joe was in the room. I asked Morrow who our other roommates were.

He looked up from his book, "Spec 4 Ron Walters has the bunk next to Pace's, and Spec 5 Wally Bunker has the one opposite mine. Walters had been a cadet at West Point, but he washed out and enlisted in ASA to meet his service commitment to the government. He's a German op. Wally is hardly ever here. He has a girlfriend in Bisch and stays down there most of the time. He's a short-timer and will get his discharge soon. I think he's going to stay in Bisch after that."

"What's Wally's MOS?"

"Wally is an 98J ELINT op – not that there's much of an ELINT mission here. But he's good at helping out with whatever needs to be done, like wrapping up courier packages and taking the burn bag detail. We call him Fritz – partly because he's a self-taught German linguist, but also because he has gone native on us. He wears German clothes and wire-rimmed glasses that he bought over in Bayreuth. Believe it or not, he even has *lederhosen* that he wears when he hikes during the warm weather. He's probably out hiking in the forest now. By the way, he's not the friendliest guy. He always seems pissed off. Oh, and don't ask Ron Walters about West Point. It's a tender subject with him."

I was glad to have the information. "Thanks for the warning, Will. I appreciate it."

Getting through the first mid shift without falling asleep on position was always a challenge. I knew that from my limited trick work experience at Herzo, so I racked out and soon slipped into a long restful nap. I must have been tired because I slept through evening chow time. It didn't really matter because I knew that the mess hall was open for midnight chow, usually a breakfast meal, to feed the mid shift before they went on duty and the swing shift after they came off duty.

A couple of the other guys were still napping, but Morrow was not in the room. I figured he had gone over to the Club to play cards.

Sure enough, Morrow as at the poker table with Jolly Ollie, SFC Rayburn, a SP4 they called Weasel, and a couple others I hadn't met yet. Everyone at the table had mugs of beer except for Morrow. He had a bottle of Coke in front of him. He looked up as I approached the table and called out, "Daniels, no beer for you. I don't have too many rules, but one of the ones I do have is that no one can drink alcohol within 8 hours of coming on duty. Is that clear?"

"Yes, Sarge. Understood." I remembered that he wanted to be called Sergeant if Ollie or the det commander was around.

Doug Broussard was behind the bar. I ordered a Fanta orange soda. It reminded me of the Nehi orange soda I'd get in the States.

Joe Parker was sitting at the bar drinking a Coke. I sat down next to him and made small talk. One of the first questions soldiers ask one another when they meet is "Where are you from in the States?"

Parker was from East Orange, New Jersey. I mentioned that I had lived in Little Falls, NJ, when I was 3 years old, but I didn't remember much about it. He was intrigued that I had also lived in Brooklyn and gone to high school there, even though I lived on Long Island during my high school years. We found that we had visited many of the same places in "The City" as we New Yorkers referred to Manhattan. We had also listened to the same radio stations, including WADO Radio, an R&B station that featured a black DJ known as Jocko Henderson and his Rocket Ship Show. We laughed as we tried our best to mimic his on-air greeting, *"Back on the scene with the record machine, saying oop-pop-a-doo and how do you do? Close the hatch and prepare to blast. Well, eee tiddle de dock. This is the Jock."*

"Hey, Joe, what's with the cook in the bunk between me and Morrow? I saw when he opened his locker that he had a bunch of hunting knives and what looked like bullwhips hanging on the inside of his locker. What the hell is that about?"

Parker just frowned and shook his head. "He's a cracker. A real redneck. We call him Whipdick. He's a misfit among misfits. A draftee from somewhere in the deep South. He's always angry and defensive to the point of being aggressive. He's got no friends on the Hill, not even among the other cooks. Keep your distance and don't piss him off. He's trouble waiting to happen."

I wasn't sure what a cracker was and didn't want to ask, but it sounded pejorative. I sat and talked with Joe until close to 10:30 pm. Morrow got up from the poker table and walked over to us at the bar. "Time to call it a night here, gentlemen. Time to get ready for work. You better have fresh fatigues to put on. I want you all looking good, at least on the first mid. Get movin'."

And we did.

****

FIRST MIDS

Whipdick was behind the grill when I entered the mess hall for midnight chow. He was making eggs to order and had bacon and sausage warming in metal pans on the steam table. Every few minutes he'd put a couple slices of white bread in the big toaster that was in continuous motion moving the bread past the red hot heating elements like the cars on a Ferris wheel and then dumping the hot toast into a tray at the base of the machine. Butter, jelly, and peanut butter containers stood nearby. A steaming cylinder of creamed chipped beef awaited those who liked S.O.S. for breakfast – a taste I never developed. I asked for some scrambled eggs, which Whipdick put on my plate without comment. A couple slices of crisp bacon and two sausage links completed my meal.

There were several Dog Trick guys sitting at three different tables. Will Morrow and Rich Roberts were at the nearest table.

"Mind if I join you guys?" I asked a bit tentatively.

Rich looked up with a big smile, "Hey, make yourself at home. Glad to have the company. Will never has too much to say."

Morrow just sorta grunted and kept mopping up egg yolk with what was left of a slice of toast. As soon as he finished his food, he lit a Pall Mall and took a deep drag.

"Is that all you're going to eat?" asked Rich. "Ya know there are no vending machines or any other sources of food in Ops or even in Topside. You're gonna get hungry long before trick change at 0800. If you're smart, you'll make yourself a peanut butter sandwich, wrap it in napkins, and stick it in your field jacket pocket so you'll have something to eat during our shift."

"Thanks, Rich. Good idea. I'll do it for sure. By the way, is there coffee up in Ops?"

"Oh yeah. There's always an urn of hot coffee. It usually has a metallic taste to it, but it'll help keep you awake and warm. Whoever drinks the last cup from the urn has to go across to the Topside building, fill it with water, and make a new batch. There's no running water in Ops. Don't let anyone catch you drinking the last of the coffee and not replenishing the urn. You'll be a marked man and have a hard time living it down." He chuckled when he said it, but I could tell he was giving me serious advice.

"Right. I'll remember that too. Thanks."

When the clock on the wall showed 2335 hours, Will Morrow got up from the table and took his tray to the pass-through window and left it on a wide ledge there. The other members of the trick followed suit and stacked their trays and silverware on top of Morrow's. I got up too and asked Rich, "Why are we going up early. Trick change isn't until midnight. Right?"

"Yeah, that's right. But we always relieve the outgoing trick at least 15 minutes before trick change. That gives them time to brief us on whatever might be going on SIGINT-wise, what radio nets are active, and anything significant that may have happened since the last time we were on duty. It usually only takes a couple of minutes, but it's an important part of the routine.

"Remember that the op you're relieving can't leave his position until you're there to take over, so don't be late. Able Trick almost never relieves us on time. They wait until the last minute before they come into Ops. I blame it on the trick chief, Riegel. He's an acting sergeant and has an ego the size of the German tower. Basically, he's a self-centered asshole, and unfortunately we can never pay them back by relieving them late because Able Trick is the only trick we never relieve."

"I remember Brett Riegle from DLI. He was an asshole there too. Married a girl from the Monterey area too if I remember right."

"Yep. He and his bride have an apartment down in Bisch. They don't mix much socially with the other married guys or with his trick for that matter. I think Riegel is counting down the days until he gets out of the

57

Army, but he acts like a lifer in the meantime. He even went to the NCO Academy down in Bad Tolz. We're relieving Charlie Trick tonight. They're all pretty good guys." Rich got up from the table and asked, "Are you coming?"

"I'll be right behind you. I'm gonna make myself a PBJ for later."

By the time I made my sandwich and started the trek up the hill, the rest of the trick was straggling into the compound and passing the guard shack. One guy peeled off from the last group and went into the shack. I figured it had to be our trick MP, Large Louis."

I tried to catch up with the group, but the steep stretch of access road from the Cabin to the guard shack left me huffing and puffing. I imagined that it would really be tough going in the winter when the road would be covered in snow and ice. I waved as I passed the MP post and then jogged the rest of the way to Ops just in time to grab the door before it closed and locked automatically. I was glad to be wearing my field jacket. Even though it was the end of April, the night air felt cold.

Joe Parker had gone into the TR hut and was being briefed by the Charlie Trick scribe. If there wasn't a lot of live intercept going on during swings and mids, the best Czech linguist on the trick would usually spend most of the shift transcribing or doing detailed gists of some of the tapes that had been recorded by prior shifts. Rich Roberts was listening to the outgoing UHF op. Things had apparently been quiet and uneventful on swings because the conversation didn't last long. It was only a matter of a few minutes before everyone from Charlie Trick had left the Ops building to us. Will Morris was reading intently from a large, green, cloth-bound journal known as the pass-on log. Every trick chief was required to make notes on any significant activity, SIGINT or not, that occurred on his shift. It was a good way to maintain continuity of operations and an effective way for the day ladies to keep track of what went on when they weren't around.

Morrow finished reading the pass-on log and called Parker from the TR hut. "You'll be working the high side for this set of mids. Roberts will be training Daniels on the low side. Mids are a good time for OJT since there's usually not much UHF comms activity until close to dawn. Daniels has a lot to learn"

Parker didn't object very strenuously, but he clearly looked a bit unhappy. "Damn, Will, the UHF position is usually dead on mids. It's boring as hell, and the time drags. When I'm transcribing, I keep busy and the time goes by quickly. But I get it. Daniels needs to learn, and Rich is a great trainer."

Parker took a seat in the swivel chair in front of the hulking UHF position and started checking out the recorders, receivers, and demultiplexers before beginning to search the UHF radio spectrum for Czech communications. The Russian and German linguists were doing the same at their respective VHF positions.

Roberts had pulled a second gray metal chair over to the Czech VHF position where he'd be training me for the next several nights. I was glad to see that the chair was cushioned. He had an earmuff-style headset plugged into one of the output jacks on the AN/TNH-11 tape recorder, and he handed me an identical set to put on. Both were grimey from the sweat and crud from all the other ops who wore them since Day One. I made a mental note to try to buy my own set if they had them in the PX.

"Why are the headsets plugged into the recorder and not the receiver, Rich?"

"Well, it's important for you as an op to be hearing what the recorder is hearing…or recording. If you were plugged directly into the receiver, you run the risk of not having audible voice on the tapes. You wouldn't want to send a blank tape back to Herzo. They'd be pissed, and they would see that you were the intercept op who screwed up. As you know, every op has a unique two-letter op sign which they use when they sign down each cut on a tape and which the TR includes on his transcript, along with his own unique digraph. My op sign is RR, as in Rich Roberts. Yours will be Delta Juliet unless that op sign has already been assigned to someone else. Ron's is Whiskey Romeo." He gestured toward Ron Walters who was plugged into the neighboring VHF position tasked with East German military coverage.

Stan Pace, the Bard, was sitting at the first Russian VHF position, and a tall bespectacled guy with a massive mustache was sitting at the other Russian pos. His mustache, shaggy haircut and low-quarter shoes were clearly not in accordance with Army regulations, but that's the way things went at most border sites, especially for trick workers. I could see why the other guys called him Walrus. His real name was Jim Cavanaugh. He was a few years older than the rest of us, and I heard that he was married, living in Bad Berneck, and had completed a few years at Marquette University,

I noticed then that each of the Russian positions had a typewriter and gray steel table sitting at right angles to the intercept and recording equipment. I didn't understand why they had typewriters; Czech and German ops didn't have typewriters. They were expected to make hand notes of the basic things they heard and then stuff the notes in the envelope-like tape jackets when they changed tapes. The ops were supposed to write the tech data on the jacket for each cut on the tape. I knew I had a lot to learn and that I should concentrate on mastering my own job and not ask about anyone else's. At least for the time being.

Rich let me familiarize myself with the GLR-9 receiver and the AN/TNH-11 tape recorder. He patiently explained, "The receiver is connected via cables to a Yagi antenna mounted on a 30-foot tower outside the Ops building. The Yagi looks a lot like the TV antennas on our chimneys back home in the States. They are directional, so they should be pointed at the source of the signal to get the best readability. You can rotate the antenna using the controls below the tape recorder. Make a note of the antenna bearing on the tape jacket, along with the frequency, time you begin recording and time you end the recording. There's a space for comments too.

"All of the tapes you see mounted on the recorders right now have to be signed off and taken down at the end of the Ray Day – the radio day. The new Ray Day or intercept day begins at 0001 Zulu time – that's Greenwich Mean Time to civilians. Zulu time is usually an hour earlier than our local time, so 2400 Zulu is 0100 hours local time here, except like now during Daylight Savings Time when local time is Z + 2 hours. Oh, and that digital clock on the wall is set to Zulu time and is calibrated to be 100% accurate. Got that so far?"

"Yeah. I think I understand So at. 0200 our time we have to take down all the tapes that have intercept on them and replace them with new blank tapes on the recorders?"

Rich continued, "That's right. At the end of the Ray Day, all tapes are signed down for the day. Each op uses the mike attached to his recorder to record a message like this: 'This is tape S2-01234-66 (or whatever its serial number is). It is being dropped due to the end of the intercept day, 23 April 1966.' Then you put the tape and accompanying hand notes in its tape jacket, move it to the shelf over there with all the other tapes in serial number order, and then mount a new tape on your recorder and sign it up with a similar announcement. Are you still with me?"

"I'm with you, Rich, but I'm sure I'll be needing some reminders as we actually do this."

"No sweat, Jerry. The tasks are repetitive, so you'll get the hang of it pretty quickly. Let's move on. As you learned in tech school, the VHF frequency range is from 30 to 300 megahertz. They used to call it megacycles, but that changed a few years ago. Anyway, our friends across the border in the Warsaw Pact only use a portion of that spectrum for their military comms. We don't care about civilian nets. We generally confine our search and collection to frequencies between 20 and 50 MHz.

From 50 to 110 MHz you're going to find commercial TV and FM radio stations.

The air forces and commercial aviation use the band from around 110 to 150 MHz. We let our zoomie friends up in Hof monitor those freqs. There's not much between 150 and 210 MHz, but it doesn't hurt to look once or twice during a shift just to make sure no new equipment is being used by our targets."

"That's a lot to remember, Rich."

"It just seems that way now. It's really easy and routine most of the time. Are you ready to get started?"

"Oh, yeah! I'm ready to go...Oh, what happens if I hear some Czech?"

"No worries. That's why I'm here. We'll sort it out together. If you think it's military, just hit the 'record' button on the control box in front of you and make a note of the time you began recording. Now let's try it. Start tuning the receiver slowly from 20 MHz upward. You'll see many spikes and junk on the oscilloscope screen. It looks like a lot of uneven green grass. Don't worry about most of it. You'll be looking for spikes that pop up and down as the Czech radio ops key their mikes and transmit from the other side of the border."

We kept up our search for over an hour without finding any Czech military signals. It didn't look as though any of the other ops were copying anything either. I was disappointed, but Rich assured me that we'd see some activity as dawn approached. "Is it okay to get up and stretch my legs and maybe get a cup of coffee?"

"Sure. As long as you're not copying any traffic. Make it quick. If you have to pee or whatever, you gotta get permission from Morrow. The latrine is over in the Topside building. The treads don't like us peeing right outside the door to Ops like we do down at the Club." Rich shrugged and laughed, "Hey, it smells bad, but if you gotta go, ya gotta go."

I got up and walked over to where Morrow was typing something at a desk just outside the Ops NCOIC's office. He looked up and asked, "How's it going?"

"So far, so good. No activity, but I think I'm learning as we go."

"Good. Just listen to what Roberts tells you. He's one of the best ops we have on the Hill."

As I walked back to my pos, I saw Fritz Bunker at the shelf-like table opposite the Russian positions. He had a big cardboard box and a lot of mag tapes in their jackets. "Hey, a little early for wrapping Christmas presents, isn't it?"

"Listen, Weed," he growled, "It's Saturday night or rather Sunday morning. The courier comes up from Herzo on Tuesdays and Fridays to pick up tapes and transcripts and whatever other classified stuff we need to send down there. And he brings classified material like working aids and admin paperwork up here. Wrapping up the courier shipment is donkey work, but I do it because I don't really have an ELINT mission here. This helps pass the time. You'll get a chance to do it when I'm not around. And you'd better learn to do it right. Understand? I heard that a few years ago a guy actually did wrap Christmas gifts for his family while he was here in Ops and that he accidentally mailed the tapes to his parents in the States and couriered the gifts to Herzo. He's probably still in Leavenworth. So, don't fuck it up! And don't bug me."

"Whoa. Cool it, man. I was just making conversation."

He didn't reply and went back to packing the thick cardboard box and making a list of everything inside. He'd be double-wrapping the box in heavy brown paper once he had sealed it with packing tape. I walked back to my pos and sat back down with Rich Roberts. "Fritz is a real charmer, isn't he?"

Rich smiled, "Hey, I warned you down in the Cabin that he's usually mad at the world and everyone in it. Don't take it personally. You'll get used to him."

"Yeah, I guess there's no other choice. By the way, what's with the M-14 rifle and loaded magazine hanging on the wall by the wrapping table?"

"That's the Ops security weapon. We're authorized to use it to keep unauthorized personnel from entering the building. Do NOT touch it under any other conditions or you will be sent back to Herzo so fast that your head will spin. You'd probably get court martialed too. Seriously. Do NOT touch it."

"Okay. I won't. I noticed another one behind Jolly Ollie's desk in the orderly room."

"Right. All the other weapons are locked in racks inside the arms room next to the orderly room. If you haven't been assigned an M-14 yet, you soon will be. We all have one in case the balloon goes up. Not that it will do us much good. Oh yeah, the comms center has a weapon too, and of course the MPs all have a loaded .45 when they're on duty in the guard shack"

"Hmmmm...That's good to know. I feel so much safer now," I added a little sarcastically.

****

At a few minutes before midnight Zulu, or 0200 local time, Rich showed me how to sign down the tape on our pos and set up a new one for the new intercept day. I could see all the other ops doing the same. Fritz soon had a new stack of tapes to box up and wrap for shipment to Herzo later in the day.

****

I was getting very sleepy around 0330, and Morrow noticed my head bobbing up and down. "Daniels, get up and come with me. I'm gonna show you how to handle burn bag detail."

"Okay! I'm with you." I had learned even before arriving at Herzo Base that every piece of classified paper had to be discarded in large brown paper bags that looked a lot like the grocery bags we'd get at the supermarkets back home. Once the bags were full, you'd staple them closed and someone would take them to an incinerator. It looked as though I was that person early that morning.

We took the 8 or 10 burn bags that were piled outside the Ops OIC's office and carried them across the street to Topside. Morrow led me down the short corridor on the right side of the building, past the heavy metal door to the comms center and into the boiler room. We left the burn bags on the concrete floor in the corner of the room while Morrow demonstrated how to open the furnace door.

As soon as he opened the steel door, the heat from the coal fire engulfed the chilly boiler room like a sirocco wind blowing off the Sahara Desert. "Damn! That's really hot, Will!"

"That's the whole point of a fire, Daniels. It heats the Topside building, provides hot water, and serves as our incinerator." He paused and grabbed a burn bag from the pile. "Watch me do this. Then it's your turn."

He tossed one of the bags through the gaping furnace door and watched as it immediately caught fire and burned up in seconds. "Just feed in one bag at a time, and let the fire do its job. Don't overload the furnace. Take your time. You should be done in about 15 minutes. I'll be back to check on you before then." Morrow turned and left me to burn the classified trash. That would be my job for the rest of the set of mids. At least I was warm and busy.

****

Morrow must have gotten sidetracked because he didn't come back to check on me. I waited a bit and then went back across to Ops once I was sure that all the classified material had burned and the boiler room was secure. Ops seemed cold compared to the boiler room, even though it was a late April morning. I guessed that the outside temperature was in the low 40s. I had read somewhere that our body temperature naturally drops in the hours just before dawn. Maybe that's why I was feeling so cold as I sat back down with Rich Roberts at the VHF pos.

We finally found some Czech radio traffic around 0630 local time and recorded a few cuts over the next hour or so. For the most part it was just Czech military radio operators doing comms checks on their networks and making sure their comrades were awake and could send and receive signals. There was nothing of any intelligence significance as far as I could tell.

One of the guys swept the Ops floor while we emptied the ash trays and cleaned up the coffee cups and other trash that we had generated over the shift. The day ladies didn't work Sundays, so we didn't have to worry about them. Baker Trick relieved us right on time at 0745. The trick change briefing only took a minute since there was nothing of note to pass on.

Most of us went down to the mess hall for breakfast, and then it was back to the Cabin to clean the latrine and sweep and buff the hallway before we were free to go to bed or do whatever we pleased. The guys who lived off the Hill, like Walrus and Wally Bunker didn't stop at the mess hall and weren't required to clean the Cabin. They went straight home after the shift ended.

That first shift turned out to be a typical mid shift. The other shifts weren't too different. The day shift on weekdays was usually the busiest time in Ops as our foreign adversaries conducted their training and exercises while we listened in and reported what they were doing to Herzo Base and NSA. The early part of the 1600-2400 swing shift could also be busy, but at least there weren't many day ladies or treads to get in the way. When things were slow, the trick chief would occasionally give someone the night off as "comp time" – compensatory time off – or CTO. I'm not sure what it compensated for, but it was always a welcome reward.

There were two days off between sets of shifts. The break from mids to swings was the best because it lasted 80 hours – from 0800 off your last mid until your first swing shift started at 1600 hours some 80 hours later. A lot of the guys used the long break to travel to Munich or even as far as Amsterdam. ASA outstations were rather lax about what we did on break, but of course travel to communist countries or through East Germany to Berlin was strictly forbidden. I hoped that one day I'd have the money to do some travelling, but my pay as an SP4 E-4 with less than 2 years of service was only $168 per month. I'd get a raise next month when I went over 2 years in service. My new pay would be $211 per month. Much better, but still not a lot of money for doing much travelling. All things considered, I knew I had it good compared to most GIs.

****

THE FIRST BREAK

Rich Roberts took off right after breakfast following our last mid shift, presumably to his beloved Munich and his university student friends. We were lucky enough that this long break spanned a weekend – an unusual occurrence for trick trash like us. A weekend break opened far more evening social opportunities than a midweek break when most civilians (i.e., girls) would be home preparing for the next day at work or school. Unfortunately for me, this break was coming at the end of the month, a few days short of pay day, and I didn't have much money – less than $20 until pay day. I already knew that Will Morrow seldom left the Hill, so I asked Joe Parker if there was anything worth doing down in Bishofsgruen.

Joe didn't have to think about it, "Reissmann's *Tanzcafe* in Bisch is the center of nightlife for most of the Amis from the Hill," he explained. "Otto Reissmann owns the place. It's a disco and bar. He started it in 1961 in a separate wing of the *Gasthof zur Post*. Last year he relocated it down the street to a new, two-story building built by another local businessman. The top floor was designed specifically to accommodate the *Tanzcafe*. There's a printing shop on the first floor, and you can tell when the presses are working overtime, because the dance floor upstairs shakes like crazy." Joe laughed as he recalled this point.

"Otto has another place called the *Milchbar* over in Wunsiedel near where he lives. He plans to open a third bar in Marktredwitz not too far from the Czech border. While he's not in Bisch, his girlfriend Herta, whom we call the First Lady, runs the *Tanzcafe*. Gerti is the waitress who serves those who prefer to sit at a table rather than at the bar. She's a truly kind soul and gets very hurt if she hears anyone refer to her as Durty Gerti. She will usually accept American money if you don't have any Marks. If she knows you and if you treat her well, she may even let you run a tab until pay day. She's been working for Otto since the *Tanzcafe* opened. Bob Day, one of the maintenance guys, lives with her."

"That name doesn't ring a bell. I don't think I've met him yet."

"Probably not, Jerry. He doesn't come into the Club or mess hall. Just goes to work on the electronic stuff upstairs in Topside and then heads back to Bisch. He drives a black VW Beetle."

I was curious about Gerti. "Does Gerti tend bar too?" I asked.

"Only occasionally. The regular barmaid is Erika. She's a pretty blonde. She's only been there a few months. She and Pete the Greek are a couple. Have you met Pete? He's a Czech Mary on Baker Trick. He's from Chicago like Will Morrow and is one of the toughest guys on the Hill, but he's also one of the nicest guys you'll ever meet. You'd want Pete and Will on your side if there was a bar fight." Joe laughed, but I got the message. They were not your typical Monterey Marys.

Joe continued his narrative, "Reissmann's sometimes has live bands on weekends. There's no cover charge when they have a band, but they make you buy a shot of cognac or Jaegermeister with whatever your first drink is. If there's no band, Gunther the DJ plays top-40 music and sometimes shows short Laurel and Hardy or Charlie Chaplin movie clips."

"Sounds good to me, Joe, except for the shots. I don't like cognac, and I hate the taste of Jaegermeister!" I replied with a grimace. "Do they serve food there too?"

"None at all, but you can get some surprisingly good *gulaschsuppe*. If you want to have a meal, try the *Post*, or if you're really hungry and have some money to spend, try the *Deutcher Adler* on the market square across from the church. They serve a huge schnitzel cordon bleu called the Bozniak. It's fantastic!" (1)

"I love schnitzel! You're making my mouth water, Joe." And I think my mouth actually was watering. I resolved to check out Reissmann's Saturday night. Now it was time to clean up the Cabin latrine and hallway and then get a few hours' sleep. The set of six mid shifts had really tired me out, but I didn't want to sleep away the break.

****

When I finally got back to the Dog Trick room, I noticed that Whipdick's bunk was stripped and stockaded and that his locker was wide open and empty. Morrow was in bed but still awake and smoking a cigarette.

I asked him, "Hey, what happened to Whipdick? He was here last night when we went on duty."

"I don't know for sure, but I think he pissed off Sergeant Rayburn. They were just looking for an excuse to send him back to Herzo. No one liked the guy, and his knives and whips were making everyone nervous, including Captain Medved. Good riddance if you ask me. I think they'll be sending up a new cook with the courier next Tuesday. He's gotta be an improvement over Whipdick."

"That's for sure. Let's hope the new cook is a better fit. A lot of us are misfits, but Whipdick was way off the charts."

Morrow just grunted, ground out his cigarette, put his Coke bottle glasses on the little table beside his bunk, and rolled onto his side to go to sleep. Ron Walters and Joe Parker were already snoring. The Bard was probably reading in the kino room Topside. I slid off my combat boots and stripped off my fatigues and then crawled into my bunk for a few hours of sleep.

****

Jack Rutherford rode along with me when I drove down to Bisch on Saturday evening to check out Reissmann's. Jack and his trick were working days, but he agreed to come with me as long as I promised that I'd get him back to the Cabin in time to get a decent night's sleep so he'd be fit for duty Sunday morning. It was barely 9 o'clock so there was plenty of room in the rutted parking lot next to Reissmann's building. We parked my vintage Mercedes in a spot that would be easy to get out of later if the lot got crowded.

We were dressed in our best civilian clothes. It wasn't a regulation – at least for our unit – but nearly all of the guys wanted to dress up and look sharp. Jack was wearing a subdued blue glen plaid sport jacket, black dress pants, and white shirt, and a solid sky-blue tie. I had on a navy-blue blazer, grey slacks, a light blue button-down shirt, and a regimental-style blue and gold stripped tie. There was no way we were going to pass ourselves off as Germans, especially with our American shoes and haircuts, but what the hell, we felt good about the way we looked.

We climbed up the wide, well-lighted stairway to the building's second level and walked through double doors and into the *tanzcafe*. The dance floor and bandstand were directly in front of us. The horseshoe-shaped bar was to the right, while the entire left side of the large room was filled with booths and tables. The band had just begun playing its first set – covers of Beatles songs for the most part. It was still relatively early in the evening, so the place wasn't too crowded yet.

Jack and I sat at the bar with Bear and Anson and ordered bottles of beer. The blonde barmaid, who introduced herself as Erika, told us that we had to have a shot of schnapps with the first drink. She served us the beer with shots of cognac on the side. I offered mine to Bear, and he eagerly accepted. Anson was drinking a Fanta orange soda. Jack gave his cognac to Bear too. Bear was off to a good start while the night was still young. He had my shot, Jack's, Anson's, and his own – plus the beer he had in front of him.

Joe Parker was sitting at a booth on the far side of the room with three girls who were obviously enjoying his company. His self-taught proficiency in German and his natural charm and self-confidence seemed to have captivated the girls. It wasn't long before he was out on the dance floor with one of them. Joe was a smooth dancer and looked like he was enjoying himself. I wondered silently if I'd ever be bold enough to ask one of the local ladies to dance. Maybe someday. Definitely not tonight.

A dark-haired guy with the body of a gymnast and the smile of a choir boy approached the bar and greeted Bear and Anson and then extended his hand to me, "Hi, I'm Pete Stavros. I think I remember you from Monterey. You're a Czech, right?" His handshake was firm with a hint of great strength.

"That I am. I'm Jerry Daniels and I'm on Dog Trick. I remember you too now that I can link your name to your face. You were a couple months behind us at DLI, but you obviously got to Schneeberg well before Jack and me."

"Right. I didn't go through special training at Ft. Meade like you. I went directly from DLI to Herzo Base and then straight to the Hill from Herzo. How do you like it so far?" Pete seemed genuinely interested.

"Oh, I like it a hellavu lot better than Herzo, Pete. We haven't been here too long, but I like it a lot so far."

Erika brought him a beer but didn't include the schnapps. I figured that Pete got his drinks for free if Erika was serving. The waitress stopped to greet Pete and give him a little kiss on the cheek. "This is Gerti. She is a great waitress and a dear friend."

Gerti smiled and shook hands with Jack and me. I liked it that German girls almost always shook hands when they were introduced. American girls seldom offered their hand unless you made the first move. With German girls, it seemed automatic. Gerti went back to waiting tables and getting drinks from a service bar in the rear of the dance hall. I noticed an older woman filling Gerti's orders there. I assumed that she must be Herta, the First Lady that Joe had told me about yesterday, Otto Reissmann's girlfriend.

Jack and I had two or three beers at the bar while we listened to the band and checked out the locals. It was a little after 10:15 pm when two girls walked through the door. One was a tall blonde who carried herself with the confidence of a woman who knows she is good looking. The other gal was a petite brunette, who I thought was attractive. When I looked over to say something to Jack, I could see that his eyes were wide and that he couldn't take his eyes off the blonde.

"Take it easy, Jack. She's probably meeting someone. Besides, she looks a little out of our league."

Jack didn't say anything at first. He just continued looking at the blonde. He wasn't leering or ogling, just looking with awe and admiration.

"Jack, are you okay?" I asked.

"Ummm...I'm not sure. It sounds crazy, but I think I just experienced love at first sight. Holy moly! She is beautiful! I think I'm gonna marry her."

I didn't know what to say, so the best I could manage was, "Uh huh. Good luck with that."

71

Jack asked Anson and Bear if they knew who she was. They didn't know her name, but they said she came in most weekends and liked to dance. Jack turned to Pete Stavros and asked him. "Oh, that's Heidi. She's a regular in here. She lives with her mother in a house just up the hill from here on Route 303. She's a nice girl. She even speaks some English. Do you want me to introduce you?"

Jack blanched, "No. No. Not tonight. Maybe next time we're in here. But thanks, I'd really like to meet her."

"No problem. She's friends with Gerti even though Gerti is several years older. I think Heidi is only 18 or 19."

Jack kept his eyes riveted on Heidi for the next hour. She danced with a couple different German fellas, but she didn't seem to have a boyfriend or anyone special.

My money had just about run out by 11 pm, and I knew Jack had to work days the next morning, so we paid our tab and drove back up the Hill to the Cabin. The couple hours we spent in Reissmann's was time well spent. We had met a few of the locals and felt comfortable and welcome in the *tanzcafe*. And Jack had fallen in love.

(1) Thanks to Ed Railsback for putting together a history of Reissmann's and posting it on Phil Ward's Schneebergvets.org website.

****

PRAYERS, POKER, AND PAYDAY

A cold rain was falling outside the trick room in the Cabin when I awoke Sunday morning. I didn't have anything planned for the day and expected to go up to the kino room after breakfast to see if anyone was going to show a movie. The Bard was waiting for me back in our room after I had showered and shaved.

"Hey, Jerry, I noticed that you wear a religious medal with your dog tags and that you've made some comments that make me think you're a Catholic. Am I right?"

"Yeah, I am, Stan, but I'm not a particularly good one. I got lazy once I enlisted and seldom go to church now. Why do you ask?"

"Well, I was wondering…actually, I was hoping that you'd do me a big favor and take me over to Bindlach so I can attend Mass there at the post chapel. I'd be willing to pay for gas. I try not to miss Mass when we're not on duty on Sundays, but I don't have a car. Any chance you'd take me? I'd be grateful."

The look in his eyes told me that this truly was important to Stan. I didn't have anything else to do, and I liked Stan and wanted to foster a friendship with him. "Sure. What the hell. What time do we have to be there?" I asked.

"Mass starts at 11 am. It takes around 30 minutes to get there, so we have plenty of time before we have to leave. Thanks, Jerry. This means a lot to me."

"No problem. It will do me good to get off the Hill."

My parents always expected me to dress up for church, so I decided to wear the same clothes that I wore to Reissmann's the night before. Traffic was light on the way to Bindlach, so we were there in less than 30 minutes and still had 15 minutes before the service began. Stan and I had a good conversation about how we wound up in ASA and on Schneeberg. He told me that he had been raised as a Baptist/Methodist on St. Clements Island, Georgia, and that he had converted to Catholicism while in college – much to the dismay of his family.

"My roommate at Georgia State was a practicing Catholic. He invited me to several Newman Club social events and eventually to come to Mass with him when I expressed curiosity. The Newman Club chaplain, a Jesuit priest, was a good guy. He shared my interest in the theater and could tell that I was searching for something meaningful on a spiritual plane. To be honest, I was inspired not only by his faith but by the way he, my roommate, and their friends led their lives. They all seemed to be genuinely good people who were trying to live in accordance with their beliefs without acting sanctimonious. After a few months of soul searching, I decided to enroll in the Rite of Christian Initiation for Adults and become a Catholic. The following Easter I was received into the Church. That was three years ago."

"How did your family react to that?"

"Well, I didn't tell them until I went home for the summer after sophomore year. At first, they were aghast, then confused, and finally angry. Terribly angry. They tried to make me change my mind, but I was firmly committed to the faith. I wouldn't have converted unless I was certain it was the right decision for me. My folks threatened to stop paying my tuition and expenses, but I wouldn't back down.

"At the end of summer, they made good on their threat. I knew I couldn't afford to go back to school on my own dime, and I knew that I'd probably be drafted as soon as my local draft board took away my 2-S student deferment. I also knew I didn't want to be drafted, so I talked to the various armed forces recruiters and decided that ASA would give me the best opportunity to gain college credits and travel to interesting places where I might even be able to pursue my interest in the theater.

"I enlisted, went to basic at Ft. Jackson, South Carolina, and then went through a 47-week Russian class at Monterey. I did well in the Russian course, sang in the Russian Department choir, and loved the arts scene in Monterey and Carmel- by-the-Sea. Eighteen months after enlisting, I was at Schneeberg sitting a Russian pos and trying to save money to go back to school after my enlistment is up in a couple of years. What about you?"

"My story isn't too much different from yours, Stan. In fact, we even have a Jesuit link. I went to a Jesuit high school in Brooklyn, New York, and then spent a year at Fordham University's School of Business, another Jesuit institution. I definitely did not distinguish myself at Fordham. The dean called me to his office in the spring of freshman year and told me that my returning for sophomore year was not an option. Frankly, I was relieved. I didn't want a career in business. I had no idea what I did want as a career, but I knew it wasn't in the business world. Like you, I was sure I'd be drafted sooner rather than later, so I shopped around the recruiting stations for the best deal I could get. ASA was it. I loved Monterey, and I like the work. The Army stuff sucks, but I really do like the intercept work."

It was time to go in for Mass. The sign outside the building indicated that the Catholic parish at the chapel was dedicated to Our Lady of the Border. That seemed more than a little incongruous to me at the time. Does Mary really recognize borders, or does she mourn them. I guess it made sense in a warped sort of way. The mission of the armored cavalry unit at Bindlach was to patrol part of the German border shared with communist Czechoslovakia. I pushed the thought from my mind and tried to focus on the service.

After Mass, Stan offered to buy me a meal at the PX snack bar, but I wanted to get back to the Hill to write a couple letters, do some reading, and maybe watch a movie.

One of the fun things about going to Bindlach was that the MPs at the gate almost always saluted us on the way in and out of the casern, even though we were enlisted guys like the MPs and didn't rate a salute. Our cars had U.S. forces license plates, but we were not required to display bumper stickers on the front and back which would show our home installation and which were color coded to indicate whether we were officers, enlisted, or civilian contractor personnel. The MPs had been trained in the concept of "When in doubt, salute," and that's what they did nearly every time we entered or left the base. Of course, we would return the salute, but we did so in a casual manner. I guess we were easily amused.

    ****

The poker players in the Club were a man short on Sunday night, and Will Morrow asked me if I wanted to join them at the table.

"I'd like that, Will, but I only have a few bucks left until pay day tomorrow."

Will was quick to respond, "No problem. We never play with cash. We use chips – white ones are a nickel, red is a dime, blue is a quarter. I keep a book on who wins and who loses, and everyone settles up as soon as we get paid. It's a fairly good system, and the stakes are low enough so that no one takes too big a hit if they lose. C'mon. Grab a seat."

I didn't want to say no because I thought that playing would give me a chance to get better acquainted with some of the other guys, including Jolly Ollie, who was a fixture at the table. I sat in and tried my best to understand the games they played. I knew five card stud and five card draw, but they were playing more exotic games with wild cards and names I had never heard before. It didn't take me long to be $10 down.

"Sorry, guys, but that's my limit. I can't afford to lose more than that – especially on my first night at the table."

Jolly Ollie was quick to agree. "Good call, Daniels. A man should never gamble with money he can't afford to lose. You paid $10 for a poker lesson tonight. I hope it was worth it. There's no one waiting to sit in on the game, so why don't you just stay here at the table and watch us play. Pay attention, and you should learn something. Morrow is a damn good poker player, and Weasel ain't bad either. I won't brag, but I'm not too bad myself. Grab another beer and watch."

"Thanks, Top. I'd like that a lot." It was the first time Sergeant Henry had talked to me off duty, and it surprised me a little that he remembered my name and that he wasn't as gruff as he seemed to be during the duty day. Of course, he had the ever-present cigar stub in his mouth and even paused to light it from time to time and take a puff. When I got myself a beer from Doug Broussard at the bar, I got one for Ollie too.

"Thanks, Daniels. I won't turn down a free beer."

I watched the game and the players for a good 90 minutes. At one point early on, Ollie took a card from the empty box that had held the deck. It listed the relative rank of poker hands ranging from one pair up to a royal flush, and it also showed the odds of getting each hand.

"Thanks, Top. I needed a cheat sheet like that."

"I could tell that from the way you were playing before," he made a sound like a quick cough which I surmised was his idea of a chuckle. "When you're bored and have some time on your hands, instead of playing solitaire, try playing five-handed poker with yourself. It's a good way to practice shuffling and dealing and to see how the cards fall. Poker is more skill than luck. Work at it a little."

"Will do. Thanks again."

Ollie resumed playing and then looked back to me when he folded a hand. "Daniels, were you in Reissmann's last night?"

"Yeah, I was there for a while, Top. I was there with Jack Rutherford, and we left around 11 o'clock so he could work a day shift today. Why?"

Ollie didn't answer my question, but he asked his own. "Did you see Bear there last night?"

"I saw him and sat at the bar with him and Anson until I left. Pete Stavros was sitting with us most of the time too."

"Was Bear drunk?"

I was surprised at the directness of the question and was unsure how to reply. I figured that the truth was better than a lie when it came to talking to the first sergeant. "I don't know about drunk, Top, but he was obviously feeling no pain. He had a couple beers while I was there, and I think he may have had a few shots of schnapps too. He seemed pretty mellow to me when we left."

"Was he being obnoxious or combative?"

I was starting to feel like I was being interrogated. "Did something happen, Sarge? He seemed okay when I was there."

"I don't want to say too much about it right now, but there've been some allegations that Bear did some serious damage to the men's room at Reissmann's. Do you know anything about that?"

"No way! I saw Bear go out to use the can once or twice, but he wasn't being loud or aggressive. He may have been a little unsteady on his feet, but like I said, he seemed mellow and even sorta happy. I can't believe that he got out of hand. Besides, Anson was with him all the time I was there, and Anson wasn't drinking."

After several minutes, Ollie threw his cards onto the center of the table, counted his chips, and said, "That's it for me for the night. I'm heading up Topside to get some sleep. As always, gentlemen, it has been a pleasure to take your money." He winked, put his field jacket and baseball hat on, and walked out the Club door.

Once Ollie was gone, I turned to Will Morrow and asked, "What the hell's going on?"

"I don't know for sure 'cause I wasn't down there last night, but the word is that someone tore the sink right off the wall in the men's room and smashed it on the floor. That would take a lot of strength, and Bear was one of the last guys seen using the can before the damage was discovered. He's strong enough to do something like that, but I've never seen him turn into a nasty drunk. He usually just gets happy and sleepy when he drinks too much. If he does gets wobbly, he'll put his head down on the bar and fall asleep. That's what Anson said he did last night."

"What about Bear? Does he admit doing it?"

"That's where it gets interesting. Bear says he can't remember doing anything like that. In fact, he says he doesn't remember anything after the band stopped playing at midnight. He and Anson mentioned that there was a table of rowdy Germans who seemed to know Otto Reissmann, but none of the Amis paid any attention to them. Reissmann's the one who says Bear did the damage, and he wants Bear to pay for it. It's gonna cost a few hundred Marks to replace the sink and install a new one."

"Wow! That's pretty close to what Bear makes in a month. Is he going to pay it?"

"He says he'll try to pay it if there's any proof that he really did it, but he honestly can't remember doing anything like that, and Anson insists that he couldn't have done it. Ollie told Bear not to say or do anything or have any contact with Herr Reissmann or his people until Ollie can talk to Captain Medved tomorrow morning."

"That's good advice. I'm glad that Ollie is trying to keep an open mind."

Morrow nodded and said, "Ollie really is a good NCO. You'll see that the longer you're here. He'll never be your buddy, but he won't try to dick you away either – unless you deserve it. Oh, one more thing. Ollie has decreed that Reissmann's is off limits and out of bounds until this matter is settled. He'll have Medved confirm that order tomorrow."

"Oh, crap. I'm sorry to hear that. I had a good time last night and was looking forward to going back soon. When Jack Rutherford finds out, he's gonna freak out."

"Why?! He's a weed like you. It shouldn't matter to him. He can drink at the *Post* instead. Some of the guys hang out in the back there. The room has a juke box, and the owner closes the door to that part of the *gasthaus,* so our people don't bother the locals in the main room."

"Let's just say that Jack saw a girl at Reissmann's last night and instantly fell in love."

"You're shitting me, right? You mean he fell in lust."

"No, Will, I don't think it's that. I think he felt some cosmic connection or something. Do me a favor and don't mention it to him. OK?"

"No. I won't. I hardly know him anyway."

****

Monday was the first business day of May and payday on the Hill. Captain Montgomery, our company commander from Herzo Base brought our pay to Schneeberg in an olive drab military sedan driven by an MP. Both the MP and Captain Montgomery were armed with .45 caliber pistols. We were all paid in cash at that time, and they were also carrying a large quantity of Deutche Marks (DM) so we could convert some of our pay from dollars to Marks for use in Bisch and elsewhere on the economy.

The captain set up a folding table in the hallway just outside the orderly room. The table was covered with a wool Army blanket. Montgomery's .45 rested on the table beside a large metal lockbox filled with cash. The MP stood at parade rest beside the captain, alert for any payroll robbers who might happen by our isolated mountain top.

Captain Medved, wearing a .45 in a shoulder holster, was at an adjoining folding table converting dollars to Marks at the going exchange rate of 4 DM for one dollar. Jolly Ollie sat next to Medved collecting the monthly assessment from everyone to pay the German cooks and helpers working in the mess hall so we junior enlisted men on the Hill didn't have to pull KP. Sergeant Gray was at the table with Ollie, trying half-heartedly to convince us to sign up for savings bonds. Will Morrow was at a small table settling the pay day stakes poker accounts, collecting from losers and paying off the winners. I paid my $10.

Doug Broussard was sitting in a folding chair several feet past Morrow with some cash and a cigar box with slips of paper in it.

"Hey, Doug! What are you collecting for? A charity or for that orphanage we help out?" I asked.

"No, nothing like that. It's a raffle. I'm running it for the first time this month. It's a dollar a chance. How many do you want?" He was a little furtive as he asked.

"Umm...I don't know. What's the prize if I win?"

"No one told you?" he asked cautiously.

"No. I don't know anything about your raffle. What's the deal?"

"Well, this is unofficial, of course, but...Ehhh...Well, you get one entry for each dollar you kick in. You fill out a slip with you name on it and toss it in the cigar box. The drawing will be held at 9 o'clock tonight at the Club. I'll pick someone at random to draw the winning name."

"OK. But what's the prize?!"

"Like I said, this in unofficial. We can't let Captain Medved know. OK?"

"Alright. I understand. Why all the secrecy? What's the prize?" I was getting impatient and less interested in buying a chance with every passing second.

Doug half whispered, "There are actually two prizes. The first one is a steak dinner with all the trimmings at the Army hotel in Nuremberg."

"OK. That sounds good. What's the other prize?"

"A piece of ass at the Wall in Nuremberg."

"What?! The Wall is off limits to all U.S. military personnel, isn't it? That's where the prostitutes work. I know it's legal in Germany, but it's definitely a no-no for us. Are you crazy?"

Doug was nonplussed, "It's no big deal. The MPs don't hang out looking for GIs there. And the ladies are happy to have the business. Whadaya say? Are you in?"

I bought a chance and hoped I wouldn't win. I don't know how many chances Doug sold that day, but I'm sure he made a nice profit. The steak dinner at the hotel probably cost less than $10, and the fee at the Wall was 40 DM or $10, plus tip if you left happy.

****

I played some pool and then read in the kino room before going down to the mess hall at the tail end of the lunch period. Anson was sitting by himself at one of the tables, so I joined him once I got my food.

"What's up, Anson? Any news on Bear?" I asked.

"Sergeant Henry talked to the C.O. as soon as the captain got in this morning. They closed the door to his office, but I could hear Medved yelling and cussing up a storm. I heard him say something about damaging German-American relations. I couldn't hear what Ollie had to say, but the C.O. seemed to calm down after a few minutes. Sarge told me that the C.O. was going to go downtown to talk to Mr. Reissmann and get his version of what supposedly happened.

"He questioned Bear in his office for 10 or 15 minutes, and Bear told him that he didn't remember much after midnight but that he honestly didn't believe he did any damage to anything. He also told the captain that he would pay for the damage if ordered to do so. I told Medved what I told Ollie yesterday. That Bear was with me all evening and that I don't believe that he did what Reissmann says he did. Pete Stavros should be able to back us up too."

"So, did Captain Medved believe Bear? Did he go see Reissmann?"

"I think he's giving him the benefit of the doubt for now. We all know that Bear's an honest guy who does his best to avoid trouble. And, yeah, after everyone got paid, the C.O. got hold of Father Pat to translate for him, and they went down to see Reissmann in Bisch. They were gone about an hour. When he got back to his office, Medved called Ollie in and did some more yelling and cussin', but this time it was all about Otto Reissmann.

"Ollie told him that he had already put out the word that the *tanzcafe* was off limits to all Schneebergers until further notice. That pleased the C.O. because he had told Reissmann that he wasn't going to allow any of us to go in there until either he or Reissmann could prove whether Bear did the damage or if someone else did."

81

"That sounds fair. If you believe Bear, that's good enough for me."

"Thanks. I don't really care one way or another about not going down there, but I know that some of the other guys are going to be pretty pissed if the boycott lasts more than a week or two. The *Post* is okay, but not too many girls go there. They like the live music and dancing at Reissmann's."

"Yeah, we'll have to see what happens. Dog Trick is working swings all this week, so we wouldn't be able to go there even if we wanted to."

Anson went back up the hill to the orderly room, and I went back to the trick room and passed the word to the guys who were hanging out and starting to get ready to go to work at 3:45 pm. Joe Parker was the only one who seemed unhappy about the boycott. I think he was developing a close relationship with one of the Bisch bunnies, and the only way he could contact her was in person at Reissmann's. He told me that her parents weren't too fond of Amis, especially African-Americans like him.

****

Swing shifts were usually hectic for the first couple hours. The day ladies and treads were underfoot on weekdays until 4:30 or 5 pm, and the communications networks we targeted generally kept our intercept positions busy until the early evening. Starting swings on a Monday afternoon was the price you paid for having the long mids-to-swings break over a weekend. Dog Trick could expect to be busy for the next five days. Spring and summer were the peak field training periods for our potential adversaries on the other side of the border. The Czechoslovak Signal Troops' motto was "*Bez spojeni neni veleni* (Without communications there is no command)." So, while the Czechs and their allies were training out in the field and conducting exercises, we could count on being very busy listening in to what they were up to and reporting that information to Herzo Base and beyond. Being busy made the time pass quickly for us, and it was even a little exciting. And so it would be for this six-day set of swings.

****

The mess hall crew was a cook short since Whipdick was sent back to Herzo. That meant no midnight chow over the past weekend or on Monday night either. If you were hungry before a mid or after a swing when the mess hall was closed, the only option was whatever C Rations were available in Ops. After Tuesday's swing shift we were happy to see the mess hall lights on as we walked down the road to the Cabin. The oncoming mid shift that relieved us had told us that midnight chow was available tonight and that a new cook was on duty. Sure enough, a dark-haired guy with acne-scarred cheeks wearing cooks' whites and PFC stripes was at the grill in the mess hall making eggs to order, pancakes, bacon, and sausages. I asked for two eggs over medium and grabbed a couple strips of bacon while the eggs cooked on the sizzling griddle.

"Welcome to the Hill. I'm Jerry Daniels, and the rest of this bunch are all on Dog Trick."

We didn't shake hands. He had a spatula in one hand and tongs in the other. "I'm John Ritter. Anson told me I'd be bunking in the Dog Trick room so I volunteered to cook midnight chow tonight so I could meet some of my new roommates. I came up with the Herzo courier this afternoon after you all went to work."

"No relation to Tex Ritter I hope?" I asked jokingly and got a curious stare in reply.

"Uh, no relation that I know of. I'm from Cleveland. Never been to Texas, and I'm not too fond of country music either, if you wanna know."

"That's fine, John. The cook you replaced was a real shit-kickin' country boy and liked to play his music when we trick trash were trying to sleep. He had a collection of hunting knives and whips too, and that made us all a little nervous. We called him Whipdick, but not to his face. There was something spooky about him – like a serial killer in waiting. I dunno. Anyway, I'm glad to meet you. I hope you like it here."

In the days that followed, we learned that Ritter had been a student at a community college in Cuyahoga County and had lived with his family in the Cleveland suburbs. He hadn't been taking enough courses to qualify as a full-time student, so he didn't meet the criteria for a student draft deferment. He was 20 years old and got his draft notice a few days after his birthday. He duly reported for induction into the Army shortly thereafter and did his basic training at Ft. Leonard Wood, Missouri.

He apparently scored high on all his post-induction tests. This, and the fact that he was a high school grad with a little college behind him, drew the attention of an ASA recruiter at Leonard Wood who tried his best to convince Ritter to sign up for an extra two years so he could get "special" training in ASA. Ritter wasn't interested, and that was the end of it. After basic, he received orders to attend cooks' school. It wasn't fun, but it wasn't too bad either. He discovered that he enjoyed cooking. Almost all his classmates received orders to Vietnam at graduation, but Ritter was sent to Germany, and some clerk at the replacement depot in Frankfurt sent him to Herzo Base. Herzo was okay, he told us, but he heard good things about Schneeberg and jumped at the opportunity to replace Whipdick on the Hill and cook in a small mess hall where he could better hone his culinary skills.

Ritter fit in with Dog Trick and the rest of us on the Hill right from the very start. He respected our need for off-duty sleep during hours that weren't always in sync with his duty schedule in the mess hall. Besides that, he was a damn good cook who took pride in his work. Not a typical draftee.

Ritter became a regular at the Club. He'd drink a beer or two, but he didn't hit it hard like so many of the others did. One evening a few nights after his arrival, he was sitting at the bar writing in a notebook when Sef, the German handyman who helped maintain the detachment, came into the Club to check that the kerosene heater was working properly. It could get cold on the Hill even in early May. Sef was an unkempt little guy of indeterminate age who wore layers of rumpled clothing, even during the warmer weather. He drove an old Fiat that was much smaller than a VW Beetle. He was famous for almost never speaking to any of the Amis. He just did whatever needed doing and went about his business. Ritter eyed him curiously and turned to Doug Broussard when Sef left.

"Who's the grommet?" he asked.

Doug gave him a puzzled look, "Grommet? I don't know what that is, but the German man who was just in here is Sef. He's the site handyman. What's a grommet?"

"You never heard of grommets?" Ritter asked incredulously.

"Well, I think it's some kind of hardware. I never heard the word referring to a person. Maybe it's a Cleveland thing."

"Maybe so. You really never heard of grommets before?

"No. What are they?"

"I thought everyone knew about them. Grommets are those scruffy guys with shaggy hair and stubbly beards who hang out in bus station rest rooms. They're usually perverts or weirdos," Ritter explained in all seriousness.

Doug cracked up and laughed heartily at the image until tears were in his eyes. I guess he could see that Sef might meet that description. He called over to the poker players and relayed what Ritter had said about Sef being a grommet. Everyone thought it was hilarious, even Ollie. And that's how John Ritter earned his Snow Mountain nickname. From then on, he was known as Grommet Cook. It was a term of endearment, respect, and acceptance.

I wondered how some of the others got their nicknames. Some were obvious – like Bear, Lurch, Jolly Ollie, Cajun, Large Louis, and even Whipdick. Other nicknames, like Weasel, Evil Crow, Whiskey Man, and Poop were a puzzle. Maybe I'd ask more questions when I wasn't a weed anymore. Maybe I'd even get a nickname of my own.

****

THE CRITIC

The most important responsibility of all our intelligence agencies is to safeguard the United States of America and its interests at home and abroad. The number one priority is to detect and report an impending attack against the U.S., its armed forces, or its allies – that includes, of course, the impending outbreak of war. The most current available Intelligence Community Directive defines critical Information as "information concerning possible threats to U.S. national security that are so significant that they require the immediate attention of the President and the National Security Council. Critical information includes the decisions, intentions, or actions of foreign governments, organizations, or individuals that could imminently and materially jeopardize vital U.S. policy, economic, information system, critical infrastructure, cyberspace, or military interests." (1)

Serious intelligence reporting deficiencies were identified in the mid-1950s. An Intelligence Community (IC)-wide study begun in late 1957 demonstrated that many critically important intelligence items were being handled in a routine manner and that they frequently required more than 24 hours to reach the White House. In terms of averages, critical intelligence information would take nine and a half hours to move from the field reporter to intelligence users in Washington, including the White House. This was obviously unacceptable in the nuclear age. The National Security Council issued a directive (NSCID No. 7) designating the Department of Defense as executive agent for creating and managing a world-wide communications system for the transmission of critical intelligence. This led to the establishment of the CRITIC system of procedures for rapid reporting over this world-wide communications net.

Under this new system, field reporting of critical intelligence was to be carried out via a special vehicle known as a CRITIC, with amplification and explanation of the initial data forwarded in CRITIC Follow-up reports which were also to be sent at the highest message precedence. Messages carrying this indicator would receive simultaneous electrical dissemination to all the main intelligence agencies, the Strategic and the Tactical Air Commands, and other key military organizations. The system was put into effect on 21 July 1958. By the end of the first year of operations the average transmission times for critical intelligence had dropped to an hour or less. The ultimate goal called for CRITIC messages handled by field facilities to be sent with an average speed of 10 minutes or less. Numerous test messages were transmitted in substantially less than ten minutes proving that the goal of "speeds approaching ten minutes" were attainable under the right conditions. (2)

Critical information may originate from (and be reported by) any U.S. government official in the IC. ASA personnel were thoroughly trained in CRITIC reporting, and it was emphasized to them that anyone, no matter rank, could issue a CRITIC and that the watchword for CRITIC reporting was "When in doubt, send it out." However, since a CRITIC would be received and read at the highest levels of our government, one could be sure that the decision to issue a CRITIC would be subject to great scrutiny and Monday morning quarterbacking. Practice CRITIC drills were conducted monthly at Schneeberg and other ASA stations to ensure that all personnel knew what they were to do in the event they recognized critical intelligence information. However, the generation and transmittal of an actual CRITIC was an extremely rare event at ASA European border sites in the mid-1960s.

The men of Dog Trick had money in their pockets after pay day and a set of six swings that ended at midnight Saturday. We had had little opportunity to spend our cash before going on the swings-to-days break on Sunday and Monday. It was a dry weekend for us. No drinking at the *Post* in Bisch or even at the Club until Sunday. And, of course, Reissmann's was still off limits. There was a rumor circulating in the mess hall on

Sunday afternoon that Jack Rutherford had been seen going into Reissmann's Saturday evening in defiance of the boycott. If it was true, he was probably trying to see Heidi, the object of his desire. Erika the barmaid may have told Pete Stavros because Pete reportedly had a quiet word with Jack on Sunday morning, during which Jack allegedly looked rattled. The word was that Pete had warned Jack not to venture back into Reissmann's until the incident about Bear had been cleared up. Even weeds knew that when Pete the Greek had a quiet word with you, you had better listen.

It was becoming apparent that something big was brewing on the other side of the border. Czech signal troops seemed to be setting up additional communications networks using procedures and characteristics we hadn't seen before, and they were expanding the ones with which we were familiar. We also began hearing far more Soviet military communications than normal and even some East German networks, which was very unusual. Just before we went off duty on Saturday night, we received a message from Herzo Base advising us that final preparations were underway for a major Warsaw Pact exercise just across the border in northwestern Czechoslovakia. The Czechoslovak People's Army and its air force would be the primary players and were to be assisted or reinforced by elements from the Group of Soviet Forces Germany (GSFG) and from the East German *NVA (Die Nationale Volksarmee der DDR)*, the National People's Army of the German Democratic Republic. It was beginning to look like Dog Trick would have an exceptionally busy set of day shifts.

Herzo Base sent up several additional Czech, Russian, and German intercept operators so that all positions in Ops would be fully manned and that more timely transcription could be done on site before tapes of the intercept were sent to Herzo. They also dispatched a special intercept van known as an RRCV-4 which consisted of a steel shelter mounted on a deuce-and-a-half truck. It had its own electrical power generator and rotatable Yagi antenna system. Doug Broussard and Don McGrew were to man it along with a couple guys from Herzo. The rest of us didn't know exactly what the van was for, but we figured it had something to do with the Soviet target. We knew that Don McGrew had helped design the equipment lay-out in the van and that he was considered the expert on its operation.

We were on break as scheduled Sunday and Monday, but we were ordered to stay within 25 miles of the Hill so we could return quickly if needed. By Monday morning we knew that the exercise had started and that Ops was a madhouse of activity. I saw Pat Riley grabbing a meal in the mess hall, and he looked frazzled and exhausted. When I asked him what was going on, he just shook his head and said, "You'll find out everything you need to know tomorrow morning. Tell Morrow to get your trick to work early because your trick will have a lot to catch up to do before you can relieve the mid shift."

****

And Father Pat was right. Our trick arrived 30 minutes early for shift change Tuesday morning and still didn't have enough time to digest everything that had been going on since oh-dark-thirty Monday when the exercise kicked off. Tapes were piled up in the TR hut, and three linguists were squeezed in there churning out transcripts of the intercept. Two analysts who had been sent up from Herzo were pouring over the transcripts trying to make sense of what was happening on the other side of the border. They were writing technical reports to send to Herzo where the information would be blended with data from other stations and sources and reported to NSA and other military and civilian organizations.

Understanding all of this was way above my current paygrade. My job was to sit the VHF position and record intercept from the networks to which the Herzo analysts had assigned the highest priority. To be honest, I didn't understand very much of what I was hearing and recording, but I did my best to try to write a basic gist of each cut. I couldn't help feeling a sense of regret that I hadn't worked harder in Monterey to master the Czech language.

The exercise activity began to slacken off around midday on Saturday when we heard some of the networks send out orders to tear down their communications facilities and prepare to return to their garrisons. That was good news to our tired ears. We were mentally exhausted from the intensive activity of the past few days, which reminded us that there was a chance that someday the communist forces might decide to cross the border and attack NATO...and us.

****

Sunday morning started out very quietly. There was very little activity on the VHF side, which was typical for a Sunday. There were still a few radiotelephone nets active on the UHF side, which Rich Roberts was monitoring. He only had one recorder rolling, and from what I could tell from looking over his shoulder at his notes, he wasn't listening to any high-level communications – just a couple of relatively low-ranking radio operators b.s.ing to pass the time of day. I went back to the VHF side to see if there was anything going on there.

A few minutes later all hell broke loose. Rich virtually levitated out of his chair screaming "Holy shit! Holy shit! I can't believe this! Holy shit!" His face was beet red, and his eyes seemed to be ready to pop out of his skull. "Holy shit! I've got a CRITIC!"

That sure got the attention everyone on Dog Trick. Will Morrow literally dropped whatever papers he was working on back by the trick chief's desk and ran over to Roberts at the UHF pos. "Calm down, Rich. What do you have? Calm down and tell me what you heard." Morrow was not an excitable guy anyway, and he exuded an inner calm as he tried to determine what had Roberts so stirred up.

"Will, no shit. I have a CRITIC!! The Czech op said that World War Three is going to start tomorrow. I know that's what he said. There's no doubt. It's a CRITIC! What do I do now?!"

"Are you sure that's what was said?"

"One hundred and ten percent. He clearly said '*třetí světová válka bude začít zitra rano...*' The third world war will begin tomorrow morning. I swear he said it." Rich was so excited and distressed that he looked like he might burst a blood vessel.

Morrow was a Russian linguist, not a Czech, so he turned to me, "Daniels! Is that what it means?"

"Yes. Absolutely!" I had no doubt either. "That's exactly what it means."

Morrow paused only a minute and then started barking orders, "Daniels! Run, and I mean RUN, over to Topside, bang on the comms center door, and tell Matt Rivington that we have a CRITIC coming his way."

I was out of my chair and heading for the door before Will even finished his sentence.

"Cavanaugh! Run to the orderly room and tell the CQ to call Pat Riley at home and tell him to get his ass up to Ops immediately if not sooner! Got that? OK, then see if Ollie is in his room. Tell him we have a CRITIC

91

situation and that he needs to call Captain Medved and the Ops NCOIC at home and get them in here pronto. If Ollie's not in his room, tell the CQ to call Medved and Sergeant Karney at home and get them here. Then see if Ollie is in the Club or the mess hall and let him know we have a big flap."

Jim Cavanaugh, the Russian op we called the Walrus, was out the door in a flash. The rest of the trick looked like they were all in shock. Morrow barked at them, "The rest of you get back to your positions and start searching the spectrum for any unusual activity! It's been quiet today. Maybe the bad guys are maintaining radio silence. This could be the real deal. Remember that Pearl Harbor took place on a Sunday. Do your jobs and pay attention to detail. Do it now!"

Morrow turned back to Rich Roberts at the UHF position and got him to sit down. His AN/TNH-11 recorder was still turning, but the two Czech radio operators he had been listening to had apparently ended their conversation while Rich was declaring the CRITIC situation."

"OK, Rich. We need to get the initial CRITIC message out within 10 minutes of recognition. The clock is ticking. Just do an extremely basic and short who, what, when, where narrative to get things rolling. I'll write down the tech details, frequency, and net designator, while you write the basic sentence or two."

Meanwhile, Matt Rivington had arrived after sprinting across the road from the Topside comms center to Ops. He was so pumped up that he seemed to be running in place as he waited for Morrow and Rich to draft the initial CRITIC report. It only took a couple minutes to draft. Morrow handed it to Matt who read it aloud as if to confirm the content, "*According to an unidentified Czechoslovak People Army radio operator, quote the third word war will begin tomorrow morning. Unquote. The operator made the statement to a second operator at 0926 Zulu this day. Additional details will follow ASAP. Tech details below.*" Matt looked at Morrow and Rich, "Is that it? This is real, Right? Not a test?"

"This is real, Matt! Send it now! It is a CRITIC. Do it!" snapped Morrow, and Matt ran for the door and headed to the comms center to transmit the message to NSA, the White House, and the rest of the free world.

Morrow told Rich to sign down the tape with the CRITIC information on it and mount a new tape on that recorder. Joe Parker was standing by to transcribe the tape so that amplifying details could be sent out in one or more CRITIC follow-up messages. Joe grabbed the tape and the tape jacket and went into the TR hut to begin a transcript.

"Rich, let's try to put the statement from the CRITIC into some sort of context so we can send an initial follow-up report." Will and Rich began writing a narrative expanding on the initial message, "*During the 0900 Zulu hour on this day, two Czechoslovak military radio operators were engaged in a routine conversation of a generally personal and relatively insignificant nature. They had commented on having just finished participating in an exercise with Russian and East German units and that there was a great deal of work to do. At that point one of the operators told the other that 'the third world war will begin tomorrow morning.' Shortly after that, they concluded their conversation. A verbatim transcript will follow ASAP. Note: No other unusual communications activity has been detected at this time.*"

Matt Rivington had returned to the Ops building while Morrow was drafting the follow-up. He reported that the initial CRITIC had been transmitted and that he would send the follow-up as soon as he got back to the comms center. Like the CRITIC itself, it would be sent at the highest precedence – FLASH. Matt was out the door a few seconds later with the first follow-up report. Will reached into his fatigue shirt pocket for his cigarettes and put a Pall Mall in his mouth. When he took his Zippo from his pants pocket to light his cigarette, I could see that his hand was shaking badly. Rich looked like he might faint.

Several minutes later, Master Sergeant Henry came into the Ops building huffing and puffing from having hurried up the road from the mess hall. Jim Cavanaugh came in with him and returned to his intercept position. Ollie was flushed but calm as he used his parade ground voice to address everyone in Ops, "OK. Listen up! Cavanaugh has explained to me what's happening. As I understand it, y'all have done what you're supposed to have done. I want you to know that Spec 6 Riley is on his way up the Hill to give you any language help you need. Captain Medved is on the way too. Sergeant Karney will probably be here in less than 30 minutes. He's on his way here from Bayreuth. Sergeant Morrow seems to have things here under control. I'm not gonna get in the way. Ops ain't my bailiwick anyway. I'll be back there in the Ops NCOIC's office until

Sergeant Karney and Spec 6 Riley get here. Carry on!" Even though Ollie didn't know much about SIGINT, it was a comfort having a calm senior NCO in the building with us.

Will Morrow had the pass on log open and was writing an account of what had occurred over the past 15 or 20 minutes. The only secure communications link between Schneeberg and Herzo was the teletype in the comms center. Herzo and NSA would certainly have questions about the CRITIC, but there was no way they could communicate easily with the site. The only telephone link to and from the detachment was a German commercial telephone line in the orderly room, but it was not secure, so there could be no classified conversations about the CRITIC. Any queries and replies would have to be via the teletype in the comms center. Matt Rivington knew he would be very busy trying to handle them, so he called in his boss, Sergeant Dean Peece, to help him since none of the Ops guys were allowed in the comms center.

Joe Parker had been in the TR hut listening to the tape for 20 minutes or so. He had begun the transcript by typing a header containing the date, the time, and tech information, but he knew it was always a good idea to listen to the entire conversation before typing the actual transcript. He was nearing the end of the intercepted conversation when he let out an audible gasp and a loud "Oh shit!" He rewound the tape a few times and relistened to what had prompted his outburst.

"Will! Get in here! We have a problem! A big FUBAR problem!"

Morrow hurried into the TR hut, banging his head as he tried to duck through the low metal doorway. "What's the problem, Joe? Tell me we didn't screw up. Please!"

"Will, I could tell you that, but it wouldn't be exactly true. The Czech did say what Rich said he said and what we put into the CRITIC. He said 'the third world war will begin tomorrow morning...'"

"OK, so what's the problem?"

"Well, that's not all he said. Rich must have gotten so excited that he didn't hear the rest. He missed the context. What the Czech said was, 'the third world war will begin tomorrow morning when the first sergeant gets here and sees what a mess everything is. The van is stuck in the mud, and the generator is about to burn out.' And then the two Czech ops just laughed, and the second Czech wished the first one good luck, and they ended the conversation. Rich must have been so shocked by the first statement that he missed the rest of it. I think you're gonna have to cancel the CRITIC and then explain what happened. Let's hope that none of us get busted over this."

Morrow's face went gray, and his left eye started twitching behind his thick glasses. He was quiet as he shakily lit another Pall Mall. "Oh, man, what a mess. Yeah, I think you're right. I've been reading over the CRITIC handbook since Rich called the CRITIC, and I think I know what we have to do next."

Will went back to the Ops NCOIC's office and gave Ollie the bad news. Ollie didn't go into orbit or start cussing. He just asked Will if he knew what to do until Father Pat and Karney got there. Will just nodded and went back to the trick chief's desk, got a message form, and drafted the CRITIC cancellation containing a short explanation that the world war three comment had actually been made but that it had been in a jocular manner which was not noted by the intercept operator. The information in the CRITIC therefore was not indicative of any threat to the U.S. or its interests. A full explanation would follow ASAP.

Pat Riley and Captain Medved arrived after the cancellation had been sent. Both were in civilian clothes and eager to hear what was going on that required their presence. SFC Karney came into the Ops building just as Will Morrow began briefing Medved and Father Pat in the Ops NCOIC's office. Ollie stood silently against the back wall. Ops wasn't his responsibility, but he was interested and wanted to understand what Rich Roberts and Morrow had done and why.

Despite his earlier case of nerves, Morrow was calm and composed as he briefed his superiors. Rich stood by looking crestfallen and probably worrying that he would wind up in Leavenworth. Morrow took responsibility for making the decision to send out the CRITIC.

"We had a statement that met the criteria for CRITIC reporting. At first glance, it seemed genuine. No, we did not have the context of the statement, but the requirement is to get the critical information out within 10 minutes of recognition. There was no time for us to have second thoughts or check the tape within that time frame. We were sure of what the Czech speaker said, so I made the decision to send the CRITIC. We are all trained in the CRITIC motto of *When in doubt, send it out.*' And

95

that's what we did. We then followed procedure, started transcribing the intercept, and found that the context of the statement showed that, if fact, there was no threat to U.S. interests. As soon as we made that determination, we cancelled the CRITIC and gave a preliminary explanation. Sir, if there was an error, it was an error in my judgement."

Captain Medved, SFC Karney, and Father Pat had all listened closely to Will Morrow's explanation. Karney and Pat looked to the captain for his reaction. Medved was quiet for a minute or two as he mentally reviewed what Will had told him.

"OK. Good briefing, Sergeant Morrow. What next?"

SFC Karney answered for Will, "Sir, we will have to issue a final follow-up to the initial CRITIC. It will be similar to the briefing we just received...except for Sergeant Morrow shouldering any blame. Either late today or more probably tomorrow morning, NSA will send Herzo and us their assessment of our performance. Based on what we know of the situation, I believe they will conclude, as I do, that our people did the right thing and acted in good faith according to existing guidance. All things considered, I think Spec 5 Roberts and Sergeant Morrow did a good job."

Medved did not hesitate, "I agree. Well done, Sergeant Morrow, Spec 5 Roberts. It may be embarrassing, but it would have been a lot more than embarrassing if what the Czech said was true and you failed to recognize and report it. Don't worry about any flak from Herzo or NSA. I'll back you up."

"Thank you, Sir." Will looked like he was about to say more, but he choked it off and just nodded at Rich Roberts. "We'd better get on with preparing the final follow-up. Pat, would you please help Joe Parker with the final version of the transcript that we'll send on the Herzo and NSA electronically. We need to have it exactly right."

Captain Medved and Ollie started to leave the Ops building, but Ollie paused as he passed Will and Rich. He clamped his meaty hand on their shoulders as he passed each of them as an expression of his support. "Good job, men. I'm proud of you."

Parker and Riley went into the TR hut to do the full transcript while Will and Rich worked on the final narrative follow-up report itself. The rest of Dog Trick went back to work and finished an otherwise quiet Sunday day shift.

As usual, Able Trick and Acting Sergeant Riegel did not relieve us until it was exactly 1600 hours. Our obligation to brief them on what happened during the day meant that we weren't able to leave Ops until 15 or 20 minutes after the hour.

Most of Dog Trick didn't bother going straight to the mess hall for dinner after the CRITIC craziness in Ops. We dragged both Morrow and Roberts into the Club to have a beer or two before having dinner across the street. As soon as Will and Rich walked in the door, they were greeted by cheers from the guys at the bar and the poker table. The story of the "third world war" had already spread throughout the detachment.

Ollie wasn't cheering, but there was a hint of a smile on his face, and that was significant in itself. There was a lot of razzing and references to Paul Revere and questions whether the invaders were coming by land or by sea. Although it hadn't made its way to Schneeberg yet, someone also joked about the newly released movie "The Russians Are Coming! The Russians Are Coming!" It was all good natured, and Will and Rich took it well. What a way to start a break!

(1) Director of National Intelligence, Intelligence Community Directive 190, 3 February 2015: https://fas.org/irp/dni/icd/icd-190.pdf (UNCLASSIFIED)

(2) Notes on the CRITIC System, Central Intelligence Agency, CIA Historical Review Program, 18 September 1995: https://www.cia.gov/library/center-for-the-study-of-intelligence/kent-csi/vol4no2/html/v04i2a03p_0001.htm (DECLASSIFIED)

****

THE BOYCOTT ENDS

Dog Trick was on break on Monday, but Will Morrow and Rich Roberts reported to Ops to help SFC Karney and Spec 6 Riley who had been tasked with replying to the multiple messages from Herzo Base and NSA about the Rich's "third world war" CRITIC. A full verbatim transcript of the intercepted conversation had been sent to both Herzo and the Agency. A special courier from Herzo was dispatched to bring the tape recording of the intercept back to the main base for re-checking there, and the courier also took whatever other tapes and classified material that had been wrapped and were ready for pick-up. The handful of extra linguists sent up to the Hill for the big exercise returned to Herzo as well. The powers-that-be decided to leave the RRCV-4 van behind for the time being to determine if there was a productive mission for it on Schneeberg. That meant nothing to us on Dog Trick since we didn't know what mission it was designed for; however, Doug Broussard and Don McGrew were happy that it would stay on and that they would have something special to do.

The break between days and mids was the shortest. In theory, we still had two days off after working six day shifts, but it seemed like only one day. We finished days on Sunday at 1600 hours. On Monday we would be off all day – 24 hours, and the same for Tuesday – another 24 fours, for a total of 56 hours off. But we would have to be back at work for mids just before midnight on Tuesday night. In contrast, the break from mids to swings was 80 hours long. It was still only two complete days off, but since you got off at 0800 after your last mid, then had two complete days off, and didn't have to be at work until 1600 on the next day, it seemed like a 3-day break. If you could afford it, that was the time to do some travelling.

****

Jack Rutherford was sitting at the bar in the Club when I went in on Monday evening. Anson was playing foosball with Large Louis, the Dog Trick MP, whose actual name was Louis Trzescianski. He wanted to be called Louis, like St. Louis the city. He emphatically disliked being called Louie or Lou. The Czech and Russian Marys on the Hill could take a stab at pronouncing his last name and assumed it was Polish. The funny thing is that we never asked him. Louis was one of the four military policemen assigned to the Hill. There was one MP assigned to each trick. They manned the gate to Topside alongside two unarmed German civilian guards who worked eight-hour shifts. The MP would periodically roam around the Topside complex looking for irregularities. Each MP was armed with a .45 automatic pistol when on duty.

Large Louis was assigned to our trick, but he bunked Topside with the other MPs and the support people rather than in the Cabin with the trick trash who worked in Ops. Michael "Mike the Cop" Floyd was a big guy too and, like Joe Parker, was one of relatively few African-Americans in ASA at that time. Louis was even bigger than Mike. Louis was somewhere a bit north of 6'3" tall and had to weigh in somewhere around 240 solid pounds. Within a day or two of his arrival, he was christened Large Louis. He was a bruiser, but a gentle giant who didn't have much to say. He seemed to be more of a watcher than a talker.

Over the course of a few weeks, Louis grew close to Anson and Bear. It probably had something to do with their all being billeted Topside and with Anson and Bear already being good friends. They were all quiet, unassuming guys. Anson was clever but not super smart. Large Louis was extraordinarily strong, trusting, and moral to a fault. They reminded some of us of Steinbeck's characters Lennie and George in *Of Mice and Men*. Lennie was a large, lumbering, childlike migrant worker. George was a small, wiry, quick-witted man who travels with Lennie. Anson and Large Louis looked out for one another in a subtle way. Louis once confided to Anson that he didn't mind being called Large Louis. In fact, he kinda liked

99

it because the nickname made him feel accepted into whatever half-assed brotherhood we had on the Hill. He may not have been as educated as some of the other ASAers, but he had street smarts and an innate kindness that others could sense. They simply felt that Large Louis was a good person. And he was.

Large Louis seldom went into Bisch like most of the others did. He preferred to stay on the Hill and watch movies in the kino room or hang out in the Club to play foosball and listen to whatever was being discussed on any particular night. He didn't drink much or say too much, and he didn't participate in the ongoing poker games. He might watch Anson if he was playing poker or sit at one of the tables with Anson and Bear sipping a Coke. He was a quiet, benevolent presence. You felt good that he was in the room with you, even if you didn't talk with him.

I greeted Anson and Large Louis as I walked past the foosball table and then sat next to Jack Rutherford at the bar. Matt Rivington was sitting on a stool by the corner of the bar with his fedora pushed down and almost covering his eyes. Doug Broussard was tending bar as usual and brought me a bottle of beer after grabbing my Frankenbrau beer mug from its peg on the wall.

I nudged Jack, "Hey, Jack! What's happening? I don't see you too much now that we're on different tricks."

"Not much, Jerry. I hang out with some of the guys from my trick. The usual stuff. I heard that Dog Trick had quite a day shift on Sunday. I'm glad it turned out okay and that no one got burned."

"Yeah, the final word from on high was that we did a pretty good job, all things considered. We're not gonna get a commendation or anything like that, but no one is going to get court martialed either." I paused for a minute and then asked the question that had been bugging me since I heard the rumor. "I hope you don't mint my asking, but there was a story going around that you were in Reissmann's over the weekend despite the boycott. Is that true?"

Jack stiffened and looked away for a second or two, "It's basically true, and I'm embarrassed to admit it, but I did go in for just a few minutes on Saturday. I was hoping to see Heidi. Just to see her. I still hadn't even talked to her, but I couldn't stop thinking about her."

"So, did you see her?"

"Yes, she was there with a few of her girlfriends. Gunther, the DJ, was at their table when I came in. He must have recognized me as one of the Amis because he waved at me and smiled. He said something to the girls too, and they all looked over at me. So, I smiled at them and waved. That's when I made eye contact with Heidi. I swear she smiled a special smile at me. Gunther came over to where I was standing by the door and asked when the rest of the Amis would be coming back. His English is decent, by the way.

"Anyway, I told him that I didn't know and that I shouldn't be in there myself and that I had just been hoping to see someone." Jack grimaced a little and then went on, "Well, Gunther is no dope. He must have noticed the way I had been looking at Heidi and how I lit up when she smiled at me. He took me by the arm and half dragged me over to Heidi's table and made me introduce myself to all the girls. I shook hands with each of them. Heidi has the nicest hands, Jerry, and the deepest blue eyes you've ever seen. We only spoke for a moment or two. My German is almost nonexistent, but she spoke more English than I could speak German. I told her I had to leave but that I hoped to see her again soon. She told me that would be nice."

"You really did have to leave, didn't you?" I asked.

"Oh, yeah. Both Gerti and Erika were giving me the fisheye from the minute I walked in. I think they support the boycott, even though it's costing them a lot of tip money. Erika must have told Pete Stavros I was there because Pete talked to me the next day and reminded me that no one was supposed to break the boycott. He was not happy with me. I won't go in again until the thing about Bear is cleared up."

"Good idea, Jack. I don't think the boycott will last much longer. Reissmann knows he needs our business."

A seat opened at the poker table as I said that, and Will Morrow called over to ask if I wanted to play. I was feeling lucky, so I joined the game and left Jack at the bar.

****

My statement to Jack turned out to be more prophetic than I could have imagined. I was sitting in the mess hall having lunch Tuesday when Pete the Greek came in with an enigmatic smile on his face. He looked around and saw Jolly Ollie eating at the table next to mine.

He walked over and said, "Good afternoon, Top. Would it be okay if I joined you for a few minutes? There's something I need to talk to you about. I'm gonna need to talk to Captain Medved, and I wanted to run it past you first."

Ollie looked puzzled but quickly replied, "Sure, Stavros. Sit yourself down. What's on your mind?"

Pete sat down and began talking quietly, "Top, I don't know if you know, but I have developed a close relationship with Erika, the bartender down at Reissmann's."

"Yeah, I know. It's no big thing unless you're getting married. Then you'll probably lose your security clearance at least temporarily. Is that why you want to see the C.O.?"

"No, it's nothing like that. At least not yet. This has to do with the boycott of Reissmann's. Otto Reissmann knows that Erika and I are close, so he asked her to ask me to be a sorta go-between between him and the captain. I said I'd try. I hope that's okay."

"I don't think that's a problem, Stavros. I think the captain will be glad to talk with you. You can come up Topside with me right after I finish eating. He should be in his office for the rest of the afternoon."

"Thanks, Top. Herr Reissmann gave me a gift to give the captain. It's in my car outside in the parking lot."

"Okay. This should be interesting. Do you know what it is?"

Pete smiled, "Not exactly, but I've got a pretty good idea."

A few minutes later, Pete and Jolly Ollie left the mess hall bound for Topside and what turned out to be round one of "let's make a deal."

****

Anson had been typing at his desk in the orderly room when Pete the Greek and Jolly Ollie went in to see Captain Medved. They didn't close the door behind them, so Anson was able to tell me later about what was going on. Pete told the C.O. that Otto Reissmann was upset about the loss of Ami business and the money they spent. Right up until this past Sunday he still believed Bear had broken up the men's room, but he was looking into the matter a little deeper and trying to determine whether one of his German acquaintances may have been the culprit rather than Bear. They were the rowdy Germans who were there that night. He did a little arm twisting and, sure enough, one of the rowdies admitted under duress that he had done the damage. The culprit and his friends had already reimbursed Otto for the cost of repairs, and now Otto wanted to make a peace offering to the Amis on Schneeberg. Pete put a large cardboard carton on Medved's desk. It was a full case of Ansbach Uralt cognac.

The captain was a little taken aback by the magnitude of the gift. According to Anson, Medved told Pete that he wasn't much of a drinker himself but that he appreciated the gesture. However, he felt that it was too much and that Pete should return it to Herr Reissmann. Pete suggested that Medved do so himself in person so they could shake hands and maybe establish a little German-American rapport at the executive level. Medved agreed. He decided to keep one bottle for himself and give one to Ollie, SFC Karney, and SFC Rayburn, and three to the Club to be meted out in moderation to the guys. He said he would return the other half case to Herr Reissmann when he saw him. Pete said he would set up the meeting for later that afternoon.

After the duty day ended, Medved got hold of Pat Riley and went down to Bisch to see Otto. Pat had called first to confirm that Otto would be there in his office at the *tanzcafe*. Erika must have been there when they met and told Pete the Greek who passed on the details to some of the rest of us. According to Pete, the session started out very formally. Otto may have even clicked his heels and bowed slightly when Father Pat introduced him to Captain Medved.

Otto was eager to explain how he had determined that Bear was not responsible for any damage to the men's room and that he hoped the captain would convey his apology to Bear. He expressed regret for misjudging Bear and hoped that the unfortunate incident could be soon be forgotten. Captain Medved was gracious and assured Herr Reissmann that he would pass the message to Bear and that no lasting damage had been done to relations between the Amis and the *tanzcafe*. He promised to tell his men that they were free to patronize Reissmann's if they chose to do so. He also thanked Otto for the case of cognac, but went on to say that the gesture of friendship was too generous and that he was returning half of the case with his personal thanks and the gratitude of the men with whom he was sharing the gift.

Otto took one of the bottles from the half empty case, opened it, and called to Erika to bring three glasses so they could drink to their *rapproachment*. Otto and Medved proceeded to talk at length in a mixture of German and English and drink more than a few shots of cognac. Father Pat excused himself after two or three shots and left the two on their own. It turned out that Otto could speak more English that we knew — alcohol has been known to relax the inhibitions that keep some of us from trying to speak, however imperfectly, in another language.

Captain Medved learned that Reissmann had served as a conscript with the *Wehrmacht* in North Africa during WW II and that he had been a POW in England toward the end of the war. The captain talked a little bit about having served in combat in Vietnam, and the two seemed to establish a bond over having shared the horrors of the front lines.

Otto was surprised to learn that the captain lived near his own home in Wunsiedel and extended an invitation for Medved to join him for dinner later in the week at a restaurant in Wunsiedel, after which Otto would show him the *milchbar* he owned there. Their cognac-fueled bonhomie seemed genuine as they parted, and with their parting the boycott was ended and the Amis were once again free to imbibe, flirt, dance, or whatever at Reissmann's *Tanzcafe* in Bischofsgruen.

It must have been at the dinner that followed that Otto Reissmann confided in Captain Medved that he was concerned about a group of motor scooter-riding young men who had recently been causing problems at the *Milchbar*. But I'm getting ahead of myself.

****

DECLINE AND FALL

Sometimes it was hard to fall asleep. Part of the problem, of course, was with working rotating shifts – six shifts on duty followed by two "days" off. Anyone who has done this for an extended period will tell you that it raises absolute hell with your circadian rhythm, the 24-hour internal clock that is running in the background of your brain and which cycles between sleepiness and alertness at regular intervals. It's also known as your sleep/wake cycle. For most adults, the biggest dip in energy happens in the middle of the night (somewhere between 2:00am and 4:00am and just after lunchtime (around 1:00pm to 3:00pm, when they tend to crave a post-lunch nap). Those times can be different if you're naturally a night owl or a morning person. However, when you're sleep-deprived, you'll notice bigger swings of sleepiness and alertness.

Outside factors like lightness and darkness can also impact it. When it's dark at night, your eyes send a signal to your brain that it's time to feel tired. Your brain, in turn, sends a signal to your body to release melatonin, which makes your body tired. That's why your circadian rhythm tends to coincide with the cycle of daytime and nighttime and why it's so hard for shift workers to sleep during the day and stay awake at night. (1)

It didn't matter what time it was when I hit the rack and tried to go to sleep. Unless I had had several beers before going to bed, it would take me as much as 30 minutes to drop off into sleep. My thoughts as I awaited sleep were often reflections on things that I did poorly in the past, sometimes even in the distant yet still clear days of early childhood. There were memories and regrets over everything from minor social gaffs to what seemed then as life-changing mistakes. The thoughts were not

105

always negative. Many times, my thoughts turned toward the near- and long- term future when things would be better. I would not be lonely. I would be doing something more meaningful and fulfilling. I would be freer. I would love and be loved. It would all work out. It would be okay. I would be okay. And then, perhaps slowly, perhaps suddenly, I would feel a certain optimism and then be enveloped by the oblivion of sleep.

There was a song about seeing things more clearly in the morning light. There were many times when I preferred to see my life through the misty haze of too many beers mixed with far too much self-pity. The harshness of the morning light would have shown me that I was extraordinarily fortunate to be swilling beer on top of a Bavarian mountain instead of dodging VC bullets in an insect-infested, dung-smelling hell hole in Vietnam. If I was lonely, it was because I was too timid to ask one of the Bisch bunnies to dance. Not to ask for more than a dance. Just a dance, a smile, a touch from someone else. The girls probably weren't much different from me. Some of them were probably lonely too. They may have wanted a friend more than an Ami who would marry them and give them a passport back to the land of round doorknobs and the big PX. They were human too. They had feelings and wants and needs. We all did.

****

A few months passed surprisingly quickly as we worked our cycle of days-to-mids-to-swings-to-days and so on. I grew comfortable and reasonably confident in my work and felt fully integrated into the brotherhood of the Hill.

It became apparent by mid-September how Schneeberg got its name. We had seen snow flurries on the 4th of July, believe it or not, but snowfall became common as autumn made its appearance. The pine forest that surrounded us on the Hill was green year-round, but the deciduous trees down in Bisch had already donned their fall colors and soon would shed their leaves. The hours of daylight were getting shorter, and the nights were getting longer and much colder. As the light and the warmth left the mountaintop and snow began to accumulate on the ground, you could sense that morale was falling too. Some were more affected than others.

A few of us on Dog Trick were growing concerned about Matt Rivington, our comms center op. We didn't see much of him while we were on duty in Ops because he would be locked away by himself in the comms center in the Topside building across the road. During off-duty hours, Matt could usually be found sitting alone on a bar stool in the Club drinking *Frankenbrau* from his ceramic mug and wearing a beat-up fedora down low over his eyes. I was having breakfast in the mess hall with Joe Parker after a mid shift in late September.

"What's up with Matt Rivington?" Joe asked me out of the blue during a break in our conversation about the world in general.

"What do you mean? He's a little quiet, but I guess he's just being himself," I replied, not really sure about what to say.

"Naw, I don't think he's okay. It's none of business, but I think Matt's head is messed up."

"How? I haven't seen any big change on him lately."

Joe thought a moment before continuing, "You probably wouldn't notice. You haven't been on the Hill as long as I have. He changed a lot right around the time you got here. He had been very friendly and a happy person. Then he got a dear John letter from his girlfriend back in Tennessee... I think it was his fiancée. She found someone new and broke off with Matt. There was nothing he could do about it. He couldn't afford to take leave and fly home to try to get her back, and he couldn't even call her on the phone from this god-forsaken place. All he could do was write her letters. She answered the first one or two, but she didn't want him back. Then she stopped writing to him all together. He went into a tailspin after that and started drinking a lot...and I mean a lot!"

"Geez, Joe, I didn't know. I just thought he was a bit of a loner, but I get along with him well. We're not super close, but I do consider him a friend. We've talked a lot since I got here. I like him."

"I like him too, Jerry. That's why I'm worried about him. I took a few psych courses when I was at Howard University before joining ASA. I think Matt's got serious textbook-style clinical depression. All of us get mopey from time to time, but Matt is living every day in a very dark place, and he's been there for too long. The other night I was on burn bag detail in the furnace room and found Matt burning letters, some books, and other personal things. I asked him what he was doing, and he tried to laugh it off, saying that it was just stuff he didn't need anymore."

"OK, but that doesn't necessarily mean anything, does it?"

"No, not as an isolated incident, but there are other things that worry me. For example, Matt has an old Opel sedan that he doesn't drive anymore. He used to drive it over to Bindlach and up to the Air Force PX in Hof. Sometimes even down to Nuremberg or Herzo. It's been sitting in the Topside parking lot for at least two months. Two of the tires are flat now, but Matt says he doesn't care. He told me he doesn't need a car. He even offered to give it to me. For free! I don't think that bodes well for him."

"I didn't know any of that, Joe. I thought it was strange that he almost always sat by himself in the Club with his hat pulled down over his eyes, but I just thought that was normal for him. Hell, we have a lot of people up here who would be considered strange back home. The Hill has more than its fair share of misfits. I'm probably one myself. But I'd rather be here than Herzo or some animal outfit."

"Yeah. Me too. I'm just sayin' that I'm worried about Matt. You're closer to him than I am, so try to keep an eye on him and maybe reach out and try to engage him in something. Anything. OK?"

"I'll do that, Joe. Thanks for the heads up. I'll let you know if I get any bad vibes from him."

****

We went on break a couple days later – the long break between mids and swings. Rich Roberts had gone off to Munich, and Joe had gone up to Hof to visit two Air Force linguists who had been in his Czech class at Monterey.

When I went into the Club on the first night of our break, Matt was at his usual seat at the bar. Ollie and Will Morrow were playing cards with Lurch, Weasel, and the Grommet Cook. Large Louis, Bear, and Anson were taking turns on the foosball table. Four Able Trick guys were sitting at a table playing some game they called Soul Search.

(Sketch by Arielle Combs)

It was a variation of Truth or Dare. Instead of players being given the choice between answering a question truthfully or performing a "dare," the players each had to write a word on a slip of paper describing one of the other people at the table. The moderator then picks a slip from the pile at random, reads it aloud, and all the players take turns trying to guess who the word best describes and why. I played it once and didn't care for it. The word that someone felt best described me was "fantasy." I honestly didn't understand how that word applied strongly to me, but someone did. I didn't listen to the explanation and really didn't care.

Anyway, Tony Phillips, my Czech classmate from DLI, was the moderator for this evening's game and was looking for another person to join in. I don't know how he did it, but he somehow persuaded Matt to leave his perch at the bar and sit in at the table. Everyone seemed to be enjoying the game for the first 10 or 15 minutes. The players were laughing and drinking their beers as they congenially ribbed each other and traded playful insults that may have been partially true. And then Matt lost his mind.

He suddenly jumped up from his chair, overturned the table, and drew a 5-inch utility knife from his belt before anyone could move.

"IS THAT WHAT YOU THINK OF ME?!" he shouted. Rage was on his face and in his voice, but something else was in his eyes. "WHO WROTE THAT WORD ABOUT ME? I'M GONNA KILL YOU!"

The Club went deadly quiet. The Soul Search players were rooted to their chairs. Matt looked menacingly at each of the young men he had been playing the game with moments before. He continued to yell, "I mean it. Whoever wrote that about me is gonna get stuck. I'm serious. I've got nothin' to lose. I hate this place. And I don't give a shit anymore about anything or anyone!"

Weasel and Will Morrow started to get up from the poker table, perhaps thinking about intervening, but Ollie grabbed each of them by their sleeves and pulled them back into their chairs. Meanwhile, Large Louis had turned from the foosball table and soothingly began talking to Matt as he ever-so-slowly started moving from the foosball table toward the Soul Search group and the outraged Matt.

"Whoa there, Matt. Take it easy now, brother. You don't want to hurt anyone, and no one wants to hurt you. We can work this out."

"Stay away from me, Louis. This is none of your business. Whoever wrote that about me has to pay."

We could almost sense Large Louis thinking about what options he had available. He was trained as an MP to disarm assailants, but he clearly didn't want the situation to escalate any further. "It's okay, Matt. I'm sure whoever did it didn't mean to upset you. It was probably just a joke. Take a minute. Think about it. Like I said, we can work this out."

Louis continued to edge toward the Soul Search group and finally positioned himself between Matt and Tony Phillips, on whom Matt seemed to be focusing most of his hostility.

"Tony! Leave the Club. NOW! DO it!" Louis urged in a low voice. Tony didn't hesitate. He backed away from Matt and went out the door of the Club toward the safety of the Cabin. The other players began to slowly move away from Matt and behind Louis."

"Louis, I've got nothin' against you. I don't want to fight you or stick you, but someone's gotta pay. Tony's the one! He thinks he's so much better than everyone else…and smarter too. Get out of my way! I'm goin' after him!" Matt's voice had lost a little bit of rage, and his eyes had filled with tears that now began to slide down his cheeks. He was still menacing Louis with the knife.

"Well, I don't want to hurt you or fight you either, Matt. I like you, and I know you're a good guy and that you've had some personal problems. It's nobody's fault. Stuff happens, and then we get together and try to fix things as best we can. You're surrounded by friends here. No one has it in for you."

There were murmurs of assent from several others, and Ollie spoke quietly from his seat at the poker table, "It's alright, son. I know you really don't want to hurt anyone…except maybe yourself. Nobody on this Hill wants that to happen. Listen to Louis. Give him your knife and then have a seat so we can have a good talk. OK?"

"I can't do that, Top. I've gone too far. I know you're gonna dick me away," Matt's tears were flowing freely now, and his voice was choking with suppressed sobs. "I just want to get out of here. I can't do this anymore. I can't!"

"I understand, son. This life is not for everyone. We all feel isolated up here on the mountain. We miss our families back home. If you put the knife down, I promise to help you find a way out of this and get you feeling better. Work with me. OK?" Ollie asked in an unfamiliar sympathetic tone.

Matt looked like he was wavering and had lowered the knife so it was pointing toward the floor. Large Louis slowly moved next to Matt. I thought he was going to make a grab for the knife and then take Matt down. But he didn't. Instead, Louis gently put his beefy arm around Matt's shoulder and drew him close to his own body. "It's gonna be okay, brother. I got you. Top and I won't let anyone hurt you. It's okay now. You're gonna be okay."

Matt dropped the knife, and Louis kicked it away toward the poker table. He then took his other arm and wrapped Matt in a huge bear hug. It wasn't a violent, wrestling-like bear hug. No, it was a hug of comfort and compassion. Matt collapsed into Large Louis's arms and sobbed. "I'm sorry. I'm so sorry. I didn't really want to hurt anyone. I'm just so tired. So done with everything." Matt wept openly, and I think I saw a drop of moisture in Large Louis' eye too.

Bear and Anson left the area by the bar where they had retreated when the ruckus began. The went up to Matt and Large Louis and joined them in a group hug while Ollie walked slowly over to their huddle and began to pat Matt and Louis on their backs. "It's okay now, son. You're gonna be fine. You and Louis and your friends Bear and Anson, y'all come on up Topside with me now and we'll talk about what we're gonna do to make this better for you. C'mon now. No one's gonna hurt you. It's alright now."

Ollie led the group out of the Club and up the road toward Topside. Those of us left in the Club started breathing again and then cleaned up the overthrown table, chairs, and the debris from the interrupted mind game.

Doug Broussard bought a round of drinks on the house, but there was no celebration or laughter. We were all shaken by thoughts of what could have happened if Large Louis had not acted as he did to control the situation. I think a few of us reflected later that night on the fragility of life and the value of human kindness and understanding. No one ever asked, and no one ever said what word in the Soul Search game had sent Matt over the edge.

****

We learned the next day that Large Louis, Bear, and Anson had taken turns sitting with Matt in his room throughout the night. Ollie didn't order them to watch him. It was just something they wanted to do to make sure Matt didn't harm himself. Ollie had Sergeant Gray make a few calls the next morning and arranged for Matt to be taken to the Army hospital in Nuremberg for evaluation. Large Louis and Bear drove him down there later in the day and helped him check into the hospital.

It was about two weeks after that when Jim Cavanaugh saw Matt down at Herzo Base. Jim had taken his wife down to Nuremberg for a pre-natal check, and they stopped at Herzo. Matt was raking leaves at the edge of a wooded area next to the base mess hall, and Jim stopped to say hello. He told us that Matt seemed happy to see a familiar and friendly face and how

112

Matt, ever the southern gentleman, doffed his cap when he got alongside Jim's car and saw Jim's wife in the passenger seat. Ollie and Captain Medved had spoken to the staff judge advocate, and Matt would not be court martialed. The shrinks at Nuremberg had decided that he suffered from major depression and anxiety and that it would be best for the Army if he were given a medical discharge, Matt expected to be back in Tennessee well before Thanksgiving.

(1) https://www.sleepfoundation.org/articles/what-circadian-rhythm

****

SHOWDOWN AT THE *MILCHBAR*

Early October snow already covered the ground and trees atop the mountain, but the towns and villages below still enjoyed temperate autumn weather. The annual Oktoberfest was winding down in Munich, and many smaller cities were conducting their own harvest fests and fall celebrations while the weather was still relatively pleasant.

Rich Roberts returned from a visit to Munich during our long break. He had obviously enjoyed his time there and was in an upbeat mood when I sat down with him in the mess hall before we began a set of swings.

"What's happenin', Rich? You look like a happy guy. Did you have a good break?" I asked.

"Hey, Jerry. Yeah, I sure did. Munich was great. The Oktoberfest was still bringing in tons of tourists from all over. The city was jammed. I was lucky to have a place to crash with friends in the Schwabing section of the city. I had a blast."

"Cool. Did you go to the Oktoberfest?"

"No, not this time. It was too crazy and crowded. I did see a play and attended a concert where one of my good friends was playing."

"Classical? I know you enjoy the real oldies."

Rich laughed, "Yeah, it was chamber music by Hayden. My friend Felix plays viola in a chamber ensemble at the University of Music and the Performing Arts in Munich. He's incredibly talented."

"I have to admit that I don't know much about classical music, Rich. I like Tchaikovsky, and we listened to some Dvořák and Smetana as part of our Czech cultural studies in Monterey. But that's about all I know."

"I think you'd probably like Hayden, and Mozart too. Too bad we're working swings this coming weekend. My friend and his group will be performing in Wunsiedel for the Luisenburg *Festspeile*. Will Morrow already said I could have Saturday's swing off so I can be there for the afternoon performance. There's no way he'd be able to give you off too if you wanted to come. You'll be covering the VHF position, and Joe Parker said he'd work the UHF side for me instead of transcribing. I'm really psyched about seeing Felix play again."

"Right in Wunsiedel? Where?"

"They'll be playing at the *Festspiele*. It's a unique natural stage at the lower end of the *Rock Labrynthe* on a hill on the outskirts of the town. It's a beautiful place for a concert...as long as the weather stays nice. Felix and the rest of the ensemble are booked in a hotel downtown, near Reissmann's *Milchbar*."

"It sounds nice. I haven't been over to Wunsiedel yet. I hope you enjoy it."

"Thanks. I'm sure it will be unforgettable."

****

Able Trick threw a *bowle* party in the Club Friday night to celebrate Fang's 21st birthday. One of the highlights of any German harvest festival (*Erntedankfestor*) or Oktoberfest party is the *bowle*. which is just another word for punch. There are many varieties of this party drink, and Tony Phillips had his own recipe which he concocted for the occasion. Fang, whose real name was Warren T. Feldman III, was Tony's sidekick. Both had been my classmates at DLI. However, after graduation, Fang had been sent directly to Germany while Tony and I had gone to Fort Meade for special SIGINT training at NSA before going on to Herzo Base six months later. Tony and Fang were sent to Schneeberg a couple months before me and had been close friends on Able Trick ever since.

Fang got his nickname almost as soon as he arrived on the Hill. He had two badly chipped front teeth which the Army must not have cared enough about to repair or replace. The Vietnam War was causing the Army to expand rapidly, and some dentists had been drafted right after dental school. Some of them didn't seem to care too much about their enlisted patients. At least that was my experience with dentists at the Presidio of

Monterey. Anyway, I never called Fang by his nickname. He didn't seem to mind the name, but I felt it was demeaning.

Tony's *bowle* recipe made for an extra strong punch that went down far too easily. German recipes for punch are often a treasured family tradition, and they can make parties so much nicer and potentially so much drunker. Tony was secretive about his recipe. I suspected that he made it up as he went along. I know that he began with cans of thawed out frozen strawberries from the commissary in Bindlach and fresh pineapple chunks. He added sugar, white wine, and a large bottle of vodka to the mix and let it marinate overnight in a big glass vat he borrowed from the mess hall. He added other ingredients, including rum and sparkling white wine, before icing the mixture down an hour or two before the party began.

The Able Trick crew were feeling no pain by the time I looked into the Club after Friday evening's swing shift. To be honest, most of them were wasted. Doug Broussard had the night off, so Tony was behind the bar. The guest of honor was out cold with his head resting on the bar. Grommet Cook and another guy were at the foosball table while a few others were playing hearts, a card game I never learned. Ollie was not at the poker table. My guess was that he left the Club when the party started getting a little crazy. People often said or did things when drunk that they later regretted. He probably left early so he wouldn't inhibit the partyers. He must have been glad they were getting wasted on the Hill instead of someplace they'd have to drive back from. I didn't want to be the only sober person in the Club, so I went over to the Cabin and went to bed.

****

Saturday night's swing shift was quiet and uneventful. Joe was manning the UHF position while Rich enjoyed his night off with his Munich friend at the music festival in Wunsiedel. The Czechs must have been enjoying a night off as well because there was hardly any radio activity on the VHF side. I still had to search the spectrum on a regular basis for signals of interest, but there just wasn't much to do. At times like that, we could read books or write letters or just b.s. with the other ops as long as we kept plugged into the receivers and searched from time to time.

The Club was already closed and locked up when Baker Trick relieved us at midnight. Grommet Cook was handling midnight chow in the mess hall. I wasn't too hungry, but I asked him to make me scrambled eggs which I put on a couple slices of white toast for an egg sandwich. Rich Roberts wasn't in his bunk when I went back to the trick room in the Cabin. I figured he stayed in Wunsiedel for the night. Maybe he and his pal Felix got lucky and met some girls who fancied classical music.

****

The next afternoon before work I was in the latrine shaving at one of the sinks when Rich came in to do the same. I was shocked by his appearance.

"Holy crap, Rich, what the hell happened to you? Were you in an accident?" He had a black eye and the left side of his face was badly bruised and had a couple of nasty lacerations that looked like they might have benefited from some stitches.

"I'm okay. It's no big deal. I don't want to talk about it. Really! Okay?" He winced noticeably whenever he tried to turn or bend. He looked like he had gone a few rounds with Muhammad Ali.

"Geez, did you get into a fight over in Wunsiedel last night? Maybe you should go to the dispensary over in Bindlach and have a medic check you out," I suggested.

"I said I don't want to talk about it, Jerry!" he snapped. "Just leave it at that. I'm okay. Just a little sore. Let it go!"

"Yeah, sure. Eh…I guess I won't ask about the concert. I'm sorry you're banged up."

"Thanks. Gotta go." Rich went back to the trick room to dress for work. I didn't want to bug him, and he apparently made it clear to the rest of the trick to give him some space.

****

Monday morning, Anson came into our room a little past 0900 and talked quietly with Rich, telling him that Ollie and the captain wanted to see him Topside as soon as he showered and dressed. I could hear Rich groan with pain as he got out of his bunk. I hoped he wasn't in trouble.

117

Rich came back 30 minutes later. He didn't say anything to any of us in the room. He just grabbed his car keys from his locker and left. I thought his eyes looked red. I figured it was because of the black eye and the bruises.

I saw Anson in the mess hall when I went in later for lunch before going to work. He was sitting by himself, so I joined him. We complained about the weather turning cold and that we were already tired of snow…and it wasn't even winter yet.

"Look, I hate to ask you this, but I gotta know. Is Rich Roberts in trouble with the captain and Ollie? I know he got called up there this morning. Is he gonna get dicked away for being in a fight?" I asked.

Anson looked around to see if anyone was nearby who might hear him. The only other person in the mess hall was Will Morrow. Anson beckoned him over, and Will took a seat with us.

"What's up?" Will asked, looking at both of us.

"I was just asking Anson if Rich is in trouble with Captain Medved." I explained.

"Morrow, you're gonna hear about this later when Ollie calls you into his office, but I'll give you a heads-up now since Jerry is friends with Rich." He paused for a moment before continuing, "This is just between us for now. Herr Reissmann went to see the captain yesterday afternoon at his apartment over in Wunsiedel. They've been buddies ever since the boycott was lifted. Anyway, Reissmann knew what happened to Roberts on Saturday and told the captain about it."

Will spoke up before Anson could go on, "No worries, man. We're not gonna tell anyone whatever you're gonna tell us. But it was just a simple bar fight or something like that, right?"

"No. It wasn't like that at all. According to Reissmann, Rich and his musician friend from Munich were jumped by a bunch of punks who hang out around the *Milchbar*. Rich and his friend were walking back from the concert where his friend had played that afternoon. I think they were on the way to the friend's hotel for dinner. Anyway, the punks saw Rich and his friend and started calling them names. They saw the friend was carrying a violin case and that the friend looked a little girlish. They called both of them fags and queers...I don't know the German words...maybe they said it in English. Who knows?

"Rich ignored the punks, but they blocked the sidewalk and kept calling them names. Rich was cool until one of the punks slapped his friend hard across the face and tried to grab his violin case. Rich stepped between them and tried to reason with the German punk. Then another punk sucker-punched Rich from behind, and the first one started punching the musician. Rich went down after a few punches, and then two of the punks kicked him in the ribs before he could get up. Rich and his friend were able to hang onto the violin and run back to the hotel. The hotel manager called the *polizei*, but the punks were long gone by the time the cops got there. The cops took a report, but Rich didn't think they would follow up. They didn't seem too interested in a beaten-up Ami and his girly friend."

"Whoa! That's really something! Did Rich confirm that that's what happened?" I asked.

"Not at first. He just told the captain that he didn't want to talk about it. That it didn't matter."

"What did the captain say to that?"

"Well, he was really angry. Not at Rich, but at whoever did this. He finally got Rich to admit that Reissmann's version of the attack was accurate. Rich was terribly upset by that time, so the captain told him he could leave. Ollie patted him on the back as he left the orderly room and told him not to worry about anything."

"So, was that the end of it?" Will asked.

Anson laughed, "Oh, no! It gets better from here on. After Rich left Topside, Ollie went into Medved's office and closed the door behind him. Even with the door closed, I could hear almost every word they said. They were both...how can I put it?...animated."

"Right. So, what did they say?"

"Like I said, the captain was really pissed. He was yelling about not letting one of our guys get kicked around by some German assholes. Ollie finally calmed him down and asked him straight out what he wanted to do about it. Ollie reminded the C.O. that the German punks thought Rich and his friend were gay and that's why they got beat up.

"Well, that sent Medved off into a rage again. I think his exact words were, 'I don't give a shit whether he's gay or straight, black, white or purple. He's a good soldier and a good friend to everyone on the Hill. If he is queer, then he's our queer, and we're not going to let anyone kick his ass and get away with it!'

Ollie liked that answer and agreed. Then he asked the captain what he wanted him to do. He told Ollie to have Bear, Lurch, Large Louis, Pete the Greek, Weasel, and a couple others, including you, Will, meet with him late this afternoon. You'll find out then what he's planning. I think the captain was going to talk with Reissmann about it."

120

"Hah! This could get interesting," Will responded with a trace of a smile on his face.

****

It's hard to keep a secret at a small detachment like Schneeberg where everyone knows everyone else's business. There were whispered questions about whether Rich was gay, but they were generally answered with a shrug of shoulders and a "who cares?" attitude. In fact, no one seemed to care one way or the other. There were a few other guys on the Hill who might be gay – Staff Sergeant Gray, the admin NCO, was one, and he was rumored to be "close" to Sergeant Peece, the comms center NCOIC. None of them ever did anything overtly gay, so no one gave a damn what they did in private.

The Monday afternoon meeting involving Captain Medved, Ollie, and the other people Anson had mentioned was supposed to be secret, but bits and pieces of information began leaking out over the following few days. We knew that something was planned for Friday evening because the Ops NCOIC, SFC Karney, asked for volunteers to work for a few of the men who were scheduled to work a swing or a mid that night. Three or four people volunteered for each slot that would be open. Everyone wanted to be a part of whatever was about to happen. Someone casually remarked that it sounded like they were forming a posse.

****

Early Friday evening the dozen or so members of Medved's posse met in the Topside pool room to finalize their plans for the *Milchbar*. They would be going to Wunsiedel in three vehicles. Bear has a VW Kombi bus that could carry 5 passengers. Pete the Greek had an old Opel sedan that could carry three or four passengers, and Weasel had a VW Beetle and could take three with him. Unfortunately, Weasel's VW wouldn't start, so I was recruited to drive since my Mercedes could carry four passengers.

Everyone was in civilian clothes, of course…even Ollie – which was a first as far as we could remember. Ollie went over the plan again and again using the pool table as his map table. The cars would leave the Hill at ten-minute intervals starting at 1930 hours. Ollie would be in the first car with Pete. They would all arrive in Wunsiedel around 2000 hours and park a block or two from the *Milchbar*. The guys would proceed in ones, twos, and threes to the *Milchbar* and scatter their seating around the main room at tables and at the bar so it wouldn't be apparent that a large group of Amis were in the disco. We could have one drink and one drink only while we waited for events to unfold.

Pete the Greek and Large Louis stood at the bar. We were surprised to see a few of our *Luftwaffe* counterparts at two of the tables in back. They smiled, nodded to the Amis, and gave us a thumbs up. They were apparently in on the plot. Maybe they were our back-up.

Sometime around 2100 six or seven of the punks came in wearing cheap *faux* biker leather. They must have seen the old Marlon Brando movie *The Wild One* and thought they were a bad-ass biker gang, even though they only rode 150cc motor bikes. Their leader looked like a member of the Hitler *Jungend* with his closely cropped blond hair. He was wearing motorcycle boots on his feet and a smirk on his face as he looked around.

The group sat at a large round table opposite the bar and ordered drinks from the waitress who seemed to be intimidated by their presence and whatever wisecracks they directed her way. Pete was seething already, probably thinking of Erika putting up with their b.s. if she worked there.

At precisely 2130 hours Ollie walked in the door with Rich Roberts. I didn't know Rich would be coming. Ollie had his arm on Rich's shoulder as they walked past the table where the punks were sitting. Rich looked over at them and then nodded to Ollie. They had only taken a few more steps when the Hitler *Jungend* jerk got up from his table and sauntered over to them, grabbing Rich by the arm and turning him around, telling him in German,

"We told you last weekend not to come back here. This is our town, and we don't like fags. Who's your fat friend? Is he a queer too?" He looked over to his punk friends as if looking for applause. They were all laughing and pointing at the trio. And that's when the fun started.

Bear, Lurch, Weasel, Will Morrow, and a few others had quietly moved from where they had been sitting and took up positions behind the punks at the table, at least one Ami for each German creep. While they were doing that, Pete the Greek and Large Louis moved away from the bar and walked silently over to the head punk. They each grabbed one of the would-be *fuhrer's* arms, making him grimace with pain as he tried in vain to wriggle out of their grasp. They half lifted him and half dragged him out of the dance floor area and into the hallway while Ollie and Rich left the *Milchbar*.

The band kept playing and people kept dancing as the scene quietly unfolded. The only patrons who seemed concerned were the punks. One or two of them tried to get up from the table to see where their *fuhrer* was being taken. The Amis behind them had their hands on their shoulders and exerted pressure when they tried to move. It was like the Vulcan death grip. Bear and Weasel knew exactly where and how hard to press to inflict maximum pain with minimum effort. Lurch towered over the table with his best Frankenstein monster imitation complete with a low growl.

Meanwhile out in the hallway, Pete the Greek was having a quiet word in German with the *fuhrer*. Erika had helped him prepare what he was now

123

telling the young German in German. Large Louis was standing with a firm grip on the young man's arm and with a scowl on his face that would have made John Wayne back off. Pete was reminding the head punk what he and his pals had done to Rich and Felix last weekend.

Pete had a mirthless smile on his face and punctuated the early part of his chat with a sharp slap across the *fuhrer's* cheek. Whatever Pete was telling him had turned him a whiter shade of pale except for the red mark on his cheek where he had been slapped. He looked like he was going to faint. I think he pissed his pants and then started crying.

Pete gave him a gentle slap on the other cheek and smiled a little more broadly and menacingly. He told the *fuhrer* to leave the disco and not come back unless he wanted the posse to come back and be less friendly next time. I could hear Pete's parting words all the way across the room, "...and don't ever mess with Amis again. Understand?!" With that, the *fuhrer* rushed out the door into the night with his not-so-merry men right behind him.

The Schneeberg posse all headed for the door a few minutes later. We were truly shocked when several of the Germans applauded.

****

The Club was unusually crowded when we got back to the Hill. Everyone wanted to know what had happened, and Ollie was only too happy to summarize the events of the evening. He even bought a round of drinks, which was another first. Rich Roberts was embarrassed by all the attention and excused himself after 30 minutes. Most of the others soon drifted away until we were down to the hard-core drinkers and poker players. I was with Ollie and Will Morrow at the poker table.

"Hey, Top, where did you go after Pete and Large Louis grabbed the *fuhrer*?" I asked.

"Don't go tellin' everyone, but I took Roberts down the street to the restaurant where the C.O. was having dinner and drinks with Otto Reissmann. Otto somehow got the Wunsiedel chief of police to join them. Everything we did tonight was worked out between the captain and Reissmann, and Reissmann made some sort of deal with the police chief to let us do our thing. I think maybe the chief is on Otto's payroll," Ollie winked and cracked a hint of a smile when he said that. "I think the chief

124

put out the word to his men that they were to stay away from the *Milchbar* unless he called them himself."

"That's fantastic, Top!" I was impressed.

"That's not all either. Reissmann bought Roberts and me some schnapps and then he had the police chief apologize to Rich for the poor treatment from the cops. This was a win-win for everyone. We evened the score for Roberts and his friend and got across a clear warning to the punks and anyone else who was listening that they'd better not mess with our people. Reissmann got something too. He doesn't think that those guys will be coming back to the *Milchbar* anytime soon to harass his customers or the waitresses. And even the chief is happy, because no one got hurt and there was no damage to the town."

"Yeah, I was a little worried that there was a chance that things might get out of hand. I'm glad they didn't."

"Me too." Ollie continued. "But all of our guys knew not to start anything and to just keep the motorbikers away from their leader so Pete the Greek and Louis could have the come-to-Jesus-meeting with him. The C.O. had agreed with Reissmann that we would pay for any damage that might occur, and the chief had said that if his men had to take any of our people into custody, they would be released to the captain for whatever discipline he saw fit to impose. But everything went off just as we hoped. It was a good night's work. And it was fun too if I do say so myself." He laughed a bit, lit his cigar stub, took a puff, and started dealing seven-card stud.

There was never another incident where one of the Schneeberg Amis, gay or not, was targeted by any of the locals. The Amis from the Hill behaved respectfully, even when drunk, and earned and kept the respect of the Germans in the nearby towns.

****

ALERTS

Detachment J was finally blessed with a new Ops officer-in-charge (OIC) on the first day of November, which happened to be a Tuesday in 1966. WO1 Brad Foster had been a Staff Sergeant 98C traffic analyst before being selected for a warrant and attending warrant officer school at Fort Rucker, Alabama. Prior to that, and after basic training, he had been through extensive analytic training at Fort Devens, Massachusetts. He then did a two-year tour of duty with the 2nd USASA Field Station at Two Rock Ranch near Petaluma, California, before serving 13 months with the 3rd Radio Research Unit (which was actually an ASA unit) in Vietnam. He was promoted to SSG in Vietnam and was selected for warrant officer upon his return.

Those warrant officers who weren't helicopter or fixed-wing pilots were usually technical experts in a specific career field. It was an ideal rank. They ranked lower than all commissioned officers and higher than all NCOs, and each of the four warrant officer grades earned just a bit less than the first four grades of commissioned officers. Enlisted personnel were required to render a hand salute to warrants when outdoors and address them as Sir or Mister. Like 2nd lieutenants, smart junior warrant officers knew that it was wise to defer to the knowledge and experience of senior NCOs before diving off the deep end of the pool.

Mr. Foster seemed like a smart warrant and was eager to get to work and establish himself on the Hill. He was single and had volunteered for the border site assignment for the very reason that he would be the officer **in charge** of operations. He believed it was better to be in charge of a small operation than to be a small cog in someone else's machine. Since

126

he had arrived on the first day of the month and was an officer, he took a spot toward the end of the payday disbursement line so he could see some of the men he would be charged with overseeing.

Mr. Foster owned a bright red '65 Mustang GT fastback that he bought new with money he had saved in Vietnam. It was a beauty, but some of us thought it would have traction problems on our access road which had been icy and snow covered for the past two weeks and which would remain that way until spring. He wore the red and yellow patch of the Military Assistance Command Vietnam (MACV) on the right shoulder of his uniform signifying that he had served in a war zone with that unit. Like the rest of us, he wore the ASA patch on his left shoulder.

Our new Ops OIC didn't waste any time before going to work. He was ensconced in his office with SFC Karney the next morning. He'd be working straight days like most of the other treads, but he let us know that we could expect him to make unannounced visits to Ops at any time of the day or night, even on weekends. He busied himself for the first few days by reading every file in Ops that he could lay his hands on. By the end of his first week, he had talked to each op on the day shift and had them explain their responsibilities. He seemed eager to learn and even made it a point to read the trick chief pass-on log so he would be familiar with what was going on during each shift.

****

One of the joys or benefits ("bennies") of an outstation assignment was that the monthly alerts were far different from those conducted at Herzo Base. Alerts at Herzo were usually called in the pre-dawn hours. If you weren't a trick worker, you'd be roused from your sleep by someone blowing a whistle or cranking a portable siren while going up and down the barracks hallways. You'd have to throw on your fatigues and boots, grab your field gear and haul yourself and your equipment to an assembly point outside the barracks building where you'd wait until a deuce-and-a-half arrived. Then you'd throw your gear into the truck, climb in, and take a seat on the wooden benches that lined each side of the bed. The trucks would move out from the barracks area and line up in convoy fashion on the long street that led from the main operations building past the consolidated mess to the main gate. It was as if the unit were about to deploy to support combat operations.

Sometimes the convoy would move out and drive around for 30 minutes before returning to base. Once the alert was terminated, you'd have to haul all your equipment back to your barracks room, get it squared away, and only then could you return to the normal morning routine of shower, shave, clean the latrine and hallway, and finally go to work.

The alert drill at Schneeberg was quite different, even though it occurred simultaneously with the one at Herzo and other bases. The alert notification came in the form of a telephone call to the CQ or in a message to the comms center from higher HQ. The CQ would immediately rouse everyone sleeping in the Topside building and dispatch someone to wake up everyone in the Cabin. Meanwhile, he had to notify the trick chief in Ops that an alert was in progress and contact the C.O. and all NCOs and enlisted men living off base who were then required to report ASAP to the Hill.

The men living on the Hill didn't have to grab their field gear like at Herzo, they just had to assemble in uniform in the kino room for a nose count until the alert was called off, usually less than an hour later. Most of the off-post guys never made it to Topside before the alert ended.

The November alert was called early on a Wednesday morning during a howling snowstorm. The off-post people were going to have a hard time making it up the mountain. I was sitting next to Jack Rutherford in the kino room waiting for the alert to be over. He had recently been on break.

"You were on break last weekend, weren't you?" I asked. "Did you see Heidi? How are you two getting on?" I was genuinely interested since I liked them both.

"It was a great break, Jerry. We had a nice weekend. We were at Reissmann's Friday and Saturday nights. She loves to dance, and I'm enjoying it more myself. I'm getting to know her friends a lot better too, and my German is improving. Father Pat has been tutoring me when he has time, and Heidi's a good teacher too."

"I'll bet," I replied, not intending to sound sarcastic or make it a double entendre.

Jack arched his eyebrows briefly and continued, "And then on Sunday she had me to her house for dinner and to meet her mother. Her mom is genuinely nice. She made me feel welcome."

"What about her father?"

"He's not in the picture at all. I think her parents split up when Heidi was very young. She never talks about him. I'm not sure she even remembers him."

"Oh, that's too bad. But at least you don't have to worry about winning over her father."

"Yeah, that's true. Her mom seemed to like me. At least she acted like she did. Heidi made *rouladen*. It's thin strips of steak rolled up like little jelly rolls around chopped onions, bacon, and pickle and served with gravy. It was delicious and reminded me of a good pot roast, although I didn't like the pickles at first. She and her mom both wore *dirndls*, those Bavarian dresses with a full skirt and a tight top. Heidi looked beautiful."

"You two are getting serious then?"

"Man, we already are serious. I know we've only known each other for a few months, but I honestly think this is the real deal. I'm gonna ask her to marry me."

I was only mildly surprised. "You're not kidding, are you? I can remember you telling me you were going to marry her the first time you laid eyes on her. Do you think she'll say yes? Do you have a wedding date in mind? You know this could affect your security clearance, right?"

"That's a lot of questions…but, yes, I do think she'll say yes. I've hinted at it, and she has too. I know I'm no great prize, but I'm fairly sure she loves me. And I love her." He paused to gather his thoughts and then went on, "The Army is something else though. I don't think I need the C.O.'s permission to marry, but I had a quiet word with Sergeant Gray, and he didn't think it would be a problem.

"The security clearance is another matter. We can sleep together, live together, whatever, and ASA doesn't seem to care. But when it comes to marrying a foreign national, guys often lose their clearance, at least temporarily. I'll cross that bridge when I get to it."

"What about money, Jack? Can you afford to get married?"

"I've given that a lot of thought and talked with Rob Gray about it as well. I'm putting in a request to attend 7th Army NCO Academy down in

Bad Tolz. If that goes through and I can survive 3 weeks of craziness down there, then Rob tells me I should make E-5 soon after. Once I make E-5. I'll reenlist for 4 years. As 98Gs we're eligible for a big reenlistment bonus and proficiency pay for being linguists once we're on our second hitch. And it wouldn't really be for 4 more years.

"What they do is discharge you from your current enlistment one day and then swear you again immediately for a new 4-year commitment. You must have already served 2 years of your initial enlistment, and I passed that point more than a month ago. So, in my case it will only mean another 2 ½ years beyond my initial enlistment. I think the re-up bonus for us is something like $4,800. They don't give it to you all at once. They pay you 25% when you re-up and another 25% each year after that. It's a pretty good deal."

"Gee, I didn't know that, Jack. It does sound attractive, at least at first glance. But what about your clearance? You can't work your MOS unless you're cleared for top secret crypto. And if you can't work your MOS, maybe they'll take your bonus back."

"I don't know, Jerry. I have to look into all of that before I re-up."

"Good luck with all of it. Say hi to Heidi for me. By the way, I'd like to meet her little brunette friend."

Jack laughed and nodded, "I'll see if I can make that happen next time we're all at Reissmann's."

The alert was terminated long before most the off-post people showed up. Mr. Foster managed to get his Mustang up the mountain despite the heavy snow, but he had to stop and put chains on the rear wheels to make the final mile.

****

Later that night I was in the Club drinking beer and playing poker with Jolly Ollie, Will Morrow, Lurch, and a few others. Large Louis and Bear were battling it out on the foosball table while Simon and Garfunkle sang "Homeward Bound" on the jukebox for the third time that night. I wished that they would change the records more often. I'm not so sure they ever changed them, come to think of it.

Many times, after an alert, some of the guys would talk about what would happen if we actually had a war on our hands. Most of us had made a conscious choice to enlist in ASA since we believed it was less likely we would see combat in an intelligence unit. But the periodic alerts reminded us that we could indeed find ourselves in battle one day.

Tony Phillips, Fang, and a Russian weed called Peeps were sitting at the bar talking in voices amplified by several beers about what they thought they'd do if the balloon went up. Tony owned an aging Porsche 356 coupe which he called the Green Weenie. He had gone to the trouble of getting an international driver's license for himself and international tags for his car. The rest of us had U.S. military licenses and tags. So did Tony, but he would put the international tags on his Porsche when he traveled to Austria or France on break or to Spain or Italy when on leave. He also had a civilian U.S. passport which most of us did not possess. We relied upon our military ID card which allowed us to travel to most NATO and neutral countries without a passport or visa.

Tony was telling Fang and Peeps that he and the Green Weenie would be heading for Switzerland if war was imminent. "My civilian license, passport, and license plates should get me past any MPs checking cars on the autobahn. My passport lists my occupation as student. I think I could make it."

"Make sure you save room for me," interjected Fang.

"Okay, but you'd better get a passport. That's the only way you'll get past the MPs."

Peeps didn't look convinced that they were serious. I wasn't sure either. Deserting one's post in the face of the enemy was frowned upon in the military…and carried profoundly serious consequences. I'm sure Ollie heard the conversation, but when I looked over at him, he was just shaking his head and chewing on his cigar.

Lurch had heard the conversation too, but he didn't comment or react. However, he must have been thinking about it as well as the alert that morning. He normally didn't have much to say while we were playing poker, but he unfortunately chose that moment to start bitching.

"There's a couple things that bug me about this place. For one thing, we don't have a medic here in the detachment. What happens if one of us gets hurt or real sick? I don't get it. And another thing, I don't understand why we have alerts and have to have all that field gear piled on top of our lockers. It's not like we're in the real Army. We're all technicians here on the Hill. All that other stuff is a lot of chicken shit." I think he had forgotten that MSG Henry was sitting at the table with him. "Uh oh, no offense intended, Top."

Jolly Ollie didn't say anything at all for at least 60 seconds. Then he put down his cards, re-lit his cigar stub, took a deep puff, and looked at Lurch with cold gray eyes and spoke with a voice that everyone in the Club could clearly hear, "Boy, you know why there's no medic on the Hill? I'll tell you why. It's 'cause they've already written us off. Why do you think they send the weirdos, misfits, and outcasts here? I know, damn it. I'm one myself. And you're probably right about alerts and field gear. You ain't never gonna need that stuff. Did you ever wonder **why** we don't do all the PT and field training that them animal outfits do? Do you, boy?! We don't even do as much as they do down at Herzo. And you know why?! Well, it's 'cause that, if or when that damn balloon does go up, every swinging dick on this damn mountain top is gonna be a dead ass crispy critter before the first day of battle has ended. You understand that, boy?! I saw my share of combat in Korea. That's ancient history to you dipshits, But I lost buddies there and served with good leaders too. Accept what it is here. All those other suckers will be just as dead as us within a few days of that balloon. That's the damn truth, so you and all these other smart-ass college boys had better get used to that idea. You got that?!"

The Club was absolutely quiet except for the closing bars of the Four Tops singing their current hit, "Reach Out for Me" on the juke box, *"Reach out for me. Hah, I'll be there to love and comfort you, and I'll be there to cherish and care for you."*

Ollie thundered out the question again, "You got that?!"

Lurch and a few of the rest of us automatically replied, "Yes, Sergeant!"

"Alright then. Let's get back to playin' cards."

And that's what we did for the rest of the evening.

****

FALSE FLAG

The mid shift can be boring, especially in mid-November when sections of northcentral Europe are already deep into winter weather. Soviet and Czech military units received conscripts into their ranks in October and November (1) and seldom conducted field training until the latest group of draftees had completed their basic military training. Consequently, the radio networks serving the Czechoslovak Peoples Army and those supporting Soviet forces in East Germany were only sporadically active during this period. The ASA intercept operators at Schneeberg sometimes had too much time on their hands, and some of them proved the adage that idle hands are the devil's tools.

One of the Russian Marys on Baker Trick was inspired by his devilish muse early one boring morning to introduce a new Russian army-level commander into our informal site order of battle for the Group of Soviet Forces Germany (GSFG). He wrote an anonymous entry in the trick chiefs' pass-on log that one Colonel General Kutchurdikov (pronounced like cut-your-dick-off) had been identified in intercept as the new commander of the 1st Guards Tank Army in Dresden (2). He found it amusing, but no one noticed at first.

Once the other Russian ops saw the note, they knew it was a joke and began embellishing the story with additional fictional information. One wrote that General Kutcherdikov's aide de camp was a Colonel Yakimov, and another identified his driver as Nikolai Alexandrovich Romanov. No one thought that these identifications would leave the Hill. They were merely a puerile attempt at humor born of boredom.

WO1 Foster was away for several days for training at Herzo Base while this creative writing exercise was unfolding in the pass-on log. He returned to the Hill on a Saturday afternoon while Baker Trick was on its long break. He wanted to be up to speed by Monday morning when the regular work week began. He spent most of that Saturday reviewing all message traffic that had been sent and received during his absence and decided to read the pass-on log before going home for the night.

He was excited to find these new order of battle intelligence nuggets on a hitherto unknown Soviet officer of flag rank. He intently pulled all the threads together into a special COMINT technical report titled "New Commander of Soviet 1st Guards Tank Army Identified" which he sent to Herzo Base. It was so well written that the on-duty analyst there decided to forward it electronically to NSA. Neither Foster nor the analyst at Herzo was a Russian linguist, and both failed to see the play on words.

In Mr. Foster's eagerness to get the scoop to Herzo, he neglected to run his report by his Ops NCOIC, SFC Karney, or any of the trick chiefs or Russian transcribers. When SFC Karney, who was a Russian linguist himself, saw Foster's report on Monday morning, he knew right away that it was bogus. One big giveaway was that the driver's name was the full name of the last Russian Tsar, Nicholas II. Karney was livid and had to tell WO1 Foster who felt humiliated. The tech report was cancelled with an apology. It was months before Mr. Foster or SFC Karney could see any humor in it.

****

The official start of winter was still a few weeks away, but almost everything atop our mountain was already covered in deep snow. After the *Bundeswehr* had taken occupancy of their new tower adjoining the American compound, they assumed responsibility for clearing the access road between Route 303 near the foot of the mountain and the sites at the summit. Before that, we Amis had struggled to keep the road clear using a snowplow attached to the front of a deuce-and-a-half. The Germans, on the other hand, had a custom-made vehicle that we had nicknamed the *schneefresser* (snow-eater). It was basically a huge snowblower mounted on the front of a truck.

The *schneefresser* was highly effective at clearing heavy snow and making the road drivable, but it was unable to strip the snow all the way down to bare pavement. There were always several inches of packed ice and snow on the road. The snow built up several feet high on the sides of the road over the course of weeks. That was good in one way because it made it almost impossible to skid off the road into the forest except at two or three bends in the road where the roadside dropped off somewhat precipitously. These were spots where it would have been wise to install a guardrail, but that never came about.

The final stretch of road from the Cabin and Club up to Topside was the steepest and most challenging for our cars to ascend without the benefit of tire chains. It could be done if you sped up just before passing the Club, so you'd have the momentum to make it up the final 100 yards. *(Photo courtesy of Phil Ward and Schneebergvets.org)*

Walking up that last stretch of road during the winter was also a challenge. The combat boots that were issued to us by the Army and which we were required to wear with our fatigues provided almost no traction on snow or ice. If you were fortunate, there would be enough powdery snow on the shoulders of the road to give you traction to get up the incline. Otherwise it was a chore climbing to Topside. Coming down to the Cabin after work was another matter. The daring few got a running start at the guard shack and slid down the steep incline like a skier *sans* skis.

****

The corrugated metal Ops building was always cold in the winter, even with six feet of snow piled up around the building's exterior and theoretically providing some insulation. It may have helped a little, but the building was still frigid and extremely drafty. The only heat in Ops came from a single kerosene heater near the center of the building. There was an electric space heater in the Ops OIC's office, but that didn't provide any benefit to the operators manning the intercept positions. The TR hut was even colder.

Most Schneebergers wore a standard field jacket over their fatigue shirts during the summer months. If Ops was warm on a sunny day, we could work in t-shirts as long as we stayed inside the building. As the weather grew colder, most of us switched over to wearing the parkas we had been issued as part of our field gear. It had a zip-in liner and came down almost to the knees. Once it got really cold, nearly everyone wore a sweatshirt or long johns under their fatigues. Even with layers of clothing, it was still cold in Ops. We would sit position wearing our parkas and still struggle to stay warm. On mids it was virtually impossible. Taking the burn bags over to the furnace room became a sought-after job. It was always toasty warm in the furnace room – and in the rest of the Topside building too.

The detachment mascot was an old German shepherd named Shadow. He had been on the Hill since he was a puppy and was considered everyone's dog. The cooks in the mess hall made sure that he was well fed, and he usually found a place to sleep in one of the Topside bunk rooms. One of his favorite places to sleep on winter nights was directly in front of the kerosene heater in Ops. When he wanted to come in for the night, he would bark outside the entry door until someone let him in. He'd walk around Ops and sniff each person there before plopping himself by the heater adjacent to the Czech UHF position and opposite the Czech and East German VHF positions.

Old Shadow had a chronic gastro-intestinal problem that produced copious amounts of gas. The UHF op was usually the first to detect one of Shadow's air bombs and could be expected to react with some colorful language as he leapt from his chair and tried to find safety toward the back of the building. The rest of us learned to follow his lead and hunker down near the OIC's office until the fart cloud had dispersed. There is no way to adequately describe a Shadow fart. They were killers. We'd cuss the old dog, but no one ever did anything to hurt him. Shadow supposedly held the rank of corporal and had medical records over in Bindlach. He was a good old dog.

****

The mess hall pulled out all the stops for Thanksgiving and set out a feast worthy of the holiday: shrimp cocktail, roast turkey with stuffing, baked ham, and tons of sides. It was everything a guy could want for Thanksgiving, except being at home with his family. Some of the married trick workers invited their unmarried coworkers over for a home-cooked meal. Others brought their wives up to the Hill for the mess hall banquet. Most of the trick trash had to work a shift over the holiday, but I was fortunate to be on break and had been invited to join a married DLI classmate and his wife for dinner at their apartment near the Herzo Base.

I got back to Schneeberg late on the afternoon after Thanksgiving and grabbed a few hours' sleep before starting a set of mids. According to the pass-on log, Captain Medved had visited Ops on Thanksgiving Day to thank everyone for their work and to deliver a big cake he bought at a bakery in Wunsiedel. WO1 Foster and SFC Karney had also made appearances; Karney brought cookies his wife had baked.

I was tired from the trip to Herzo and from working the first mid, which was always tough, so I didn't go into the Club until early Sunday evening.

I had to go to work in a few hours, so I ordered a Fanta instead of a beer. The Club was unusually quiet. No one playing poker or foosball. Tony Phillips was tending bar because Doug Broussard was TDY at the Gartow border site with the RRCV-4 van and Don McGrew. I started playing the nickel slot machine just to pass the time. The dime and quarter machines were too rich for my pay grade.

Not long after that, the door to the Club opened, and Anson and Bear escorted Ollie into the room. As usual, he was wearing fatigues and his field jacket, but his head and face were wrapped in bandages. I think he could see well enough, but Anson and Bear had their hands under his arms. They guided him into the room and sat him down at his usual seat at the poker table. He looked like a chubby mummy except where a stub of a cigar poked through from where his mouth was. There were holes in the bandages for his eyes and nose, but nearly everything else above his neck was covered. I went over and sat at the table.

"Holy crap, Top, what the hell happened to you? Were you in an accident?" I asked with genuine concern.

"I don't want to talk about it, Daniels. It was an accident. Yes. Let's just leave it at that." It was not a suggestion, but an order.

"Right, Sarge. Sorry. I hope you're feeling okay."

"Thanks," he grumbled. "I'll be good as new in a couple days. How about getting me a beer."

It was clear that he wasn't feeling conversational, so I got him a beer, drank my Fanta, and went back to the Cabin to read for a bit before midnight chow and the second mid shift.

Once we took care of the usual trick change routine and settled in for the night's work, I went over to where Will Morrow was sitting outside the OIC's office.

"I saw Ollie in the Club tonight. What happened to him? Do you know?" I asked.

Will rolled his eyes behind his thick black plastic Army-issued glasses and then replied, "I'll tell you what happened, but if Ollie asks you, you didn't hear it from me. Okay?"

"Sure. No problem. I was just shocked to see him all bandaged up. He said he had an accident."

"Yeah, you could say it was an accident. This is what went down. Ollie was in the Club Thanksgiving night. There were only a handful of us there. Tony Phillips was tending bar because Doug Broussard was cooking a Cajun-style Thanksgiving meal for his girlfriend Evi and her family in Bisch before he left for Gartow early yesterday morning. Anyway, it was a lot colder than usual in the Club. That single kerosene heater there doesn't work any better than the one here in Ops. Tony had fiddled with it for an hour or more trying to get it to work, but he wasn't having any luck with it. It just wouldn't stay lighted."

"Yeah, they can be hard to get going. Sometimes you gotta be a little creative to make it work," I added."

"Tony had tried everything he could think of. I think he might have even squirted some lighter fluid into the fire box hoping that would get it going, but it didn't work. Tony gave up, and then Ollie went over to see if he could do something. He had the top cover off the heater and was poking around inside it. He leaned in to try to get a better look, and next thing we knew there was a flash and a little explosion. Then Ollie staggered backwards holding his face and collapsed on the floor."

"Geez, what did you do?!"

"We were all frozen for a few seconds until we realized that he was hurt and not just screwing around. Ollie tried to tell us he was alright, but we could see that his face was all red and that his eyebrows were burned. He was in pain and just yelled at us to leave him alone. He was trying to sit up on the floor, but he couldn't quite make it. Bear ran across the street to get his VW bus in the parking lot, and Anson and Large Louis did their best to assess the injuries as Ollie kept waving them away. They finally were able to get Ollie on his feet and into Bear's bus. They took him over to Bindlach to have a medic look at him. We had the CQ call ahead so maybe a doctor would be there at the dispensary when Ollie arrived."

"So, what did they do at Bindlach?" I asked.

"Not a lot. They looked him over and then decided to take him by ambulance down to the hospital in Nuremberg for treatment. Anson rode down with him to keep him company. He told us later that Ollie pissed and moaned all the way there."

"How bad are his burns?"

139

"He was lucky, Jerry. Most are relatively mild first-degree burns. He has a couple small areas of second degree burns on his forehead and near one of his ears. That's why the bandages are on, He has to go back to the medics in Bindlach this week, and they'll probably take most or all of the bandages off then. He's gonna have some pain – like a bad sunburn – but he'll be fine before long."

"Does anyone know why it happened?"

"Not for sure, but you know how he always has that cigar stub in his mouth? Well, we think he forgot that it was there and that he had lit it just before he went over to look at the heater. We think that he took a puff on the cigar when he had his head in the heater and that was enough to ignite the fumes that were in there. It was just a freak accident, but he definitely doesn't want to talk about it or hear anyone else talking about it. Remember that."

"Right. I'm glad that he's gonna be okay."

(1)https://www.globalsecurity.org/military/world/russia/cccp-personnel.htm

(2)https://en.wikipedia.org/wiki/List_of_Soviet_military_sites_in_Germany/

****

THE DEFECTORS

I was finishing my dinner in the mess hall several days after Thanksgiving when Jack Rutherford came in to grab something to eat. The entrée was spaghetti with meat sauce and wasn't too bad, but nowhere near as good as my girlfriend's mother made using the family's Sicilian recipe. Jack sat down next to me.

"What's up, Jack? How was your Thanksgiving?" I asked.

"It was fantastic! I bought a turkey at the commissary over in Bindlach, and Heidi's mother cooked it perfectly. The stuffing didn't come out quite right, but everything else was wonderful. Stuffing is a little like chili in that everyone has their own recipe. I miss my Mom's stuffing. Anyway, Heidi's aunt and uncle were there for Thanksgiving too."

"And...?" I could feel that he wanted to make an announcement.

"I asked Heidi to marry me, and she said yes. We're engaged! Man, I am so damn happy!"

"That's great news, Jack! Congratulations!" And I meant it sincerely. "How does her mother feel about Heidi getting married?"

"Well, honestly, I think she had some misgivings at first because we're both so young. Heidi's only 19, and I won't turn 21 until February. But I think she's coming around and is sharing in our happiness."

"That's good. Have you set a date yet?"

"Not yet. It'll probably be in the spring. There are a few things I have to take care of before we can set an exact date."

I knew there would be a lot of paperwork involved, but I was curious what Jack meant. "Like what?"

141

"There are two big things. First, I'll be heading to the NCO Academy in Bad Tolz next week. Ollie somehow got me a slot in the class that begins Monday December 5th. I think he used his network of senior NCOs and pulled some strings for me. Of course, not too many people want to be in Bad Tolz for three weeks right before Christmas."

"Yeah, that's for sure. Bad Tolz is in the mountains south of Munich and not too far from Innsbruck, Austria. I think the 10th Special Forces Group has its headquarters at Bad Tolz. Are you gonna try for a green beret?"

"Hell no, Jerry. I'm more of a technician than a warrior, but Ollie pretty much guaranteed me that I'd be promoted to E-5 as long as I successfully completed the academy. I'm counting on that. Once I get promoted, I'll reenlist, like we talked about a few weeks ago. The re-up bonus will help Heidi and me get started on our own. And I'll start drawing pro-pay once I've re-uped."

"Sounds like a good plan, Jack. I'll know who to see if I need to borrow some money." We both laughed. "Let me know if there's anything I can do for you while you're away. I hope everything goes smoothly and that this all works out. I'm happy for you, man."

"Thanks. I hope my family back in New Jersey accepts Heidi. I really do love her."

"I know you do, Jack. She's a good one. A keeper."

****

Doug Broussard and Don McGrew left Schneeberg with the RRCV-4 van a few days earlier, just before dawn on the Saturday after Thanksgiving. The RRCV-4 was a one-of-a-kind SIGINT collection resource that was still semi-experimental. Its precise mission was never revealed to me, but I know it had something to do with some new technology that Soviet signal troops had been using in East Germany and elsewhere. Will Morrow told me that Doug and Don would be deployed to the ASA site at Gartow for about 14 days. Herzo believed that the Soviets were going to be conducting a communications exercise (COMEX) and that the RRCV-4 might be able to prove its worth during the COMEX if its equipment functioned correctly. Doug and Don would certainly do their best to prove the van's value.

Gartow was the northernmost outstation belonging to Herzo Base's sister unit, the 319th USASA Battalion at Rothwesten, and was in the British sector in northern West Germany approximately 80 miles southeast of Hamburg. The intercept site was on a mountainside overlooking East Germany. Unlike Schneeberg, it was not a permanent site. It operated out of shelters mounted on deuce-and-a-half trucks. Most of the ASA personnel assigned to the site were billeted in *pensions* in the town of Gartow at the foot of the hill and adjacent to the Elbe River, which marked the border between East and West Germany.

The border was one of the world's most heavily fortified frontiers, defined by a continuous line of high metal fences and walls, barbed wire, alarms, anti-vehicle ditches, watchtowers, automatic booby traps, and minefields. It was patrolled by 50,000 armed East German guards. A plowed strip 10 m (32.8 ft) ran along the entire length of the border. An adjoining "protective strip" (*Schutzstreifen*) 500m (1,640 ft) wide was tightly controlled. Only people holding a special permit could live or work within the adjacent 5 km (3.1 mile)-wide "restricted zone" (*Sperrzone).* When the communist authorities constructed the fortifications, they cut down trees and brush to clear lines of sight for the guards and to eliminate cover for would-be defectors. Houses adjoining the border were torn down, bridges were closed, and barbed-wire fencing was put up in many places. Farmers were permitted to work their fields along the border only in daylight hours and under the watch of armed guards, who were authorized to use deadly force if their orders were not obeyed.

The border zone was monitored by East German guards stationed in concrete, steel and wooden watchtowers constructed at regular intervals along the entire length of the frontier. Each of the larger ones was equipped with a powerful 1,000-watt rotating searchlight (*Suchscheinwerfer*) and firing ports to enable the guards to open fire without having to go outside. (1)

****

Broussard and McGrew came back to the Hill from their two-week TDY to Gartow in mid-December after making an overnight stop at Herzo Base for debriefing and a maintenance check of the RRCV-4. Once they secured the vehicle in the Topside parking lot, they came down to the Club where a dozen of us had gathered for drinks, cards, foosball, and socializing. Tony Phillips was behind the bar and bought Doug and Don their first round of beers. We were all eager to hear about the TDY and about life at another ASA border site. Tony got the narrative going, "So, how was Gartow? Better than here?"

Doug responded with a snorty laugh, "It was definitely THE most bizarre TDY I've ever been on, and I've been on quite a few. It's a long story, so bear with me. It started out like a normal deployment. It took us a good 12 hours to drive there, even doing 60 miles per hour on the autobahn most of the way. The roads to Gartow are well marked, but finding the site itself was a challenge. It was after dark when we arrived, so we just secured the vehicle in the operations compound and borrowed a jeep to go down to the village to get a meal and a room for the night. We spent most of Sunday back on the mountainside setting up the van for the intercept mission. The site looks down on the village of Gartow and the Elbe River, which is the border with East Germany. The site gave us a good line of sight into the area of East Germany controlled by the Soviet 3rd Shock Army at Magdeburg (2) (3), but I can't talk about that here.

145

"Most of the detachment lives in *pensions* in the village. That sounds good, but the accommodations are kinda spartan. As it turned out, one of the non-Morse intercept ops was a friend of mine named Johnny whom I knew from training at Fort Devens. He and six or seven other ops had leased a fully furnished vacation home a few hundred yards from the Elbe. Their combined housing allowance more than covered the rent and utilities, and their subsistence allowance paid for food and copious amounts of beer, wine, and booze. Two of the housemates had recently rotated back to the States, so Don and I were invited to stay at the house in return for paying a share of the rent from our TDY money. We jumped at the chance.

"We didn't know until later that the house had the reputation as THE party place in the local area. Everyone, including the Germans, referred to it as the Chateau. It's little more than a stone's throw from the Elbe, but that's not a problem since there are no 5K zone restrictions (4) on us there. The town and the site are in the British sector and outside the jurisdiction of USAREUR MPs."

Don continued the story, "We worked our asses off that first week, putting in 12 to 14 hours per day. I think we collected some good stuff for Daddy DIRNSA. The Russians kept us hopping until late Saturday morning, and then things went quiet. We decided to take the rest of the weekend off. We grabbed a late lunch at a *gasthaus* and then went back to the Chateau to relax. Little did we know what we were in for."

Doug took up the story again, "Saturday night was the big party night at the Chateau. By 10 pm the beer and wine were flowing freely. Music was blasting from a huge stereo system that one of the guys bought at a British PX. A few couples were dancing in the living room, and no one was feeling any pain at all. Don and I were feeling good too. I know I had a good buzz on at that point.

"I thought I heard someone banging on the front door, but I ignored it. The banging got much louder, like someone was hitting the door with something metallic. I got my buddy Johnny to turn down the stereo, and we both went to the front door to see what was going on. We thought that

146

a neighbor might have complained to the *polizei*, but it seemed unlikely since most of the nearby homes were unoccupied during the winter.

"Well, we half staggered to the front door, opened it, and nearly crapped our pants. There were two East German border guards standing there staring at us with AK-47 rifles in their hands. It's funny in retrospect, but Johnny and I both threw up our hands at the same time and shouted, 'We surrender!' The two East Germans looked at each other in puzzlement until one of them said in English, 'No, we surrender to you. We come across from DDR. We defect to you.'

"Johnny and I didn't know what to say. We were both three sheets to the wind, so we told the two border guards to leave their weapons outside the door and to come inside while we figured out what to do. It soon became apparent to us that these two guys were just as scared as we had been when we first saw them at the door. Johnny and I both speak German well, thanks to our girlfriends, so we told them not to worry and that no one would hurt them. Hell, they were as young as we are, maybe only 18 or 19 years old. We got them to take off their heavy coats and field equipment and come into the living room to get some food and drinks.

"The room went quiet when they walked in wearing their East German uniforms. Johnny explained to everyone that the two border guards were defecting to the West and needed our help. All the Amis and most of the locals gave them a big welcome. People kept bringing them beer and schnapps as well as sandwiches and junk food. You could see the apprehension fade from our new friends' faces.

"The border guards told us that they had been assigned to one of the nearby watch towers across the river. There were three men assigned to their tower. They had talked among themselves for weeks about defecting to the West while the river was frozen over. Two of them finally decided to do it, but the other one didn't want to go. However, he also didn't want to shoot his comrades as they escaped – or be shot by them. So, the three of them agreed that the two defectors would tie up the third guard who, when he was discovered, would say that the other two had overpowered him and made their escape. They put their plan into action that night. The Elbe River was frozen solid, so they were able to walk right across into West Germany. They knew that there were Americans nearby, and it didn't take them long to find the Chateau and surrender."

Don piped in, "While everyone else was getting ripped and fraternal, I went outside and unloaded the two AK-47s and then hid them in a shed around the back of the house."

Doug resumed his tale, "As the night turned into early morning, the Gartow ASAers bartered with the defectors for parts of their uniforms and field gear. One of them had brought his flare pistol with him along with a few flares. It probably wasn't a good idea, but sometime around 2 am everyone went outside, and we fired off a few flares over the Elbe toward East Germany.

"The partying continued into Sunday as folks drank themselves silly, passed out, and then rallied for more fun. By Sunday evening, the two defectors were dressed in Levis, cool t-shirts, and other American clothes. They helped us clean up the Chateau while we figured out what to do next.

"The Gartow ops took the defectors to the ASA compound on the mountain on Monday morning and kept them waiting 'under guard' in a car while Johnny went to the admin hut to notify their commander that they had two East German defectors in custody outside the gate. The C.O. got excited and ran out to see if this was for real. Johnny acted as his translator and relayed the story of how they walked across the river and gave themselves up at the Chateau. Johnny explained that they had no way to notify the C.O. until Monday morning, so they kept the two Germans in custody at the Chateau until that morning. The captain was skeptical and had lots of questions. He particularly wanted to know where the defectors' uniforms and weapons were. The ASA guys all shrugged and told the C.O. that the defectors were dressed in American clothes when they came to the door. Finally, the commander had Johnny call the local *polizei*, and the two defectors were taken off for interrogation and eventual resettlement in West Germany."

Most of us in the Club that night spent the rest of the evening debating among ourselves whether such a crazy story could be true. We decided in the end that we believed it. Maybe Doug embellished a bit, but we decided that the story itself was essentially true and that it would live on as an ASA legend for years to come.

****

Jack Rutherford was gone from the Hill for three weeks while he was at the NCO Academy. During that time, a few of the guys snickered about having seen cars belonging to SP6 Wayne Moore, the senior German linguist on site, and Captain Medved parked outside Heidi's mother's house at different times. They suggested that Heidi was entertaining those men while Jack was away.

Jack returned from the NCO Academy looking far more fit and squared away than I had ever seen him – and I had known him for two years at that point, going all the way back to language school. His starched fatigues had razor-sharp creases, and the tips of his Corcoran jump boots were spit-shined to a mirror gloss when I bumped into him Topside after he signed back in to the detachment in the orderly room.

"We're gonna have to start calling you Strack Jack if you keep looking that sharp. How was Bad Tolz?" I called out as I greeted him.

"It was really rough for the first week. Like being back in basic training again. There were a lot of chickenshit inspections and petty harassment, but the real killer was the PT. We've got it so easy here, but this was the real Army. Running at least three to five miles every morning up and down mountain roads. It's good to be back on the Hill."

"Have you seen Heidi yet?"

"You bet. I stopped at her mother's house a little while ago before signing in. She was glad to see me. So was her mother."

"Really? What have they been up to while you were gone?" I asked, hoping for a positive response.

"Oh, they've been working on some of the things that'll need doing before, during, and after the wedding. There's a lot to do, even though we haven't set a firm date."

"I'll bet."

"Yeah. I had told Heidi that Wayne Moore is an excellent photographer and that he has full access to the dark room in the Cabin. Before I left for Bad Tolz, I asked him to stop in and see Heidi and her Mom to talk about doing the wedding photography for us. He was there a week or ten days ago and spent a lot of time with them showing them samples of his work and planning for what he could do for the wedding. He's gonna give us a really nice package of photos at a great price."

"Terrific! Anything else?"

"No, not from Moore…but Captain Medved surprised them with a visit one afternoon around the same time. He heard from Ollie and Sergeant Gray that Heidi and I are planning to be married, so he stopped by to meet Heidi and to talk about some of the things she and I will have to do. It's a good thing that Heidi's English is fairly decent because his German is poor at best. Anyway, he explained that she would have to fill out a lot of forms and that her background would be thoroughly investigated. He also mentioned that if anything unfavorable turned up, I'd probably lose my security clearance. He even gave her a DD-398 form so she could start compiling all the personal history data the Army will need. It's almost like she'll be getting a clearance too."

"Yeah, in a way she will. She probably already knows more than she should just from hanging around with you and the rest of us Amis."

Jack bristled, "I never tell her anything classified, Jerry. You should know that."

"I do know, Jack. Relax. I didn't mean that you had. I just meant that she is a smart girl and that it would be natural for her to deduce what we're doing up here on the Hill. I don't think anyone in Bisch believes the cover story that we are part of STARCOM, the Strategic Army Communications System."

"Sorry. I see what you mean. But she has never asked me anything about my work. She knows I can't talk about it, and she respects that."

"Good. You know I like her. I think you and she will have a great life together."

****

While Jack was at Bad Tolz and while Doug and Don were at Gartow, Det J had an early Christmas present in the form of a USO show. We were all stunned when we heard that a USO show would come to such a small outpost. Bob Hope was taking an all-star troupe with him to Vietnam to entertain the military personnel there. He was bringing Carroll Baker, Anita Bryant, Joey Heatherton, and others with him that year. I was a Joey Heatherton fan because she grew up one town over from mine on Long Island and because her father Ray hosted a kids' show called *The Merry Mailman* on New York TV for as long as I could remember.

The USO show that came to Schneeberg that winter was far from spectacular, but much appreciated. Our guest of honor was George Jessel, the actor and comedian whose skill as a speaker earned him the honorary title of Toastmaster General. His co-stars were a dozen members of the chorus from an all-girls Catholic college in Indiana. There was a lot of discussion among the treads as to where the performance could be held. The Topside kino room was too small, and the mess hall just didn't seem to be an appropriate venue for a song, dance, and comedy show. The Club was the only viable alternative, and we had only one week to prepare it for the show.

Everyone knew that Stan "The Bard" Pace had experience staging college shows and that he hoped for a career in the theater after the Army. He was tapped to be the liaison with the USO people and plan the visit with help from Sergeant Gray, SFC Rayburn, Rich Roberts, and a couple of the straight days electronic maintenance men who could help with sound and lighting, if needed. Ollie was in overall charge.

Ollie's primary concern from the get-go was that the Club-Cabin-mess hall area be as nice looking as possible. He made it clear that something had to be done about the deep pits of yellow snow on both sides of the door to the Club where drinkers would void their bladders instead of using the latrine in the Cabin across the road. Another priority was to ensure that dressing and bathroom facilities were available for our guests. Since there were no women on the Hill, there was no ladies room either.

The Bard's committee decided to give Mr. Jessel the dark room in the Cabin as his dressing room. The girls would get the room next to it which Wayne Moore shared with SP6 Karl Waldgruen, a CARRYBACK Czech linguist. Wayne was almost never in the room because he usually stayed with his girlfriend in Wunsiedel. Karl agreed to give up his room for the day of the visit so the girls would have a dressing room too. Blankets could be placed over the windows for privacy. Sharing the latrine with the girls presented another problem, but the committee worked it out so that the latrine would be for ladies during the first 30 minutes of each hour and for men the second half.

Mr. Jessel was on the downward slope of his career when he visited Schneeberg, but most of us had heard of him or seen him on *The Ed Sullivan Show* or one of the other TV variety shows that aired in the 1950s and early 1960s. Stan Pace did some research and told us that Jessel traveled as much as 8,500 miles each year to make 200 appearances at the height of his career. He had journeyed overseas to entertain U.S. servicemen  for many years. When he was visiting Korea during the war there, he reportedly jumped out of a helicopter, was injured, and supposedly received the Purple Heart. That seemed unlikely to us, however. By late 1966 he was already an outspoken supporter of the American war effort in Vietnam. He frequently appeared in a military uniform during performances, calling it his U.S.O. outfit.

Jessel and the chorus arrived in an Army bus with USO banners. It had been converted into a tour bus for the group's trip to U.S. military installations in West Germany. The girls used it as their dressing room and were happy that we had worked out a way for them to share our bathroom facilities. They were all girl-next-door types whom we welcomed warmly. They put on a good show and finished up with a sing-along series of Christmas carols that helped remind us of the impending holidays. They were chaperoned by a stern middle-aged lady whom we all guessed was either a nun or a former nun. Mr. Jessel was both funny and charmingly endearing. We were all sad to see the troupe depart. Afterward, the only complaint I heard was from Jolly Ollie who took exception to Jessel wearing a Combat Infantryman's Badge and airborne wings on his "uniform."

****

About 10 days before Christmas, Rich Roberts took me aside in Ops with an unexpected opportunity. He was supposed to fly home for Christmas in a couple of days on a Davis Agency charter flight from Frankfurt to New York. He told me that he had decided not to go and to spend the holiday with his friend Felix instead. He offered the roundtrip ticket to me for a bargain $200, and I jumped at the chance. All I had to do was clear it with our trick chief, Will Morrow, and with Ollie. They approved my leave, and a few days later I was headed home to surprise my family and my girlfriend.

****

(1) https://en.wikipedia.org/wiki/Inner_German_border
(2) https://en.wikipedia.org/wiki/List_of_Soviet_military_sites_in_Germany
(3) https://www.3ad.com/history/cold.war/cold.war.sectors.2.html
(4) Most US personnel were not allowed within 5 km of the West German border with communist countries during the 1960s.

****

153

THE MUTINY

My charter flight back to the States left from Rhein/Main Airport in Frankfurt on the morning of Christmas Eve, which was a Saturday, and arrived at Kennedy Airport in New York early that afternoon New York time. I took a cab to my home in Baldwin which was less than 15 miles from the airport. My 80-something year old grandmother answered the front door when I knocked. She just about fell over with surprise and delight. My parents were happy to see me too, and I was exceptionally happy myself to be home to celebrate Christmas and New Year's with family and friends – especially my girl, who was home on winter break from her college upstate New York. Two weeks went by in the blink of an eye, and before I knew it, I was back at JFK waiting to board my charter flight back to Frankfurt.

Rich Roberts had timed the return to the Hill to coincide with Dog Trick's beginning days on Tuesday January 10th, which was perfect for me since we were on the same trick. I got back to Schneeberg Monday night and managed a few hours' sleep before getting up at 0600 to get prepared for work. All the guys in the trick room were unusually quiet. Will Morrow approached me as I was sitting on my bunk blousing my boots.

"I think the shit's gonna hit the fan this morning," he began. "The C.O. called a mandatory formation at 0730 outside Ops. Everyone who works in Ops must be there. Even the day ladies and the people on break. None of the maintenance techs or the others who work outside Ops have to be there. Just Marys and anyone who is involved in SIGINT collection. I hear the C.O. is really pissed."

"What the hell is going on," I asked.

154

"The less you know the better," replied Morrow. "The treads at Herzo want to dick away Fang for something he said New Year's Eve when he signed down the tapes at the end of the intercept day. He was screwing around, and they're accusing him of being drunk on duty."

"Was he? We all know he likes to drink. Just like the rest of us."

"No. That's the thing. He wasn't drunk at all. He hadn't even had one drink, but he deliberately slurred his speech when he did the sign down, and when he gave his op sign 'Whiskey November,' he said something like 'Your operator has been Whiskey November…and tonight it's been a lot more whiskey than November. Happy New Year! Hiccup.'"

Morrow continued, "Well, the tapes weren't checked or transcribed here where someone might have erased the stupid sign-down recording. Instead, the tapes were couriered back to Herzo. One of the transcribers there heard Fang's sign down and thought it was pretty funny. He called a couple other scribes over to listen to it, and they were all laughing…."

"That's when the NCOIC of the Czech shop happened into the TR room. You probably know him. SFC Waldron?"

"Yeah, I know him. He's a hard ass and doesn't have much of a sense of humor."

"That's what we heard. Anyway, he wanted to know what the TRs were laughing about. The scribes who had been laughing tried to hem and haw and avoid answering. Finally, Waldron grabbed a pair of earphones and listened to the sign down himself. From what I'm told, he went batshit crazy after that. Ranting about drunks at the outstations, lack of discipline, no dedication to duty, and so on.

"The scribes tried to calm him down and explain that it was probably just Fang screwing around, but Waldron wouldn't buy it. He wanted blood. He sent a report up the chain of command to the Ops Officer, LtCol Brown, and Brown called Captain Medved and gave him hell. Medved called Fang into his office and read him his rights under Article 31 of the UCMJ. Fang admitted to screwing around, but he insisted …even swore…that he had been sober. Medved reamed out Fang and told him he was considering giving him an Article 15. Meanwhile, Fang was not to leave the Hill or drink any alcohol."

"I'm not too surprised at the C.O.'s reaction," I replied. "I remember that he had put out the word a few days before Christmas that he wouldn't tolerate any drinking on duty or being drunk or hungover on duty during the holidays."

"You're right, but the thing is that Fang wasn't drunk. He just can't prove that he wasn't." Morrow paused for a moment before continuing, "Well, you know how word gets around quickly on the Hill, so everyone knew what was going on. People were grumbling about it being a railroad job and that Fang was being screwed for nothing. The grumbling got angrier as a handful of the short-timers started to ask themselves, 'How do you fight back at the treads? You can't go on strike…or can you?'

"They hatched a plan and spread it with whispers from one op to another. Everything would appear to be normal. We would all go to work and go through the motions as usual, but there would be no intercept, no recordings, no nothing. Everyone would suddenly be deaf."

I could see right away that this plan was perilous. "Oh, man, this is some serious shit!"

"You're right. And looking back on it now, it was a bad idea. But that's how it began a few days after New Year's. First one trick, then another went through their shifts without intercepting anything and without recording any signals, even the ones that were active like clockwork every day year-round. We trick chiefs were aware of what was going on, but we turned a blind eye and a deaf ear to it all. We simply entered 'Nil heard' in the shift pass-on book and left it at that.

"This went on for at least 48 hours before Herzo Base sent a message to the site asking about the lack of intercept. They thought it might represent radio silence by the Czechs and others. If so, what were they up to?" Morrow shook his head ruefully, "And then came the message from DIRNSA on Friday. It was carefully worded, but it was clearly 'Whiskey Tango Foxtrot? Over.' And that's when the shit started flying. I don't know what the C.O. has to say this morning, but it won't be good. We'd better get up to Topside now. It would be a bad day to be late."

****

All the Ops people assembled in the road outside the main Topside building opposite the flagpole. We fell in according to our tricks. Able Trick was in the front rank, and Dog Trick was in the rear. A few of the day ladies, like Father Pat and SP6 Moore, were interspersed with the tricks. MSG Henry called the formation to attention, and the men assumed that pose with a lackadaisical attitude.

The formation stayed at attention for a minute or two. MSG Henry had executed an about face and had his back to the group. He was facing the Topside building awaiting Captain Medved. A moment or two later, Medved came storming through the door and out into the frigid January morning. He was wearing his dress greens and dress hat. He was not smiling. He took a position in front of Ollie, who saluted him and reported, "Detail formed as ordered, Sir."

"Thank you, First Sergeant. Take your position behind the formation."

"Yes, Sir."

Medved stood and glared at the assembled Ops contingent. His face was red, and it wasn't due to the cold air. He was clearly furious. "You men look worse than a bunch of girl scouts!" he barked. "Stand at attention the way a soldier stands at attention, goddam it!"

The men straightened their posture and stood more rigidly.

"You men are in deep shit, and you're too goddam stupid to realize it. Do you hear me?"

There was a muffled "Yes, Sir" and maybe a nervous giggle or two.

"I can't hear you!" he screamed, with veins bulging at his temple and on his neck. "Do you hear me?!"

"Yes, Sir!" the men replied with much greater amplitude.

"Now listen up and listen good." He wasn't screaming, but his voice could probably be heard all the way over at the *Bundeswehr* tower. "I know what you have been doing…or, more accurately, what you have **not** been doing. What you don't understand is how you have roiled the powers-that-be, not only at Herzo Base, but at NSA HQ. You should know by now that in the Army, shit flows downhill, and this detachment is near the bottom of that hill. You people are the ones who are **really** at the bottom, and you're about to be covered in shit. And you know who's to blame? It's you! It's your shit that is about to smother you. Does that make you happy?! Does that solve anything?!" He was shouting again, and I was getting nervous about what might come next.

The formation replied softly to his rhetorical question, "No, Sir."

"What was that?! I can't hear you!"

"Sir. No, Sir!!!" came the desired reply.

"Alright then. But I don't think you men fully understand the shitstorm you have created. I'm thinking about reading all of you your rights under Article 31 of the UCMJ. That's what we do before we charge you with an offence that could be brought before a court martial or an Article 15. Did I see a smirk there, specialist?!"

I knew he wasn't talking to me. I wasn't smirking. In fact, I think my jaw was clenched in dread...

Captain Medved continued in his parade ground voice, "I had better not see any smirks, and you'd better hope I don't because right now your collective ass belongs to me. There's a slim chance that you people are too stupid to realize what you have done and what the consequences could be. I'd like to think that's true, even though I hear that you think you're supposed to be the top 10% of the Army. God help us if that's true. So, just to make this goddam situation perfectly clear to all of you, I have asked Staff Sergeant Gray to enlighten you by reading appropriate excerpts from the UCMJ. Sergeant Gray, please proceed and read the sections I have highlighted."

SSG Gray took a position next to the C.O. and began to read from a leather-bound tome which looked like a law book. "Listen up, and listen very carefully!" he barked in a voice that none of us had ever heard from him before.

"Article 94 UCMJ: Mutiny and Sedition states, and I quote:

(a) Any person subject to this chapter who—

(1) with intent to usurp or override lawful military authority, refuse, in concert with any other person, to obey orders or otherwise do his duty or creates any violence or disturbance is guilty of mutiny;

(2) fails to do his utmost to prevent and suppress a mutiny or sedition being committed in his presence, or fails to take all reasonable means to inform his superior commissioned officer or commanding officer of a mutiny or sedition which he knows or has reason to believe is taking place, is guilty of a failure to suppress or report a mutiny or sedition."

Gray paused briefly and then continued very slowly and loudly, "Listen real close to this part!

"A person who is found guilty of attempted mutiny, mutiny, sedition, or failure to suppress or report a mutiny or sedition shall be punished by death or such other punishment as a court-martial may direct."

158

There was an audible gasp from the formation. SSG Gray continued:

"Elements
(1) Mutiny by creating violence or disturbance.
(a) That the accused created violence or a disturbance; and (b) That the accused created this violence or disturbance with intent to usurp or override lawful military authority."

He paused again for effect and shouted, "This next one definitely applies to you men!

"Mutiny by refusing to obey orders or perform duty.
(a) That the accused refused to obey orders or otherwise do the accused's duty;
(b) That the accused in refusing to obey orders or perform duty acted in concert with another person or persons; and
(c) That the accused did so with intent to usurp or override lawful military authority.

"Listen carefully now. This next part applies to trick chiefs and others in authority!" He continued reading.

"Failure to prevent and suppress a mutiny or sedition.
(a) That an offense of mutiny or sedition was committed in the presence of the accused; and
(b) That the accused failed to do the accused's utmost to prevent and suppress the mutiny or sedition.
Failure to report a mutiny or sedition.
(a) That an offense of mutiny or sedition occurred;
(b) That the accused knew or had reason to believe that the offense was taking place; and
(c) That the accused failed to take all reasonable means to inform the accused's superior commissioned officer or commander of the offense.
Attempted mutiny.
(a) That the accused committed a certain overt act;
(b) That the act was done with specific intent to commit the offense of mutiny;
(c) That the act amounted to more than mere preparation; and
(d) That the act apparently tended to effect the commission of the offense of mutiny."

159

Gray paused again and turned a page in the UCMJ book. "Now listen to this explanation of what I have already read to you.

"(1) Mutiny. Article 94(a)(1) defines two types of mutiny, both requiring an intent to usurp or override military authority.

(a) Mutiny by creating violence or disturbance. Mutiny by creating violence or disturbance may be committed by one person acting alone or by more than one acting together.

(b) Mutiny by refusing to obey orders or perform duties. Mutiny by refusing to obey orders or perform duties requires collective insubordination and necessarily includes some combination of two or more persons in resisting lawful military authority. This concert of insubordination need not be preconceived, nor is it necessary that the insubordination be active or violent. It may consist simply of a persistent and concerted refusal or omission to obey orders, or to do duty, with an insubordinate intent, that is, with an intent to usurp or override lawful military authority.

The intent may be declared in words or inferred from acts, omissions, or surrounding circumstances.

Failure to prevent and suppress a mutiny or sedition. 'Utmost' means taking those measures to prevent and suppress a mutiny or sedition which may properly be called for by the circumstances, including the rank, responsibilities, or employment of the person concerned. 'Utmost' includes the use of such force, including deadly force, as may be reasonably necessary under the circumstances to prevent and suppress a mutiny or sedition.

Failure to report a mutiny or sedition. Failure to 'take all reasonable means to inform' includes failure to take the most expeditious means available. When the circumstances known to the accused would have caused a reasonable person in similar circumstances to believe that a mutiny or sedition was occurring, this may establish that the accused had such 'reason to believe' that mutiny or sedition was occurring.

"Sir, that concludes the reading of Article 94."

Thank you, Sergeant Gray." Medved paused and scanned the now ashen faces of the assembled Ops personnel. "Do you all understand the seriousness of what you have apparently done?" His voice was quieter now, but his anger was still apparent. "Do you?!"

"Sir, Yes, Sir!" The answer was clear. I think I heard a couple guys sniffle a bit as they responded. Maybe it was prompted by the frigid wind...or maybe not.

"Alright then. I want you all to get back to work **immediately** and resume your duties with the diligence you know I expect from you while I'm deciding how to deal with you and the mess you created. First Sergeant! Take charge of this formation."

MSG Henry came to the front, saluted the C.O., and watched him march back to the Topside building and enter. He kept us at attention for a minute or two and then gave the order to stand at ease. There was a huge collective sigh. Everyone still looked straight ahead and watched Ollie and waited for him to speak.

"You college boys think you are so damn smart. God's gift to this Army. You don't know shit from shinola when it comes to being a soldier. Your C.O. is one of the finest officers I've served with in over 20 years in this man's army. You've seen that MACV patch on his right shoulder. He's been to Vietnam and seen and done things that you can't imagine. He has led men in combat – lost a few and saved a lot thanks to his own courage and smarts. You think he sits in his office and doesn't do squat. He does more than you can dream about, and he does it for the mission and he does it for **you**.

"While you dickheads were deciding to play deaf and pull off some crazy-ass strike or whatever, Captain Medved was at Herzo doing his best to get that idiot Fang off the hook for his New Year's Eve stupidity. And, you know what? He convinced the Herzo people that it was all a misunderstanding. They agreed to let Fang off with an unofficial reprimand that won't affect his chance for promotion later this year. How about that, assholes?! And while he's doing his best for Fang and the rest of you, you decide to have a mutiny. Holy shit! I can't believe how stupid you all are! Even now, the Captain could nail all your asses to the wall and send you to Leavenworth. How'd ya like that, college boys?!"

Ollie's question was met with stunned silence.

"Now here's what you're going to do. Each and every one of you dipshits, listen to me. Day shift, you will assume your duties in Ops as soon as I dismiss you. The rest of you will resume your duties as scheduled. Your hearing will miraculously return. You will work harder than you have ever worked. You will do your best. Your absolute best! You will do it to redeem yourselves. You will do it to convince me that you are worthy to wear that uniform. You will do it to show Captain Medved that you are worth the trouble that he has gone to supporting you. And you will do it for me, because if you don't, I will kick each of your asses all the way down the road to Bischofsgruen and back. Is that crystal clear?! I want to believe you when you reply, so answer me like soldiers. Is that crystal clear?!"

The response echoed through the chilling wind. "Yes, Sergeant!"

"OK. That's it. Ten Hut! Dismissed!" Ollie turned on his heel and went back into the Topside building.

The formation broke up very quietly. The duty trick and the day ladies went into Ops. The rest of us straggled down the hill toward the Cabin and mess hall. The club would be incredibly quiet this evening. No one wanted to see Ollie anytime soon. I think most of the guys were ashamed, but no one talked about it. Not later that day. Not ever again that I can recall. Until now.

****

The next day, we learned from our trick's comms center man that Captain Medved sent out a message to Herzo a few hours after he read us the mutiny act. In the message, he advised Herzo that "After a thorough investigation, our maintenance personnel found that a heavy accumulation of ice on and around the antenna cabling systems may have caused the recent three-day interruption of intercept. Appropriate corrective measures have been taken to prevent any future occurrence. Signed, John Medved, CPT, Detachment J Commander."

****

RUTHERFORD'S RUIN

Winter on Schneeberg could be truly beautiful…when the howling wind wasn't blowing snow and ice that stung your face and limited visibility to less than 30 yards…when snow wasn't piled so high against the walls of the Ops building that it reached the roof… when it didn't felt like you were entering a snow tunnel walking from the Topside road to the door of the Ops building…when a rare day of warm sunlight didn't melt just enough snow on the access road that it turned to an ice rink after dark...or when it wasn't your turn to climb a tower in the middle of a blizzard to knock accumulated ice off the antennas.

January seemed hopelessly without end as it ever so slowly unfolded. Deep snow hid all but the top of the 8-foot barbed wire fence enclosing the Topside compound. Clear sunlit days were rare but most welcome. It was only then that we could appreciate the incredible beauty of the snow-covered forest that surrounded us and the breathtaking vista of the valleys below the mountain.

The arctic weather compounded the feeling of isolation that characterized the winter months on the Hill. Morale sagged as low as the temperatures outside. The only truly warm place at the detachment was the furnace room in the Topside building. The mess hall was tolerable due to heat generated by stoves and steam tables. The sleeping rooms in the Cabin and Topside weren't too bad either; we had heavy woolen Army blankets to keep us warm. The Club was...well, it was the only place to drink on the mountain, so the one kerosene space heater would have to do as long as we kept our parkas on. However, Ops was almost unbearably cold in winter. The corrugated metal building was not designed for a polar environment such as ours. Long johns, sweatshirts, and parkas kept us from freezing to death. Depression, cabin fever, and short tempers were the rule rather than the exception. Only a few men took advantage of skiing on nearby Ochsenkopf. For the rest of us, the only respites were movies in the kino room, beer and poker in the Club, and weekend evenings at Reissmann's *Tanzcafe* in Bisch. Despite our complaints about conditions on the Hill, we knew that we were truly fortunate to be there rather than in the midst of the widening war in Vietnam. (*Photos courtesy of Phil Ward and Schneebergvets.org.*)

****

Jack Rutherford was aglow with happiness after receiving word from Captain Medved in late January that his promotion to SP5 had been approved and would take effect on 1 February. I was genuinely happy for him, even though I had more time in grade than he did, but I knew he deserved it, especially after enduring the NCO Academy in December.

"Congratulations, Jack! That's terrific news about your promotion. You deserve it, my friend."

"Thanks, Jerry. I appreciate that. I'm sure you'll get yours before too long," he answered graciously.

"That'd be nice. But I'll have to stay out of trouble. Sometimes I think I have a knack for finding it…either that, or I have a magnet for attracting trouble." We both laughed, and I continued, "So does this mean that you and Heidi will be setting the date for your wedding?"

"Absolutely! I already talked to her, and we've tentatively settled on Friday May 19th at the *rathaus* in Bisch, the town hall. She's not too religious, and I was thinking that maybe we'd wait until we get back to the States next year before we have a church wedding."

"Good idea! Then your family and stateside friends could celebrate the marriage, meet Heidi, and bring presents too. What about reenlisting? Are you gonna do it?"

"Yep. Heidi and I talked it over. To be honest, we'll need the reenlistment bonus to get started here on the right foot. I just talked to the

C.O. and Ollie about it, and they're having Sergeant Gray put in the paperwork. If all goes according to plan. I'll re-up on Valentine's Day. Captain Medved can administer the oath here, but I'll have to go to Darby Kaserne in Fuerth-Nuremberg to collect my bonus."

"Re-upping is a big step, Jack, but I know you've given it a lot of thought. By the way, I just read *in Stars and Stripes* that the variable reenlistment bonus for us 98Gs is a factor of 4. I think that's the max."

"That's right. I did some rough calculations and figure that the first installment on my re-up day will be around $2,000 before taxes are withheld. And then on each anniversary of my reenlistment for the following 3 years I'll get another $1,000. That's right around 4 month's base pay for an E-5 with over 2 years of service. Of course, once I'm married, I'll draw quarters and subsistence allowances, plus I'll start getting language proficiency pay as soon as I re-up. Things are looking good."

"I'm really happy for you, Jack. And for Heidi too. Say hi for me when you see her."

****

Depression, bad weather, immaturity, and alcohol are a mix that often leads young men to make bad decisions, especially when a measure of testosterone is added to the recipe. Fortunately, they usually gain a dollop of wisdom from their ill-advised choices. Such was the case with a quartet of Schneebergers who set off on a road trip to the brothels in Nuremberg early one February morning after drinking all night at the Club. Doug Broussard told me about it one evening when he and I were alone in the Club.

"Did you hear about Dick Proust and Charlie Trick's trip to the Wall?" he asked me out of the blue. Dick Proust was an acting sergeant and a Czech Mary who was the trick chief for Charlie Trick. He was always ready to party and perpetually had a devilish grin on his face. He was a good intercept op and linguist despite his strong dislike of the Army and great affection for alcohol.

"You mean the Wall in Nuremberg where the whore houses are? No, I haven't heard anything about it. Did the whole trick go?"

"No, not the whole trick. Just Dick, Whiskey Man Smythe, the Grommet Cook, and a weed they've decided to call Peeps – SP4 Darrel Price, a Russian Mary on Charlie Trick."

"So, what happened?" I asked.

Doug opened another beer for each of us and leaned forward as if confiding, "All I know is what Grommet Cook told me. He said that the four of them started drinking in the Club one night about a week ago when Charlie Trick was on break. Tony Phillips was tending bar and decided to stay open as long as they wanted to keep drinking. I think he was enjoying their company. Dick and Whiskey Man are always fun to be around. Anyway, sometime well after midnight it somehow came out that Peeps was a virgin. The other three harassed him about it off and on for at least an hour. And then Dick had a brainstorm. They would all get into Dick's VW and drive to Nuremberg so Peeps could get laid at the Wall.

"There was a lot of back and forth as they discussed the pros and cons of the idea. They all knew that the Wall is off limits and out of bounds for American military, but they figured the odds would be against any MPs being around early in the morning. None of them had to work in the morning, so that wasn't an obstacle to their plan. Money was a minor concern, even though the going price was only 40 DM ($10), but Dick said he'd put up the money if anyone needed a loan. The funny thing was that none of them seemed concerned that Dick would be doing the driving and had already had a lot to drink."

"So, everyone went along with the idea?" I asked.

"Yeah, but Dick was the most enthusiastic. I think he thought that it would be a big favor to Peeps. As usual, Whiskey Man was willing to go along with whatever Dick had in mind. Grommet Cook was neutral at first and then adopted a 'what the hell' attitude and agreed to go. Peeps was the only hold out. They had to do a lot of arm twisting before he finally agreed."

"Did they actually go to the Wall and get the deed done?" I was thinking that they might have sobered up on the drive down to Nuremberg and changed their minds.

"They did it alright, Jerry, but I don't think it went as they had hoped. Grommet Cook told me that it was a little past dawn when they got to Nuremberg. They found the Wall easily enough. You know, the red-light district is actually just inside and opposite the old city wall and not far from the *hauptbahnhof*."

"Sounds as though you've been there, Doug," I teased.

"Just as a sightseer, not as a patron. But back to the story...The guys were supposedly hungry and wanted to get breakfast first. They found an open *gasthaus* around the block from the Wall, parked outside, and went in to eat and, in my opinion, muster their courage. After eggs and sausage, Grommet said they walked around the corner to the two-block stretch of buildings that make up the zone. Normally, there would be women showing their wares in the windows, but it was the beginning of the day shift, and there weren't many of them looking for business.

"The guys found a place that had four girls available, and in they went, agreeing to meet back by Dick's car when they finished their business. Grommet told me that none of the women was good looking and that one of them looked old enough to be his mother. He said he wasn't turned on by the one he got, but he paid her, did what he was supposed to do, and was back outside heading for Dick's car within 15 minutes. He expected to have to wait for the others. The funny thing was that the other three guys were already waiting for him at the car. I guess it was a 'wham, bam, thank you ma'am' experience for all of them – certainly not the auspicious initiation into manhood that Dick imagined for Peeps. I think they were all embarrassed by the experience and maybe even a little ashamed, based on what Grommet told me."

"I can only imagine, Doug. It doesn't sound like my cup of tea." I took a swallow of beer and then asked, "Do you know how Whiskey Man got his nickname? I'm simply curious. I've never seen him drink whiskey here or down at Reissmann's. What's the story?"

A smile crossed Doug's Cajun face, "It doesn't have anything at all to do with what he drinks. He got the name a few months ago after Dick and the rest of Charlie Trick watched a western movie in the kino room. The name of the movie was *Ride Beyond Vengeance*. Chuck Connors and Michael Rennie had the lead roles. Rennie was a corrupt banker, and one of his henchmen was played by Claude Akins. The Akins character had a serious drinking problem and had a permanent hallucination of a companion whom he called Whiskey Man. Chuck Connors shoots Akins at the end of the movie, and as the Akins character dies he turns to his imaginary friend and says something like, 'Whiskey Man, he done killed us both.' Well, I think the Charlie Trick guys thought the relationship between Dick Proust and Walt Smythe resembled the one between Akins and his hallucination, so they christened Walt as Whiskey Man, and it stuck."

"Good story. I like it. Thanks."

****

Jack took the oath of reenlistment as planned on the morning of February 14th. He invited me to witness the brief ceremony in Captain Medved's office with Ollie, Sergeant Gray, and Anson looking on. I was happy to attend since I was working days and only had to walk across the road from Ops to Topside to observe. Heidi couldn't attend because German civilians were not allowed inside the Topside compound. I congratulated Jack and wished him well as he began the new 4-year hitch.

"What next, Jack?"

"I'm heading down to pick up Heidi at her mom's house, and then we'll be driving down to the finance office at William O. Darby Kaserne. I think it's about a quarter mile from the main PX in Fuerth."

"I know the area pretty well. I bought my Mercedes from a used car dealer across the street from the PX. There's an American Express military banking branch next to the PX. It would be a good place to deposit your bonus."

"It would be if I were stationed at Herzo Base, but there's no American Express office near here, although Hof Air Station might have one. No, I'm gonna deposit my money in the *Deutsche Bank* down in Bisch. That way it'll be handy for local expenses related to the wedding and setting up an apartment with Heidi."

"I guess that makes sense. You'd better be careful carrying that much cash. I hear that the finance office doesn't issue checks. Instead, they pay the bonus in 20-dollar bills. That'll be a huge wad of cash to carry."

"Yeah, but I'm not worried. I'll have Heidi along to protect me." We both laughed.

"Right. Well, be careful. As the locals say, *Gute fahrt*! Safe travels."

****

I didn't see Jack again until 48 hours later. He looked very downcast and didn't respond when I greeted him in the Cabin hallway. I happened to run into his trick chief, SSG Jim Hall, outside the orderly room later.

"Hey, Sergeant Hall, how's it goin'?"

"Doing well, thanks. How about you?"

"I'm good. I'm glad I ran into you. I saw Jack Rutherford earlier today, and he looked like hell. Is he okay?"

"He's not too okay right now, but I'm hoping he'll come around in a few days. I really can't tell you about it. I think Jack wants to keep quiet about what happened to him. Just try to be a good friend to him and be patient if he's in a crappy mood. I'd be down too if I were he."

"Heidi didn't break up with him, did she?" I asked.

"No, they're still on track to get married in a few months. I can't say anything else, Daniels. Gotta go. Seeya."

I was very curious, naturally, and concerned for my friend too. I figured that if Jack wanted to talk, he'd seek me out. If not, then it was better to respect his privacy and give him a wide berth, if that's what he wanted.

It's virtually impossible to keep your personal life private at small detachments like Schneeberg. Someone will discover one bit of information, and someone else will stumble upon another tidbit until a story starts to take shape. After all, intelligence people are supposed to be good at connecting dots and analyzing data. Enough bits and pieces emerged over the next few days for the story to be told at the poker table in the Club.

Lurch had overheard Anson talking to Sergeant Gray about it in the orderly room, and he was eager to share what he heard with those of us at the card table. Luckily, Jack wasn't there. He was working swings that night.

"Hey, I think I've got the skinny on what happened to Rutherford last week. He's really screwed if you ask me," Lurch began.

Weasel perked up, "What's the deal? Is he in trouble?"

"No. Nothing like that. Not as far as trouble with the Army. It's worse than that. He lost his reenlistment bonus on the way back from collecting it down in Fuerth. From what I heard, he had a flat tire on the autobahn on the way to Bisch from Nuremberg, He pulled off onto the side of the road somewhere south of Bayreuth to change the tire. It was wicked cold, but he had to do it. His girlfriend Heidi was with him and got out of the car to help him. They changed the tire and got back on the road to Bisch, but when they got to Bisch, they realized that the thick envelope of reenlistment cash was gone. Rutherford had it in his fatigue shirt when he left Darby Kaserne, and the only stop they made was to change the tire."

"What did they do once they realized the money was gone?"

"They panicked and drove back to the spot by the side of the autobahn where they changed the tire. They searched and searched, but they couldn't find any trace of the money. Rutherford is absolutely crushed by the loss. Hell, who wouldn't be?! He just signed away the next 4 years of his life."

I had to ask, "How did Heidi react?"

"I heard that she's trying to be upbeat and help Rutherford accept it. He offered to cancel or postpone the wedding, but she wouldn't hear of it. I guess they'll have to adapt their plans."

Ollie had come into the Club and sat down at the table just as Lurch finished his story. He looked unhappy and glared at Lurch, who just shrugged and looked away.

Weasel, on the other hand, couldn't resist, "I'll bet his girlfriend took the money. He probably dropped it when he got out to change the tire. She's just another German gal looking to get what she can from an Ami."

Ollie barked, "That's enough! Change the topic."

"But Sarge, I was just sayin…."

"I heard what you were sayin', Weasel. And you heard what I said. That's enough. Either change the subject and play cards or get the hell out of here now! Give Rutherford a break!"

Weasel didn't say anything else for the rest of the night. Some of the other guys speculated along the same lines in the days that followed, but they were the same people who wanted to believe Heidi had been fooling around with SP6 Moore and Captain Medved when Jack was at NCO Academy. I didn't understand how they could be so mean, so lacking in empathy. Maybe they were jealous. Heidi was a beautiful girl. Why was it so hard for them to believe that Jack was just a lucky guy who somehow won her love? At least that's what I believed.

****

171

TRAGEDY STRIKES

Bear burst through the door of the Club and staggered into the room. He was screaming for help and was covered in blood from facial lacerations and other wounds we couldn't readily see beneath his parka. He was out of breath and sweating despite the frigid temperature outside. His left wrist was hanging at an odd angle, probably broken. His shouting was nearly incomprehensible. The only words we could understand were "Anson! Help! Blood...Help!...Sand Pit...Crash."

As usual, several of us had been sitting there playing cards, drinking beer, and playing foosball or shuffleboard. Will Morris, Ollie, Lurch, Grommet Cook, and I were at the card table. Large Louis and Frank DiMartino, the MP from Charlie Trick, were playing foosball. Doug Broussard was tending bar.

Large Louis and Ollie tried to calm Bear down so they could understand what he was trying to say. They couldn't even get him to sit down. He was like a man possessed. He kept waving his right arm around and screaming about Anson and blood. We were able to determine that Bear had been in an auto accident on the access road down near the sand pit and that Anson was gravely injured.

We knew that the location could be dangerous. The road is a straight shot downhill from the Club and mess hall area for a half a mile or so, but then there's a relatively sharp bend to the right near the sand pit access road where the RRCV-4 was sometimes positioned so it could "look" toward East Germany rather than Czechoslovakia. Although snow berms lined both sides of the access road from Route 303 to Topside during the winter, there was a sharp drop-off on the right side of this turn where there was virtually no berm. The plowed snow went down the embankment rather than lining the right side of the road. Bear confirmed that the accident had occurred there.

Ollie sent DiMartino up Topside and told him to get the three-quarter to use as an ambulance to take Anson to the dispensary in Bindlach for medical help. He told Doug to run over to the Cabin and use the field phone in the hallway to call the CQ and tell the CQ to alert Bindlach that we'd be bringing in a casualty in approximately 30 minutes.

I ran across the road to the Cabin parking lot and got my old Mercedes. Ollie, Large Louis, and Bear piled in. Bear was bleeding onto my upholstery in the back seat, but I didn't even think about it or care about it at that moment. Lurch, Grommet Cook, Will, and some weed I hadn't met yet squeezed into Lurch's Opel which happened to be parked outside the mess hall. We made our way down the snow-covered road to the curve as quickly as we dared. Bear's VW bus had apparently slid off the road sideways and tumbled down the embankment coming to rest on its side with the front of the bus crushed against a large pine tree. We had maneuvered our vehicles so that the headlights illuminated the accident scene. There was no sign of smoke or fire, thank goodness.

We could hear Anson moaning as we slid down the embankment to the bus. The passenger side door was hanging open and must have been Bear's exit point. The driver's side was resting on the snowy ground and had clearly taken the full force of the impact with the tree. The windshield glass on both sides of the center divider was broken, and a few jagged edges marked where Bear must have cut his face on impact.

Ollie, Will, and Large Louis were doing their best to get to Anson who was pinned in the vehicle by the steering wheel. He was bleeding from his scalp and nose, and his left trouser leg was soaked in blood that seeped into the snow. We needed bandages and a tourniquet right away. DiMartino brought down a first aid kit from the three-quarter and gave it to Ollie. Ollie used the web belt from his fatigue pants as an improvised tourniquet. I watched as he worked it around Anson's left thigh. Anson was whimpering, "I'm hurt bad, Top. I'm bleeding. Please don't let me die. Please."

Large Louis backed away briefly from Ollie, Will, and Anson and just shook his head. "He's hurt really bad. He's lost a lot of blood already. Ollie got the tourniquet on and got the flow of blood down to an ooze."

The first priority was to get Anson out of the wreck. The lacerations on his face and scalp were deep, but the leg wound was more serious. Will told us that Anson could move his toes and fingers, so spinal damage seemed unlikely, but we figured that his leg was probably broken and that there were also internal injuries from the steering wheel being pushed into his gut.

Ollie directed all of us to get by the front of the bus and then try to slide it away from the tree to give better direct access to Anson. That task was easier than I expected. We only had minimal tools with which to free him. DiMartino used the tire iron from the bus to clear away the windshield glass and the metal strip that divided the windshield in half. Will retrieved some metal bars from the bed of the three-quarter as two more cars arrived at the curve and several guys from Topside slid down the slope to help with the rescue. Large Louis, Lurch, DiMartino, and Ollie were all big strong guys, as were a couple of the others. Brute force would have to be the primary tool to free Anson. The group struggled, trying to pry the steering wheel away from Anson without injuring him further. After a few minutes they got him free and gently removed him from the twisted wreckage. We used a tarp from the three-quarter as a stretcher and somehow clawed up the snowy incline and stretched him out in the back of the three-quarter. He was in and out of consciousness and was shaking from the cold or from shock. We piled our coats on and under him to try to warm him up. Ollie and Louis climbed into the back of the truck beside Anson and Bear. DiMartino, with Will Morrow beside him, started down the hill intending to head for Bindlach and the dispensary.

Almost as soon as they started rolling, Ollie shouted and told them to stop at the *krankenhaus* at the bottom of the road. "I don't think we have time to make it to Bindlach. Our best bet is the *krankenhaus*. They should have a doctor or nurse there. Morrow, get out of the truck and send Lurch Topside to tell Bindlach to send their ambulance to the *krankenhaus*. Maybe we can get him stabilized by the time the ambulance gets there."

I got into my car and followed the three-quarter down to the *krankenhaus*. DiMartino was banging on the gatehouse door and ringing the bell when I pulled up. We knew that this wasn't a full-service hospital. It was a sanitorium – a place where TB patients were once treated, but now it was used more as a convalescence center for people needing long-term treatment for physical and mental disorders.

An orderly and a security guard came to the door. We explained the situation as well as we could in our *gasthaus* German. It was apparent that we urgently needed medical help. They summoned a nurse, who took one look at Anson and paged the doctor on duty. She told the orderly to call for a civilian ambulance from Bisch or Wunsiedel.

We brought Anson into the gatehouse building, and within a minute or two a doctor and nurse supervised his transfer to a gurney. They moved him into a room just inside the gatehouse. Luckily, the doctor spoke excellent English. Another nurse brought a crash cart. Ollie told DiMartino to stay outside and look for the Army ambulance from Bindlach.

The nurses cut away Anson's clothes while the doctor examined him and worked feverishly on the thigh wound. Ollie stood to the side ashen faced.

"We need blood! What is his blood type?" shouted the doc.

Ollie drew alongside and took Anson's dog tag in hand. "He's O Negative, according to his dog tag…I'm O Neg. You can use mine if you need it."

"We only have a couple units on hand. I hope we won't need more." said the doc as he turned to one of the nurses and barked an order at her in German. She ran from the room, presumably to get blood.

Anson was unconscious. The doctor and nurse continued to work on him with a growing sense of urgency. Before they chased us from the room, we could see from the monitors attached to him that his vital signs were worsening and that his hands and feet were turning white.

We could hear the doctor shouting something in German, and Ollie was calling Anson's name, telling him loudly to "Stay with us, Tim! Stay with us!" And then it was noticeably quiet. One of the nurses opened the door. She was crying. Ollie was holding Anson's hand and looked disconsolate as he turned toward those of us who were waiting outside the room. "He's gone. We lost him…. Oh, Jesus!"

We stood there in shocked disbelief as Ollie brushed away a tear and tried to compose himself. The nurses were removing the IV line and electrical sensors from Anson's body as the doctor came out of the room and closed the door behind him. "I am deeply sorry that we could not save your friend. We tried our best. He was young and strong, but he lost too much blood. He had serious internal injuries also. He needed more than we could give him here. I am so sorry."

We could say nothing in response. We just nodded, and Ollie mumbled a quiet "thank you."

The Bindlach ambulance finally arrived, and the medics confirmed that Anson was dead – not that we doubted it. They began treating Bear for his injuries. I think Bear was in shock. He wasn't answering the medics' questions. He just sat there weeping silently in a chair as they treated him.

The Bindlach people told us that they would be taking Anson's body to the military hospital in Nuremberg for autopsy and preparation for its return to U.S. We watched incredulously as they loaded him into the ambulance. They took Bear too so he could be thoroughly examined and treated in Nuremberg. They drove off and turned west on Route 303. We watched until the vehicle was out of sight. Ollie ordered us all to go Topside and meet him in the kino room.

****

Captain Medved was in the orderly room with Ollie and Sergeant Rob Gray when we went into the Topside building. Ollie was briefing the C.O. on what had transpired and simply waved us toward the kino room where several of the electronic maintenance and comms center techs were silently hanging around. It hadn't taken long for the tragic news to get from the *krankenhaus* to Topside

Medved, Ollie, and Gray came into the kino room. No one called us to attention, and none of us made any move to rise. Medved didn't notice or didn't care. We were all quiet. He looked shaken.

"Alright. Listen up!" he spoke to us quietly. "We all know what happened tonight. This is a tragic loss for the entire detachment. As I said, we know what happened, but now we need to determine how and why it happened. I've asked Sergeant Gray to take statements from all of you who were in the Club when Spec 4 Martin...umm, Bear...came crashing through the door. If you weren't there or at the accident scene or the *krankenhaus*, please go back to your rooms and let Sergeant Gray begin gathering information. Meanwhile, I have phone calls to make to Herzo and to the hospital in Nuremberg. If Spec 4 Martin is sedated or anesthetized at the hospital, Herzo will have to send someone there to be with him in case he inadvertently reveals classified information while he's out of it. There will probably be an MP accident investigation team coming up to do their thing. Make sure you fully cooperate with them when they arrive. Master Sergeant Henry will let you know if we need anything else from you. Carry on."

Medved left the room followed by the men who did not need to give statements. Ollie and Rob Gray had clipboards and legal pads on which they had already begun to make their accounts of what had happened.

****

Bear returned to the Hill a few days later via the courier run from Herzo. His broken left wrist was in a cast, and there were bandages protecting the stitches that closed the wounds on his face and neck. He had a couple of broken ribs too and was weighed down with terrible but undeserved guilt. He spent an hour or more with Captain Medved, Ollie, and Rob Gray going over what he could remember of the accident and

177

what he had told the MP team investigating the crash. He didn't want to talk with anyone else on the Hill, at least for the time being, and Ollie put out the word to give him whatever space he needed to deal with his grief and guilt.

Ollie came into the Club that evening and took his regular seat at the card table. He didn't want to play cards. No one else did either. No one was playing foosball, and no music came from the jukebox. The place was unusually sober, despite the presence of a dozen regulars. Will Morrow was seated at the table with Ollie and finally turned to him and asked, "Top, can you tell us anything more about the accident? We all know the result, but there are so many unanswered questions."

"Understood. There's not a hellavu lot to say, but I'll fill you in as best I can." Ollie paused to light his cigar stub and then began his account.

"Bear and Anson decided they were going to go down the hill to Bisch for dinner at the *Deutscher Adler*. They both loved the specialty there, a *Lustige Bosniak*. Y'all have probably ordered it yourselves -- that huge schnitzel cordon bleu that covers the entire dinner plate. Anyway, Anson had been after Bear for a long time to let him drive the VW bus. He couldn't explain why it was so important to him. It was just something that he wanted to do. You know, maybe it had a hippie feel to it. Or maybe he liked the idea of sitting right over the front wheels with a horizontal steering wheel in front of him. Bear knew Anson could drive a stick shift, but he warned him that the gear shift on the bus was nothing like the ones in standard Beetles. The pattern was the same, but the top of the shifter had to travel a couple of feet as you shifted from one gear to another. It was more like driving a three-quarter or a deuce-and-a- half. Bear finally relented and agreed to let Anson drive his bus to the *Adler*.

"They set off from Topside around 6pm. It was dark already. They weren't worried about encountering any other vehicles since trick change had been at 4pm, and the straight-day people left the Hill at 5pm. Of course, the road was snow-covered and icy in spots, but they weren't going too fast, according to Bear.

"As they approached the sandpit curve, Anson tried to downshift to slow down for the turn. He evidently got confused with the shift pattern, looked down at the shifter, and tugged at the wheel as the bus started to slide. Bear says Anson hit the brakes instead of going with the skid and steering out of the slide. There was a total loss of control, and the bus went over the embankment and tumbled over.

"Bear blames himself, but there's no evidence that he did anything wrong. Neither one of them had had any alcohol whatsoever, so no disciplinary action will be taken against Bear. He's punishing himself enough as it is. He wanted to accompany Anson's body back to the States and stay for the funeral, but the docs say that he could get blood clots on a long flight. The C.O. wouldn't let him go. Staff Sergeant Gray is the escort."

No one thought the winter moods could get any darker, but they reached a new depth after the accident. Not even drinking helped. Everyone was moping around. After he got back from the funeral, Rob Gray would be taking up the slack as detachment clerk until a new man was assigned. No one was in a hurry to see a replacement. It was going be tough for whoever came up to take Anson's place.

****

Sometime in mid-March we learned that Anson's mother was coming to the Hill. She wanted to see where he died, how it happened, where he lived and worked, and meet his friends. She told Rob Gray after the funeral ceremony that she wanted to come here, and he promised to do his best to help fulfill her wish. All the guys on the Hill wanted to have a tangible memorial, but not a side-of-the-road religious shrine that was often erected in Bavaria to mark the site of a fatal crash. A few options were proposed to the C.O. who eventually decided that a small memorial mural and plaque in the mess hall would be best. A few of our resident artists volunteered to work on it so it would be finished and ready for unveiling when Anson's mother visited.

The result was tasteful and as upbeat as a memorial can be. They started with a three-foot by four-foot section of plywood that Sef, the site handyman, had been keeping in his workshop. They sanded, stained, and varnished the wood until it shined like the toes of a strack trooper's boots. Father Pat found an artisan in Bisch who fashioned a large brass plague on which he inscribed Anson's name, hometown, date of birth, and date of death. SP6 Moore worked his own magic in the darkroom and produced several photos of Anson both in uniform and in civilian clothes. He was smiling and looked happy in each photo.

Mrs. Anson arrived during the last week of March. Rob Gray, Captain Medved, and Ollie met her at the train station in Bayreuth and escorted her to the Hill. They brought her up Topside and showed her Tim's room and the orderly room with the desk her son had worked behind. She was introduced to Bear and spent an emotional 30 minutes with him in the privacy of Captain Medved's office. She did not hold him responsible for the accident and emerged from the office holding his hand and comforting him.

Nearly everyone who wasn't working in Ops came to the mess hall for the unveiling ceremony and a short memorial service led by a chaplain from Bindlach. Otto Reissmann came up from Bisch with the First Lady, Erika, and Gertie. A few of the wives and girlfriends were there too. A *Bundeswehr* captain and a senior *Luftwaffe* NCO came to represent our German counterparts from the tower.

The chaplain led us in prayer and gave a short homily on the Christian belief in the promise of eternal life. He finished with the Lord's Prayer, and then Captain Medved spoke of what an important role Anson had played at the detachment and how he always went out of his way to help the other men whenever possible. He also announced that he had promoted Anson posthumously to the rank of corporal. He said with a smile that he thought Anson would have liked that since as a corporal he'd be an NCO and would technically outrank all the SP4s and SP5s on the Hill.

Stan "The Bard" Pace asked if he could recite one of Shakespeare's sonnets in tribute to Anson. Mrs. Anson nodded her agreement. I don't think Stan realized that not everyone shared his appreciation for the original Bard.

Stan rose from his seat and began to speak, "To our friend Tim Anson. Shakespeare's Sonnet 55.

"Not marble nor the gilded monuments
Of princes shall outlive this powerful rhyme,
But you shall shine more bright in these contents
Than unswept stone besmeared with sluttish time.
When wasteful war shall statues overturn,
And broils root out the work of masonry,

Nor Mars his sword nor war's quick fire shall burn
The living record of your memory.
'Gainst death and all-oblivious enmity
Shall you pace forth; your praise shall still find room
Even in the eyes of all posterity
That wear this world out to the ending doom.
  So, till the Judgement that yourself arise,
  You live in this, and dwell in lovers' eyes"

Father Pat Reilly got to his feet when Stan finished his recital and ended the ceremony with a traditional Irish blessing:

"May the road rise up to meet you. May the wind always be at your back. May the sun shine warm upon your face, and rains fall soft upon your fields. And until we meet again, May God hold you in the palm of His hand.

"And as St Thomas Moore said, *'Pray for me, as I will for thee, that we may merrily meet in heaven.'*

"God bless you, Tim. You were our brother and we loved you."

Many of the guests answered with a quiet "Amen" to close the formal ceremony. Nearly all of them lined up to speak with Mrs. Anson, pay their respects, and share memories of Tim. I was near the end of the line and was moved by her graciousness and composure. I learned that her name was Helen. She had a sadness in her eyes that I had seldom seen in anyone else. I guess that's indicative of the unbearable grief a parent feels when they have to bury a son or daughter.

After most of the crowd had drifted away, I heard her telling the C.O. how heartened she felt by the display of fraternal affection she witnessed on the Hill. She said that she was confident that her Tim would be remembered, appreciated, and missed. She went on to say that he had written to her often about how much he liked being on Schneeberg and what a great group of men he served with. As she left the mess hall with the escort party that would soon take her back to Nuremberg, she saw Bear standing alone in the parking lot. She walked over to him and wrapped that bear of a young man in her arms with all the love and kindness of an understanding and forgiving mother.

181

****

FATEFUL APRIL

Returning to normal is difficult and often impossible after losing a close friend or loved one. Such was the case on Schneeberg after we lost Tim Anson. In show business they say the show must go on, and it is the same in the Army Security Agency. The mission was still there, and we were obligated to execute it.

Captain Medved's mood and demeanor changed dramatically after Anson's death. He was spending less time on the Hill and, when he was there, he was usually in his office with the door closed. Staff Sergeant Gray told us that Medved was expecting to be transferred to ASA HQ at Arlington Hall Station, Virginia, in June or July and that he was looking forward to the change. For all practical purposes, Jolly Ollie oversaw the detachment while Medved distanced himself from day-to-day activities.

The C.O. called a series of meeting in the kino room a few days after Mrs. Anson visited the site. All site personnel were required to attend one of the meetings and sign a form afterward affirming that they had attended and understood the topic. The captain made it absolutely clear at these sessions that he would have zero tolerance for anyone who drove under the influence of alcohol. He knew that Anson's death was not attributable to drunk driving, but he was also aware that it was not unusual for detachment personnel to drive back up the Hill after a night of drinking at Reissmann's or anywhere else. He decreed that anyone who had been drinking in Bisch should ride back in the three-quarter that made the run from Bisch to Topside every night at midnight as it shuttled the German guards to and from Bisch. He promised that any violation of this policy would be punished severely.

****

Early April weather had begun a warming trend that soon affected the higher regions of the Hill. Small stretches of asphalt became visible again on the access road after being covered for months in several inches of ice and hardpacked snow. However, vestiges of winter remained in new snow that fell a few days each week and in the occasional windstorms that chilled us to the bone. The change in seasons was more pronounced at the foot of the mountain where flowers had begun to bloom in Bischofsgruen's gardens and fields.

A young man's fancy supposedly turns to love in the spring. There was clear evidence on the Hill to prove that adage. Jack Rutherford's May 19th wedding date was rapidly approaching as he and Heidi made final preparations to tie the knot. Doug Broussard announced that he had asked Evi to marry him and that she had accepted. Rumor had it that Pete the Greek and Erika would be the next couple to become engaged.

Change was also in the air for ASA, but it had little direct effect on the Hill. Herzo Base had been re-designated as the 16th USASA Field Station. Detachment J at Schneeberg was under the command of Co. A, 16th USASA Field Station. Company A was also responsible for the manning and operation of Detachment K on Hohenbogen, some 80 miles south of Schneeberg in the Bavarian Forest (*Bayerischer Wald*). Det K was a temporary site that was only operational during warm weather months. Unlike Schneeberg, there were no permanent American SIGINT-related structures on Hohenbogen. Instead, ASA personnel operated out of truck-mounted vans like the RRCV-4. The vans were positioned near the summit of one of the mountain's ridges, approximately 1,000 meters above sea level. Its location provided an unobstructed view across the Czechoslovak border roughly five miles in the distance. The ASA personnel and a handful of USAF Security Service technicians assigned to the site were billeted in a hotel and *gasthaus* in the village of Rimbach in the valley at the western foot of the mountain.

During the winter months, many of the men who manned Det K in the summer remained at Herzo Base maintaining the vans, generators, and other equipment that would be redeployed to the site for the summer. Most of Det K linguists, however, either worked in operations at Herzo during the winter or, in some cases, were reassigned to Det J.

184

As the designated date for spring deployment neared, Herzo sent a message to the Hill asking for volunteer Czech voice intercept operators and a few Russian 98Gs to man Det K starting in early May. The message also ordered Doug Broussard and Don McGrew to move the RRCV-4 to Hohenbogen no later than 1 May. Doug was expecting the move but was clearly unhappy to have to leave Evi behind. He was thankful to have his Porsche 356 coupe to ease his anticipated weekend commutes between Det K and Bisch.

Dick Proust and his sidekick Whiskey Man Smythe were among the first to volunteer. Dick had been at the site the previous summer and looked forward to being a trick chief at Det K. SP6 Karl Waldgruen also volunteered, as did Joe Parker and Rich Roberts, both of whom were scheduled to be discharged from the Army at around the same time that Det K would close down for the winter in late September. Stan Pace asked to be one of the Russian 98Gs sent to the site. I was ambivalent about going. I was content with my assignment on the Hill and figured that I would be getting more responsibility and maybe a promotion to E-5 when the more experienced ops and transcribers went down to Det K, leaving me to train the weeds who would be sent up to Schneeberg as their replacements. I did not volunteer.

****

A decent band was playing that late April Saturday night at Reissmann's. Most of their songs were top 40 covers that we'd been hearing on Radio Luxembourg, Radio Caroline, and even on *Der Bayerische Rundfunk.* I enjoyed listening to the band even though I was still too uncomfortable to ask one of the local girls to dance. My German was too poor to sustain even a casual conversation. And, besides, I had a girlfriend back in the States who wrote to me almost daily. I wrote to her almost as often. It didn't seem right trying to cultivate a relationship with a German girl when my heart was telling me that I genuinely cared about the girl back home. I guess I'm old fashioned that way or maybe it's just an excuse for not overcoming my shyness and chatting up a Bisch bunny.

I was sitting at the bar with one of the weeds who had recently come up the Hill as a replacement for one of the more experienced ops who were deploying to Hohenbogen. His name was Pete (actually Pedro) Alonso and he was from somewhere near San Antonio. His trick chief on Baker Trick, Jim Hall, began calling him Yaqui almost from the get-go. Pete immediately took exception to the nickname, pointing out that he was not a Native American but a Mexican-American, that his family had lived in Texas for at least 200 years, and that he believed that calling him Yaqui was racist as well as wrong. That stopped SSG Hall in his tracks. Since Pete the Greek was already on Baker Trick, Hall decided to differentiate the two by calling Pete Alonso "Texas Pete" like the hot sauce brand used in the mess hall. That met with Pete's approval and soon became his official nickname.

Texas Pete, my pal Jack Rutherford, and the rest of Baker Trick had to work a day shift in the morning, so Pete was going easy on the beer that night. He gave me his dose of the schnapps we had to buy when there was a live band, and I drank his as well as my own with beer chasers. I think I was gradually learning to like the taste of cognac. I realized that I was starting to feel pretty hammered as the magic midnight hour neared.

Jack had been dancing with Heidi earlier in the evening, but he left to walk her back to her mother's house on Route 303 a little before 11 pm. I was on break and didn't feel restricted by any Sunday morning obligations. Jack and Texas Pete planned to catch the three-quarter shuttle back up the Hill when it made its scheduled stop at Reissmann's around midnight, and which actually departed closer to 12:15 am.

Jack came back into Reissmann's a little before 11:45 and sat with us at the bar.

"Hey, Jack! I see you got Heidi home. How about a drink? On me. We should be celebrating. It's only a few weeks until your wedding."

"No thanks, Jerry. I've already had a few, and I've gotta work in the morning. I'm done for tonight. I'm just waiting for the three-quarter to come down for the guards' shift change. I'll ride back up the Hill with them. What about you?"

"I've got my car outside, Jack. I'll be driving up right after the three-quarter leaves."

"You should ride with us. I think you've had too much to drink."

"Naw, I'm not too messed up. And I don't want to leave my car in the parking lot overnight. The door locks are broken, and I'd hate to have someone trash it."

"Look, I don't think you should drive. Remember what Captain Medved said. If you get caught drunk driving, you're gonna get screwed big time."

"Really! I'm okay. Okay?!" I was becoming irate.

Jack was unconvinced. He could be stubborn when he thought he was in the right. "Listen. I'm not gonna let you drive tonight. You may think you're okay to drive, but I know you're not. Either come with me in the three-quarter or give me your keys. Either way. You're not driving."

"Ha! And you're gonna stop me? How?"

"Don't be a jerk, Jerry. I'll do what I have to do to keep you from getting behind the wheel. I mean it."

I could see that he was dead serious. I didn't want to get into a fight with him over this, so I gave in and reached into my pants pocket. "Alright already, Jack. Here are the keys. But I still don't want to leave my car outside Reissmann's overnight. How about if you drive me up the Hill in my car?"

"Oh...I dunno. I've had a few beers and I've got a little buzz on myself. And I've never driven your Merc before," he said as he was thinking it over.

"C'mon. Be a pal. You're fine. I'm the one who's drunk."

Jack was still thinking about it when one of our MPs came into the bar and announced that the three-quarter was waiting outside for anyone going up the Hill. An MP always drove the guards' shift-change shuttle.

"C'mon, Jerry. Let's go up in the three-quarter. Your car will be okay overnight. Hell, this is Bisch, not New York. Come with me and Pete. Please."

"Nope. I'm not ridin' the three-quarter. Go ahead and ride with Pete. I won't be far behind in my car."

Jack was getting pissed at me. "Damn! Alright. I'll drive your car. But we have to leave now. I gotta work in the morning, and you're gettin' to be a royal pain in the ass. Let's go!"

"Awww...you're such a good friend, Jack." I think I was slurring my words at this point. I beckoned Erika over and paid my tab. I left a generous tip too. She earned it. She always put up with a lot of crap from us Amis.

Jack and I made our way down the stairs and out to the parking lot. All the winter's snow in the lot had melted, even though there was still quite a bit on the Hill. I asked Jack one more time to let me drive, but he was adamant. He got in behind the wheel, adjusted the seat for his taller build, fastened his seat belt, and started the engine. The Merc was larger and older than the early 1960s VW Beetle that Jack owned, but Jack seemed comfortable behind the wheel. We made our way out of Bisch, crossed Route 303, and drove past the *krankenhaus*.

Jack was concentrating on his driving and was watching the road carefully as we transitioned from the older, rough roadway onto the smooth asphalt of the *Bundeswehr*-maintained access road. Jack was accelerating as we started uphill and was getting ready to shift from third to fourth gear when a deer suddenly appeared in the headlights and froze. I'm not sure what happened next. I think Jack slammed on the brakes and yanked hard on the steering wheel.

The next thing I knew, my car was upside down. I was sprawled on the car's ceiling, and Jack was hanging upside down from his seat belt. It must have been the alcohol, but I found the sight of him amusing at that moment.

"Jack, are you hurt?"

"No, I don't think so. What about you?"

"I think I'm okay. I hit my head on the windshield or something, but I'm not bleeding. I've got the window on the passenger side open. I think I can crawl through it and get out. Can you get the seat belt off?"

"Ummm…let me try…Yeah, I've got it now." He plopped down onto the ceiling beside me. It was very dark, so I couldn't see if he was bleeding. I wiggled toward the open window.

"C'mon. Let's get out of the car!"

We were able to squeeze through the window, exit the vehicle, and climb to our feet in the darkness. We could see enough to know that we had driven off the access road and down an embankment. This wasn't the same spot that Bear had had his fatal accident. We were at another curve a half mile or so downhill from Bear's curve. Somehow, neither Jack nor I had been injured. I guess this proved the old saying about God taking care of drunks and babies.

We saw two sets of headlights approaching from up the mountain. The lights from the Merc were still on and would be visible to an oncoming vehicle, but Jack and I climbed the embankment and stood by the side of the road to flag down whoever was coming. Both cars stopped when they reached us. I was dismayed to discover that one was driven by my nemesis, Acting Sergeant Riegel, trick chief on Able Trick. Three of his people got out of the second car. I think they were on their way to catch last call at Reissmann's. We stood in the glare of their headlights and confirmed that we were not bleeding and that all our body parts were in place. I realized too that I was suddenly sober.

"What happened?" asked Riegel. "You guys driving drunk?"

"Hell no!" I replied. "We swerved to avoid a deer and went off the side of the road."

"Sure you did," replied Riegel with obvious sarcasm. "Are you hurt?"

"No, we're both okay," Jack responded. "But I think the car may be totaled."

"Let's take a look," one of the Able Trick guys suggested.

All six of us made our way down the embankment and looked at the Merc which was now illuminated by the headlights of the Able Trick cars. The driver's side of the Merc was banged up, but the rest of the car didn't look too bad.

"Let's see if we can turn it right-side-up. I think we might be able to do it," I almost pleaded.

The six of us began pushing on one side of the car and got it rocking back and forth on the roof. "C'mon. We almost have it. One more big push now!" I shouted.

The car got to a tipping point and then continued its motion, coming upright again with sounds of crunching metal.

"We did it!" I yelled as I got into the car and behind the steering wheel. Miraculously, the engine started when I turned the key. I was feeling happy at that point. The reality of the situation had not yet sunk in through my addled skull. I assured our Able Trick comrades that we were okay and that I could get the car back up the Hill to the Cabin. I thanked them for helping, and they were soon on their way.

Meanwhile, Jack was freaking out. "Oh, shit. Oh, shit! Oh, shit!! I'm screwed. I'm a dead man. Medved is gonna kill me and make an example of me. Oh, shit! Maybe I'll get an Article 15 or a court martial and get busted. Oh, shit! This is gonna mess up the wedding too. Oh, shit." I think he was close to crying.

I tried to reassure him, "Relax, Jack. This wasn't your fault. There was a deer, and you tried to avoid it. It was a natural reaction. Don't sweat it."

"Yeah, but we both know that I had been drinking at Reissmann's. I'll bet Riegel could smell it on me. He's a prick. I know he'll try to dick me away first chance he gets."

"Jack, try to relax. It was my car, and you were trying to do me a favor by driving it. No one knows you were driving. They will all assume it was me."

"I dunno. I'm screwed. Oh, what am I gonna tell Heidi?!"

"Jack! You don't have to tell her anything. We had an accident. It was because of a deer. It was my car, and I'm not telling anyone that you were driving. I'm the one responsible. I got drunk and stupid. If anyone gets screwed, it'll be me. C'mon now, let's get up to the Cabin so you can get some sleep. This will be okay. Trust me."

The Merc, or what was left of it, was able to make it up the access road to the Cabin. I found a parking spot at the far end of the lot in an area away from the well-trodden paths that linked the Cabin, mess hall, and Club to the rest of the installation. I went to sleep that night with the naïve hope that no one would find out about the accident or discover my wrecked Mercedes.

****

BANISHED

They say that things usually look better in the light of day, but that wasn't the case with my Mercedes. There wasn't much doubt that it was a total loss when I checked it out on Sunday morning. The passenger side looked fine, but the driver's side was badly dented and scraped and the windshield was cracked where I banged my head. If it were a newer car and not an '51 model, maybe a body shop could restore it to a roadworthy condition. But it was 15 years old and only worth a couple hundred dollars when I bought it. Besides, I didn't have collision insurance -- just the mandatory liability coverage.

Grommet Cook came up to me when I went into the mess hall for a late breakfast. "I saw your car outside. What happened? Did anyone get hurt?" he asked.

"A deer surprised us on the way up the Hill, and we went off the road. Jack Rutherford was with me. The gods must have been watching out for us because neither of us got hurt, except for this bump on my forehead."

"You guys are lucky. But the car is a goner, I'm sure. Too bad. I really liked that car. The C.O. liked it too. He's gonna have a shit fit when he hears about the accident. Were you drunk?"

"Ummm...well, we were on our way back from Reissmann's. I had a few, but I don't think I was really drunk."

"Right. Well, good luck with that." He went back to making eggs, bacon, sausage, and pancakes on the grill.

I finished breakfast and went back to the Dog Trick room to try to think of a way out of the jam I was in. The car would run, but I had no idea where to take it to junk it or hide it. I thought about trying to cover it with

191

a tarp, but I knew that wasn't the answer. This never would have happened if I had listened to Jack and ridden the three-quarter back from Reissmann's. This was all my fault.

****

Sergeant Gray came down to the Cabin Monday morning and woke me up shortly after 8 am. Dog Trick was on break until the next morning's day shift.

"Daniels, wake up and get dressed. The C.O. wants to see you immediately, if not sooner. I gotta warn you. He is really pissed. I've never seen him this angry before." Rob Gray looked worried.

"Okay, Rob. Just give me a minute to pull myself together. I knew he'd be unhappy with me."

"Unhappy?! You have no idea. I hate to say it, but your ass is grass and he's got the lawn mower."

Not exactly words of comfort, but I knew he was right. There was nothing to do but get dressed and face the music.

A few minutes later I was standing at attention in front of the C.O.'s desk. "Specialist Daniels reporting as ordered, Sir." I rendered and held a crisp salute while staring at a spot to the right of the C.O.'s head. Captain Medved was looking at some papers on his desk and did not return my salute for a full 10 seconds. When he did, it was more a wave of the hand than a proper military salute. He did not tell me to stand at ease, so I remained at attention a few feet in front of his glass-topped desk. MSG Henry silently stood in the doorway behind me while Rob Gray tended to admin work at his desk.

"Daniels, I hope you know that you're in a heap of trouble. I was driving up the access road this morning and saw some skid marks and glass on the road by that curve between the *krankenhaus* and Bear's curve. It looked like someone went off the road last night."

"Yes, Sir." I piped up.

"Shut your mouth!" he snapped. His face was red with anger. "I'll tell you when I want to hear from you. Now, where was I?...Oh, yeah. I could tell someone went off the road over the weekend and I wondered who it was. I pulled into the Cabin parking lot, and what do I find? I find your old Mercedes way in the back of the lot where you were hoping to hide it. I liked that car, you know. It was sad to see it all banged up, especially after my warning about drunk driving."

I was about to respond when he barked, "Quiet! Now listen to me closely because I am going to read you the appropriate sections of Article 31 of the UCMJ. Before I ask you any questions, you must understand your rights.

"Number 1, You do not have to answer my questions or say anything.

"Number 2, Anything you say or do can be used as evidence against you in a criminal trial.

"Number 3. You have the right to talk privately with a lawyer before, during, and after questioning and to have a lawyer present with you during questioning. This lawyer can be a civilian you arrange for at no expense to the government or a military lawyer detailed for you at no expense to you, or both.

"Number 4. If you are now willing to discuss the offense or offenses under investigation, with or without a lawyer present, you have a right to stop answering questions at any time, or speak privately with a lawyer before answering further, even if you sign a waiver certificate like the one here in front of me.

"Do you want a lawyer at this time, Specialist Daniels?"

"No, Sir. I do not want a lawyer at this time," I replied, trying to conceal the quaver in my voice.

"At this time, are you willing to discuss the offenses under investigation and make a statement without talking to a lawyer or having a lawyer present with you?"

"Yes, Sir. I am."

"Alright then. Let's continue. Tell me what happened to your car."

"Yes, Sir. Spec 5 Rutherford and I were returning to our quarters in the Cabin after spending the evening in Bischofsgruen at Reissmann's *Tanzcafe*. We were approaching the first major curve on the access road, that's the one about a half mile below where Specialist Martin had his accident several weeks ago. Just as we started steering into the turn, a deer...I think it was a sika deer...jumped in front of us and then froze in the headlights. We braked and tried to avoid hitting it, but we went off the road instead, and my car flipped over. We were able to exit the vehicle and

193

determine that we were not injured. At that point, some men from Able Trick, who were on their way down from Ops, stopped to help us. We were able to right my car. It was still operable, so I drove it to the Cabin and parked it in the rear of the parking lot so it would not be in the way of any other vehicles. I intended to report the accident to Sergeant Gray this morning, but I was called Topside before I could do so. That's all I can tell you, Sir."

"Neither you nor Rutherford was injured?"

"No, Sir. We were very fortunate."

"Had you been drinking while you were in Reissmann's?"

"Yes, Sir. I believe I had schnapps and a few beers over the course of the evening."

"Were you drunk, Daniels?"

"I don't think that I was, Sir. I remembered your warning about punishing anyone caught driving while intoxicated. If I thought I was too impaired to drive, Sir, I would have left my car at Reissmann's and ridden up the Hill in the three-quarter with some of the other men. I did not think that was necessary, Sir."

The C.O. had been taking notes as I spoke, and he paused now to read over what he had written. I was still standing at attention. He finally looked up at me. Some of the anger seemed to have dissipated from his face, but he was far from mollified. "Stand at ease while I think about what to do with you, Daniels."

"Yes, Sir. Thank you, Sir." I assumed a posture more like parade rest than at ease.

"Alright. Here's what's going to happen. You are relieved of duty effective immediately. You will not return to the Operations building. You will go to your room in the Cabin and pack up all your personal and field gear. I'm sending you back to Herzo Base. You will ride there with the courier run tomorrow. When you arrive at Herzo, you will report to the Company A orderly room. They will be expecting you and will arrange billeting for you in the company area while I decide what to charge you with. Right now, I think the charges will be disobeying a direct order, insubordination, and driving while intoxicated. You are confined to the detachment area until you depart for Herzo. You are forbidden to drink

194

any alcoholic beverages during this period. Do you have anything further to say for yourself?"

"No, Sir."

"Very well. Dismissed."

I came to attention, saluted, did an about face, and marched from the room in as military a manner as I could manage. I glanced at Ollie on my way out, and he nodded slightly as I passed. I thought to myself, "What does that mean?" and then went down to the Cabin to start packing.

I was devastated at the prospect of leaving the Hill and returning to Herzo under a cloud. I was very sad about my wrecked car too. I consoled myself a little by telling myself that my statement to the captain was not a lie. Maybe I didn't tell the whole truth about how much I had had to drink Saturday night, but it wasn't a bald-faced lie. And he had assumed I was driving when the accident occurred. I didn't tell him otherwise. Jack's good deed might well go undiscovered and unpunished. I recognized my responsibility for the accident, and it was right that I should bear the blame and whatever punishment resulted.

Wasn't it Charles Dickens who wrote, "It is a far, far better thing that I do than I have ever done"? I figured that I'd probably get busted down to PFC at the very least, but Jack and Heidi's wedding would go on as planned, but without me. Someone had to get screwed, it might as well be me.

****

I did go to the Club that night, but not to drink. I wanted to say goodbye to as many of my friends as possible. The regulars were at the poker table, except for Ollie. I didn't feel like playing, but I needed to settle up my account in the payday stakes ledger that Will Morrow kept. This month was unusual. I was ahead by twelve dollars which Will paid me from his wallet after he made a note in the ledger that I had been paid off and that he was owed the $12. I shook hands with Will, Grommet Cook, and Weasel at the table and with Doug Broussard behind the bar. I was starting to feel emotional, so I made a quick exit and went back to my bunk and went to sleep early.

The next morning after breakfast I brought all my belongings and my field gear to the Cabin's front porch so it would be ready to load into the

195

courier van. I walked slowly up the steep incline to Topside and said my farewells to Large Louis who was the MP on duty for the day shift. I was relieved to see that Captain Medved's car was not parked in its usual spot outside Topside. I walked into the orderly room and began signing out of the unit. Rob Gray came over and shook hands with me, saying he hoped we'd cross paths again before long. Ollie looked up from his desk and stared at me for a few seconds and then rose from his swivel armchair and beckoned me into the captain's office, closing the door behind us.

"Daniels, I know what you did."

"Yeah, Top, I know you do. I fucked up."

"Yes, you did. There's no arguing that point. You definitely screwed the pooch this time. The C.O. was ready to hang you by your balls yesterday. I'm still not convinced that that's not in your future, but I think it is possible...just possible, mind you...that you might survive this mess you created."

"That would be great, Top, but I recognize that I messed up."

"You're right about that. Do you want to leave the Hill?"

"No, Sarge, I don't. I'm really sad about it. I regret the mistakes that I made on Saturday night."

"I'll bet you really do, Daniels. We can hope that you've learned something. I know I have."

"Yes, I really did learn from this. But I don't understand what you could have learned, Top. You've been around the Army just about forever. I figure you've learned everything there is to learn. What did you learn if you don't mind my asking?"

"I don't mind at all. I already told you that I know what you did."

"Yes?..."

"I mean I really know what you did. I know that you were drunk, but I also know that you weren't behind the wheel when your car went off the road."

"But Sarge..." I began, but Ollie put his finger to his lips beside his cigar stub and shushed me.

"Daniels, you're pretty smart for a college boy. You didn't lie to the C.O. when you made your statement, but you didn't exactly tell the whole truth and nothing but the truth either. I know that Rutherford was driving and that you're taking the blame so he doesn't get in trouble and have to postpone or cancel his wedding."

"Sarge, I can explain…." But he silenced me again.

"Quit while you're ahead, Daniels. I know what happened, and Sergeant Gray knows too. But the C.O. doesn't know and doesn't need to know. He'll be PCSing out of here in a few weeks and heading to Arlington Hall. He'll forget all about you. Sergeant Gray and I will do our best to sit on the paperwork charging you with the offenses the captain mentioned yesterday. With a little luck, they will be 'lost' once the captain PCS's."

"Sergeant Henry, I don't know what to say," I stammered.

"Don't say a damn word. Not to me or Gray or anyone else. Just count your lucky stars that someone told me what really happened and that I respect a man who stands up for his friends and accepts responsibility when he screws up.

"I've talked to First Sergeant Savage down at Company A and have fixed things with him. You report to him when you get to Herzo. You're gonna be assigned to the group that's getting the vehicles ready for deployment to Det K at Hohenbogen. When that group deploys, you'll be going with them, college boy. You're going to be living in a hotel this summer and working on a different hill. And then…. when summer is over, if I am still first shirt here at Schneeberg, you can expect to come back here. I'll save a seat for you at the poker table. Now, get the hell out of here before the C.O. comes back!"

I was genuinely overcome by his understanding and kindness…not to mention the possibility of returning to the Hill I loved and hated. "Top, I can't thank you enough. Thank you!"

"Get out of here, Daniels, before I change my mind," he growled with a wink of his eye and a hint of a smile."

****

The courier van arrived around 10am and dropped off the classified mail and supplies at Ops and Topside before the driver gassed up the vehicle by the guard shack and stopped to pick me up outside the Cabin. I loaded all my stuff in the back and climbed into the back seat. I had a quick last look at the Cabin, the mess hall, and the Club. There were still small piles of snow in the parking lot and beside the road. I had to smile when I noticed that there was still yellow snow outside the door to the Club.

It was cloudy with a bit of fog as we headed down the access road. I said a silent prayer for Tim Anson as we passed the site of his crash, and I said a prayer of Thanksgiving when we drove by the curve where we went off the road Saturday night. Just as we reached Route 303, the sun came out.

We turned right onto 303, passed Heidi's mother house on the right side of the road, and headed for the autobahn interchange the other side of Bad Berneck. I had mixed feelings. I would miss Schneeberg and its misfits, but I knew that I'd be seeing some of them again at Det K in a few weeks. One adventure comes to an end, at least for the time being, but a new one was about to begin on another mountain 80 miles to the south. It would prove to be an interesting summer. But I'll tell you about that another time.

****

EPILOGUE

Doug Broussard married Evi. After his discharge from the Army, Doug and Evi resided in southern Louisiana where Doug owned and operated a successful business. Doug passed away in 2010.

Jerry Daniels followed Jack Rutherford's example and reenlisted for a generous bonus so he could marry his stateside sweetheart. He served almost 7 years in ASA and later worked almost 30 years as a Department of Defense civilian.

Oliver Henry retired from the Army as a MSG (E-7) and is believed to have returned to his home in Texas or Oklahoma to continue in civilian life as an advisor, counselor, and role model for young men who had a tendency toward anti-social and sometimes self-destructive behavior.

Don McGrew left ASA after his 4-year enlistment and returned to North Carolina where he enjoyed a long and successful career with a regional telecommunications company.

John Medved remained in the Army and retired as a Lieutenant Colonel in the late 1970s or early 1980s.

Joe Parker returned to the States after his discharge and earned his baccalaureate degree. He later earned an MBA and had a successful career in business, working as president and chief operating officer of a southern bank and later as an independent consultant.

Tony Phillips traveled Europe after his discharge from ASA and eventually settled in the Midwest where he is a noted photographer and artist.

Dick Proust returned to southern Ohio after his military service and had a long career as a high school social studies teacher. He passed away in 2006, but prior to that made a return visit to Schneeberg, Hohenbogen, and Herzo Base. He also reunited a few years before his death with Doug Broussard, Don McGrew, Tony Phillips, Jerry Daniels, and another Schneeberger for a weekend of German food and drink in Columbus, Ohio.

Otto Reissmann continued to operate his entertainment business until he died in an automobile accident in 1975. Herta, the "First Lady," continued to run the *Tanzcafe* after Otto's death. At the beginning of the 1980s Herta married a local businessman and sold the *Tanzcafe*, thereby ending an illustrious chapter in the history of this small resort town. The new owner renamed the establishment "Dancehall Joy" in an attempt to capitalize on the disco trend. But with similar establishments popping up all over the area, competition was tough. The "Joy" was never able to latch onto the success of the original *Tanzcafe*. Opening hours were scaled back to 3 days a week, but the disco ultimately had to be shut down for lack of business. Around 1996 or 1997 the establishment was reopened under its original name. People who visited the *Tanzcafe* during that period reported that the interior was virtually unchanged from the day it was built. The "new" Reissmann's, however, failed to replicate its successful past and closed a year or so later.

Pat Riley stayed in the Army for at least several years after his Schneeberg days. He was last sighted in southern California as a senior citizen surfer.

John "Grommet Cook" Ritter is believed to have returned to Ohio after his discharge from the Army. There is no record of any detective mysteries having been published by a John Ritter, but he may have used a *nom de plume* to publish the stories he was working on at Schneeberg.

Jack Rutherford married Heidi and stayed in the Army, although not in ASA. They had a daughter and remain together more than 50 years later. He retired as an SFC (E-7) and then worked as a Department of the Army civilian until retiring in the early 2000s.

Pete "the Greek" Stavros remained in Germany following his discharge from the Army. He married Erika and lived in the Wunsiedel area where he worked as a carpenter. He passed away in 2005.

Walter "Whiskey Man" Smythe remained in Germany after his discharge from the Army. He was living in Berlin as of the date of publication of this book.

Corporal Shadow, the site German shepherd, lived out his life on the Hill and is buried there.

The story of the **East German border guards** defecting to the ASA border site at Gartow is one of the tales in this book that is essentially true. However, the incident actually occurred in 1970 and not December 1966. One of the ASA soldiers involved in the defection married a girl from Gartow and remained in the area after his discharge from the Army. He always wondered what happened to the defectors, so 50 years after the fact, he set out to try to find them, apparently with the sponsorship of a German TV channel. He found them and talked to them on the phone. He also found out the identity of the guard who had been left behind and organized a reunion. Sadly, it turned out that the East German authorities did not believe the story told by the guard who was left behind. He wound up serving one year in an East German military prison, during which time he was unable to communicate with his parents or the outside world. All three border guards were only 18 or 19 years old at the time. The ASAers in the Chateau reportedly kept at least one of the AK-47s. One of the ASAers purportedly hid the weapon in a large stereo speaker which was eventually shipped back to the States when he got out of the Army. The story was documented in a program broadcast on German TV. (https://www.ndr.de/lost-found/johnny125.html)

****

GLOSSARY

05H – Morse Intercept Operator
05K – Non-Morse Intercept Operator
98C – SIGINT Analyst
98G – Voice Intercept Operator
98J – ELINT Operator
AAFES – Army, Air Force Exchange Service; organization which ran the PXs on military bases
Ami – German slang (sometimes pejorative) for an American
A-Slash – Acting sergeant
ASA – Army Security Agency
ASAE – ASA Europe, Frankfurt
Bundeswehr – West German Armed Forces or Army
CARRYBACK – a cover term formerly used for a small group of German and Czech linguists born in Germany or Czechoslovakia and displaced after WW II. Their native-level language proficiency made them valuable members of ASA, but they were only cleared for Secret-level material, which excluded them from access to the most sensitive intelligence. Most reached the rank of SP6 (E-6) or SP7 (E-7) and worked primarily as transcribers.
Casern – a military garrison
C.O. – Commanding officer
COMINT – Communications intelligence
CONUS – Continental United States; home; land of the round doorknobs

CQ – Charge of Quarters; an enlisted man designated to handle matters in a unit after duty hours

Deuce-and-a-half – Army 6X6 truck with a cargo capacity of 2 ½ tons

DIRNSA – Director, National Security Agency

DLI – Defense Language Institute, Monterey, California

DERUS – Date of estimated return to the U.S. (going home date)

ELINT – Electronic intelligence, often derived from the analysis of radar and other non-communications signals

ETS – Estimated date of separation (the date one's enlistment was up)

FIGMO – F**k it! Got my orders! Describes a short-timer's attitude toward work and the Army

FUBAR – Fouled up beyond all recognition

GIRB – G.I. rotten bastard

K.P. – Kitchen police (mess hall duty usually involving the most onerous tasks)

Lifer – Career Army personnel

Luftwaffe – West German Air Force

MACV – Military Assistance Command, Vietnam; a joint service command that served as an umbrella organization overseeing all U.S. forces in Vietnam

Mag tapes – Magnetic tapes used to record radio traffic on reel-to-reel recorders

Mary – An ASA linguist trained at DLI (also Monterey Mary)

MIL – Manual typewriter that typed only in capital letters; some typed in Cyrillic alphabet

Milchbar – Originally an ice cream parlor or dairy store; many later served alcoholic beverages and became dance halls

MOS – Military occupational specialty code (e.g., 98G was a voice intercept operator)

MSG – Master Sergeant

NCO – Non-commissioned officer (e.g., a sergeant)

NCOIC – NCO in charge

NSA – National Security Agency

OIC – Officer in charge

PCS – Permanent change of station; a permanent transfer to another post

Pos – Intercept position

PX – Post exchange, a store run by AAFES; large ones were like department stores; most were small

RRCV-4 – Special purpose signal intercept van mounted on a deuce-and-a-half

SFC – Sergeant First Class (E-7)

Short-timer – One who is within 100 days of discharge or return to CONUS

SIGINT – Signals intelligence, combining COMINT, ELINT, and other related disciplines

SP5 – Specialist 5th Class (E-5), same pay grade as a buck sergeant, but not considered an NCO

SP6 – Specialist 6th Class (E-6), same pay grade as a staff sergeant, but not considered an NCO

SSG – Staff Sergeant (E-6)

Strack (also can be rendered as Strak or Strac) – describes a soldier who is well turned out in his uniform beyond the strict requirements of regulations

Three-quarter – A military equivalent of a 4x4 pick-up truck with a ¾ ton cargo capacity

TR – Transcriber of intercepted voice communications

TR Hut – where tapes were transcribed by TRs

Tread – Career Army personnel, especially someone who maintains military discipline

UCMJ – Uniform Code of Military Justice; a body of federal law, enacted by Congress which defines the military justice system and lists criminal offenses under military law.

USAFSS – U.S. Air Force Security Service (ASA's USAF counterpart)

USAREUR – U.S. Army Europe

Warsaw Pact – Communist equivalent of NATO led by the USSR.

WO1 – Warrant Officer one; lowest of the four warrant officer grades in 1966-67

Zoomie – USAF member

Zulu – Greenwich Mean Time (GMT)

****

BALLAD OF THE A.S.A.

(Sung to the tune of "Ballad of the Green Beret")

Drunken Soldiers, always high
Dropouts from old Sigma Phi
Men who bullshit all the way,
These are the men from the ASA

Plastic cans upon our ears,
We've been cleared and we're not queers
One hundred men we'll test today,
But only three make the ASA

Trained to go from bar to bar,
That's the life that's best by far
Men who drink will seldom fight,
And the ASA drinks through the night

On a mid, a trick chief waits,
Four of his men are coming late
Men who drink among the best
Another drink, their last request

A teal blue scarf 'round my son's neck
Makes my son a nervous wreck

205

One hundred men re-upped today,
But not a one from the ASA

Black is for the night we fear, (1)
Blue the water we don't go near.
White is for the flag we fly,
Yellow is the reason why.
Red is for the blood we've shed.
As you see, there is no red! (2)
One hundred men reupped today.
Not a one for the A-S-A!

(With sincere apologies to SSG Barry Sadler who wrote and sang "The Ballad of the Green Beret")

(1) The colors refer to those on the distinctive ASA unit shoulder patch worn on the uniforms of ASA personnel and reproduced on the cover of this book.
(2) A significant number of ASA soldiers did indeed make the ultimate sacrifice for our country. Their names are enshrined on the National Security Agency's Memorial Wall with the names of nearly 200 other cryptologists who died in the line of duty.

****

CAST OF CHARACTERS

CPT John Medved, Detachment Commander
WO1 Brad Foster, Operations OIC
MSG (E-7) Oliver Henry, Det NCOIC/First Sergeant
SFC William Rayburn, mess sergeant
SSG Robert Gray, detachment admin sergeant
PFC Timothy Anson, detachment clerk
STRAIGHT DAY WORKERS
SFC Kenneth Karney, Ops NCOIC
SP6 Patrick "Father Pat" Riley, Senior Czech linguist
SP6 Wayne Moore, Senior German linguist
SP6 Karl Waldgruen, CARRYBACK Czech linguist
SGT Dean Peece, Comms center NCOIC
SP5 Doug "Cajun" Broussard, 05K and Club manager
SP5 Robert Day, senior electronic maintenance tech
SP4 Don McGrew, 05K and RRCV-4 expert
SP4 Barry "Bear" Martin
SP4 George "Lurch" Oakjones
PFC Harlan "Whipdick" Thomas, cook
PFC John "Grommet Cook' Ritter, cook and aspiring writer
ABLE TRICK
A/SGT Brett Riegel, Trick Chief, Czech 98G
SP5 Bill Pierce, Russian 98G and PX manager
SP4 Tony Phillips, Czech 98G
SP4 Warren T. "Fang" Feldman, III, Czech 98G
SP4 Herbert "Weasel" Beasely, ELINT Op

SP4 Michael "Mike the Cop" Floyd, MP
BAKER TRICK
SSG Jim Hall, Trick Chief, Russian 98G
SP4 John "Jack" Rutherford, Czech 98G
SP4 Pete "the Greek" Stavros – Czech 98G
SP4 Pedro "Texas Pete" Alonso, Czech 98G
CHARLIE TRICK
A/SGT Dick Proust, Trick chief, Czech 98G
SP4 Walter "Whiskey Man" Smythe, Czech 98G
SP4 Darrel "Peeps" Price, Russian 98G
SP4 Frank DiMartino, MP
DOG TRICK
A/SGT Will Morrow, Trick Chief, Russian 98G
SP5 Richard Roberts, Czech 98G
SP5 Joe Parker, Czech 98G
SP4 Jerry Daniels, Czech 98G
SP5 Wally "Fritz" Bunker, ELINT Op 98J
SP5 James "Walrus" Cavanaugh, Russian 98G
SP4 Stan "The Bard" Pace, Russian 98G
SP4 Ronald Walters, German 98G
SP4 Matt Rivington, Comms center technician
SP4 Louis "Large Louis" Trzescianski, MP

****

Made in the USA
Middletown, DE
23 November 2020